D1604208

Murder
Checks
Out

Also available by Victoria Gilbert

Hunter and Clewe Mysteries
A Cryptic Clue
Booklover's B&B Mysteries
A Fatal Booking
Reserved for Murder
Booked for Death

The Blue Ridge Library Mysteries
Death in the Margins
Renewed for Murder
A Deadly Edition
Bound for Murder
Past Due for Murder
Shelved Under Murder
A Murder for the Books

Mirror of Immortality Series
Scepter of Fire
Crown of Ice

Murder Checks Out

A BLUE RIDGE LIBRARY MYSTERY

Victoria Gilbert

CROOKED
LANE

NEW YORK

Copyright © 2023 by Vicki L. Weavil

Published in the United States by Crooked Lane Books, an imprint of The Quick Brown Fox & Company LLC.

Crooked Lane Books and its logo are trademarks of The Quick Brown Fox & Company LLC.

Library of Congress Catalog-in-Publication data available upon request.

ISBN (hardcover): 978-1-63910-520-5
ISBN (ebook): 978-1-63910-521-2

Cover design by Griesbach/Martucci

Printed in the United States.

www.crookedlanebooks.com

Crooked Lane Books
34 West 27th St., 10th Floor
New York, NY 10001

First Edition: November 2023

10 9 8 7 6 5 4 3 2 1

In loving memory of my aunt:
Charlotte King Clatterbuck
1936–2023

Chapter One

Ask a group of people a random question and most of them will either shrug or toss off an answer, factual or not. But ask a librarian the same question and they'll research it until they can provide a definitive response.

"Okay, I found something on the website sponsored by Clarion's folklore department," I said, holding up my cell phone. "It seems that sugarplums have nothing to do with fruit, plums or otherwise. They are a type of sweet that was popular from the seventeenth through the nineteenth century. They were relatively small orbs, created by layers of candied sugar built up around a small center, like a cardamom or caraway seed or an almond. Also called a comfit."

"So something like a jawbreaker or other simple, sugar-based candy?" My friend and library codirector, Sunny Fields, gazed down at me from her perch on a stepladder. "I guess the typical costumes for the Sugarplum Fairy in *The Nutcracker* are appropriate, then. Lots of small glittering baubles sewn into the tutu would be like old-time sugarplum candies."

"Yeah, who knew?" I pocketed my phone. "You about done up there?"

"One last ornament." Sunny held up a black pipe-cleaner spider liberally dusted with silver glitter. "Really more suitable for Halloween than Christmas, wouldn't you say?"

"I bet it's meant to represent *Charlotte's Web*." I stepped back to survey the artificial pine tree we'd set up in a corner of the Taylorsford Public Library's reading room. A shaft of light falling from one of the library's tall, deep-set windows illuminated the handmade bead garlands that draped the branches.

The tree fit the space perfectly, its star-topped tip just brushing the beams of the vaulted ceiling. It was a gift from one of our wealthier patrons, and its branches and needles looked uncannily real. All it lacked was the scent of actual pine. But I'd never use a real tree, especially one decorated with lights, in our 1919 building. As Ethan, my firefighter brother-in-law, would say, *that would be foolish as well as illegal*. The Taylorsford Public Library was a heritage building, one of the many libraries built in the late nineteenth and early twentieth centuries with grants from industrialist Andrew Carnegie. I'd be devastated if its intricately carved wood trim was ever scorched by flames.

"I know we've always used traditional ornaments in the past, but I think it was a great idea to have our kids make them this year," Sunny said as she descended the stepladder.

"Well, if anyone makes negative comments, we'll just tell them we're encouraging creativity along with reading." I moved closer to the tree to tap a square ornament made of brown popsicle sticks enclosing an image of the moon in a night sky. I was glad that our younger patrons had embraced the challenge to create ornaments based on their favorite books or stories, even if some of their efforts were less than perfect. "I'm guessing this one is an homage to *Goodnight Moon*."

"Maybe." Sunny twisted a strand of her long blonde hair around one of her slender fingers. "We should've asked them to add a tag with the title."

"I don't know. I think guessing is half the fun." I examined a miniature shield painted in vibrant colors. "This must be from a fantasy series, but I haven't figured out which one yet."

Sunny crossed to stand beside me. "I bet I can guess which ones Nicky and Ella made, with a little help from you or Richard." She pointed toward another section of the tree. "A nutcracker prince and a mouse king. Pretty much a dead giveaway."

"They are a teensy bit obsessed," I said, unable to repress a sigh. "It makes sense, of course. Richard's new production of *The Nutcracker* is their first time onstage, and it seems they both have inherited their father's love for performing."

"And his talent, I hope," Sunny said, shooting me a wicked grin.

I was sure she meant *rather than your lack of it*. I wrinkled my nose at her, not really upset about her comment. I knew my limitations and was honestly glad that my five-year-old twins, Nicholas and Elenora, took after my husband when it came to athletic ability. "Thankfully. Although I do feel like the odd person out sometimes, since my dancing skills are mediocre at best."

"Oh, I don't know, Amy. You do okay dancing with Richard." Sunny studied the tree, her blue eyes sparkling with good humor.

"As would anyone. He's a great partner," I said. "Anyway, now that Nicky and Ella are going to be in the *Nutcracker* party scene, they've been listening to the score nonstop. Which was okay the first hundred times . . ."

Sunny cast me another grin. "Kids that age don't mind repetition, do they? I know our story-time kids are always asking me to read the same picture books over and over. I can recite several by heart."

"You and me both." I smiled, once again grateful that Sunny, who'd completed her master of library science degree shortly after my children were born, had agreed to share the position of library director with me. It was an arrangement that allowed me to continue working and still have enough time for my unexpectedly expanded family.

Fortunately, it was beneficial for Sunny as well. With her grand-parents, Carol and P.J. Fields, now in their eighties, she'd taken over management of Vista View, the family's organic farm. The funds the farm generated were enough to supplement the director's salary she shared with me, especially since she lived rent- and mortgage-free in the family home.

Although the director's salary isn't that much, I thought. It was fortunate that my husband had a successful career as a choreographer and teacher. And that he'd inherited our historic 1920s farmhouse, so we were also mortgage-free. It was the only way I'd been able to afford halving my salary.

"I agree with you about changing the decorations this year, though," I said. "The vintage ornaments are beautiful, but it seems more appropriate to showcase our patrons' talents during the town's new festival."

"Building community spirit. Wasn't that the whole point of Winterfest to begin with?" Sunny stepped back, her gaze fixed on the decorated tree. "Even if some people seem to have forgotten that part."

"You mean the festival chair?" I shook my head. "I don't know what the mayor was thinking, placing Wendy Blackstone in that position. He had to know what a pain she can be, if only from her antics when she's addressed the town council."

"Well, Marty hasn't really been a resident of Taylorsford that long, even if he has lived in the area for years." Sunny dusted glitter from her hands. "And you know how it goes. Wendy was probably the only person who volunteered. It's a pretty big job, setting up a town festival. Most people wouldn't want to take that on."

I was sure Sunny was right. Before going to grad school, she'd served as mayor of Taylorsford for a few years. She knew all about the difficulty of getting people to step into volunteer positions.

Sunny flicked Nicky's mouse king ornament with her finger, making the wooden spool-and-pipe-cleaner figure bounce like it was dancing. "Speaking of *The Nutcracker*, I picked up tickets for opening night yesterday."

"Will Fred be back in town by then? Or is it just you and your grandparents?"

Sunny glanced over at me. "We're all going, although it will only be Fred and I on opening night. The grands are going closing night. They said they wanted Fred and me to have our own date night, and they wanted one for themselves as well. The grands adore Fred, you know." She rolled her eyes. "They've been dropping little hints about a holiday engagement for months."

I offered her a sympathetic smile. Sunny, who'd been dating private investigator Fred Nash for several years, still insisted that she had no plans to get married. I believed her, but it seemed her grandparents, once flower children living a vagabond life, had turned more traditional in their old age.

"I keep telling them they're devolving into fuddy-duddies, but I know they just want me to be happy. Which, as I also inform them regularly, I am." Sunny tossed her silky hair behind her shoulders. Although she was now forty-two and a few laugh lines fanned out from the corners of her lovely eyes, most people assumed she was still in her thirties. Especially since time hadn't changed her slender figure.

Unlike me. Of course, for me, it's time and twins, I thought, ruefully tugging down the hem of my emerald-green tunic top. Several inches shorter than Sunny, I'd always been curvaceous, which made it difficult to find clothes that didn't make me look heavier than I actually was. Not that I hadn't put on a few extra pounds since my pregnancy with the twins. It was a situation that no amount of walking or other exercise seemed to rectify. But I wasn't too concerned. I was healthy, and my husband still thought I was beautiful. Which was all that mattered. At forty-one, I'd decided I was old enough to ignore other people's opinions.

"Well, that's done. And just in time, I guess." Sunny picked up the box that had held the handmade ornaments. "Thanks for coming in this afternoon to help."

"No problem. Richard and the kids are at a rehearsal this afternoon, and Aunt Lydia's at the garden club's booth at the festival, so it worked out. Besides, I didn't want you doing everything by yourself. You already worked after closing yesterday to put up the other decorations."

Sunny lifted her down-filled winter coat off the back of one of the reading room chairs. "Seemed like a good time to do it. Fred was out of town, and the grands were planning to get takeout, so I wasn't needed to help prep dinner."

"According to Wendy Blackstone, we're already a day late." I shrugged as Sunny turned to me, her golden eyebrows arching. "She sent me a text this morning reminding me that the festival actually started yesterday."

"That woman." Sunny yanked her arms through the sleeves of her coat. "We had to wait until today, because the library is only closed on Sundays. Surely she understands that."

"Which is why I didn't bother to respond," I said as I slipped on my own, more-tailored, cinnamon-colored woolen coat. Sunny looked adorable in her puffy turquoise jacket, but I knew that wasn't a style I could pull off. "The last time I checked my phone, it was already below freezing, so we'd better bundle up if we're going to walk up to the town square," I added, pulling an ivory knit cap over my dark-brown hair. "Now I wish I'd driven today. I thought the exercise would be worth the extra walk, but I didn't figure on the temperature dropping so rapidly."

"Why are you headed that way? It's the opposite direction from your house." Sunny adjusted her fuzzy blue earmuffs. "I have to meet some friends at the festival to help hand out flyers, but I didn't think you were volunteering for anything."

"I'm supposed to take Aunt Lydia and Zelda some soup and coffee before I walk home. I left my canvas tote with the thermoses in the workroom." I tugged on my chocolate-brown, plush-lined leather gloves. "You have gloves, I hope?"

"Absolutely. Brought my arctic mitts." Sunny held up her hands, displaying a pair of chunky mittens knitted in a Nordic pattern.

"All right, well, since we didn't unlock any of the public doors, we can just switch off the lights and go," I said, leading the way through the stacks.

When we reached the library's main entrance area, we walked behind the circulation desk, where we switched off all the lights except for those in the staff workroom, located just off the desk. Crossing the workroom, I grabbed a large canvas tote from the floor and allowed Sunny to push through the staff exit ahead of me before I turned off the workroom lights and made sure the door locked behind us.

A brisk wind brought tears to my eyes as soon as Sunny and I walked around the side of the library. "It's freezing out here," I said, wiping the moisture from my face with one gloved finger.

Sunny's breath coiled up like smoke. "It's supposed to be colder than usual all week," she said, increasing her stride when we reached the sidewalk that ran parallel to Taylorsford's main street. "Good for some of the festival activities, like the ice-skating, I guess, but I feel bad for the people manning the booths on the square."

"That's why I'm toting this bag. Aunt Lydia and Zelda are in charge of the garden club's booth this afternoon, which they agreed to before seeing any weather predictions."

"I'm sure they'll appreciate some warm liquids." Sunny glanced over at me, her ivory skin now tinged rose pink by the cold. "But you're going to have a longer walk home. Better grab a cup of coffee for yourself before you head off."

"I might do that." I switched the straps of the canvas bag from one shoulder to the other. "This feels a lot heavier than when I carried it to the library earlier."

"It's the wind. It picked up while we were inside, and now we're walking right into it." Sunny gripped her arms against her chest. "It's probably a good thing that the festival shuts down earlier today. Eight o'clock will be late enough in this weather."

"Did you leave your car at the town hall lot?" I asked, raising my voice to be heard over the wind.

"Yeah. I wanted to park there before everything got started today. Figured I might not find a spot otherwise." Sunny shoved her hands into her pockets. "I'd offer you a ride home, but I promised to stay until things close down."

"It's fine." I yanked my hat down, unrolling the cuff so it covered more of my ears. "At least I won't be walking into the wind."

As we approached the large lawn that stretched out in front of the Taylorsford town hall, I stopped for a moment to appreciate its transformation. A series of wooden facades had been set up to form an alley that replicated a vintage village street. Colored lights, strung overhead, glowed against the twilight sky. Behind the festively decorated openings cut into the facades, local businesses and organizations had set up tables to display information or sell food and crafts. The aroma of hot chocolate mingled with the scents of fried dough and grilled meats filled the air.

Murder Checks Out

Sunny said good-bye before jogging off to join a group of people clustered around a lamppost at the edge of the town hall property. Instead of manning a booth, they were standing in the open air, handing out flyers as visitors walked in from the parking lot. A few held up placards that read *Stop Blackstone Development*, *No Clear-Cutting*, and *Protect Our Forests*.

It was an eclectic assortment of people—moms in puffy down jackets pushing strollers filled with blanket-wrapped toddlers, teens braving the cold in ripped jeans and hooded sweatshirts, twenty- and thirty-somethings in heavy jackets and boots, and even a few older folks bundled up in layers of knit and wool. In the center of the group, a young man with silky, shoulder-length dark hair and a close-trimmed beard and mustache lifted one quilted flannel-clad arm and held his black-gloved hand, palm out, to silence the chatter of the crowd. A young woman stood beside him. A mass of rose-gold curls framed her round face, mirroring the circular frames of her royal-blue glasses.

Sunny was welcomed with smiles and claps on her back and shoulders. I didn't recognize many of the other participants, although I did spy local poet Emily Moore and noticed Candy Jensen, a young designer who was creating the costumes for Richard and Karla's new *Nutcracker*, standing off to one side.

"Ah, I see the opposition's troops are out in force," said a familiar voice behind me.

Glancing over my shoulder, I had to tilt my head to look up into the rugged face of the speaker, and not only because I was rather short. Unlike many men of his age, seventy-nine-year-old Kurt Kendrick hadn't lost any of his impressive height over the years. Nor had time taken his hair—it was as thick and as snowy white as when we'd first met several years before.

"Opposition to what?" I asked, looking away from his commanding blue-eyed gaze.

"The new development on the mountain," Kurt said, moving to stand beside me. "You must've heard something about that, since the planned subdivision butts up against Ethan Payne's property."

"Oh, is that what this is all about?" I frowned. Ethan owned a house and a few acres of land just outside of town, farther up in the Blue Ridge Mountains. It was the home my brother, Scott Webber, shared with him when Scott wasn't off on some clandestine mission for the secretive government agency he worked for. "I guess it makes sense that Emily, like Sunny, would support efforts to block the project."

"As former and current hippie flower children, you mean?" Kurt laid a hand on my shoulder. "I suppose that does come into it. Although I think Emily, like many others, is simply distrustful of Wendy Blackstone's promises. As am I."

"How ironic," said a clipped female voice behind us. "As if anyone would ever trust you, Kurt Kendrick, any farther than they could throw you. Which, as we all know, is no distance at all."

Chapter Two

Kurt and I turned to face the speaker, a tall, slender woman whose hazel eyes seemed almost too large for her narrow face. She flicked her fingers through her expertly feathered cap of hair. I knew Wendy Blackstone was at least fifty, but with her slender figure, finely tailored clothes, and artfully applied makeup, she could easily pass for a woman in her thirties. At least, as long as one didn't get close enough to notice the telltale signs of facelifts and Botox and the fine line of silver streaking the roots of her burnished gold hair.

"Hi, Ms. Blackstone," I said.

"Hello, Ms. Muir." Wendy adjusted the ivory silk scarf she'd tucked into the collar of her caramel-colored wool coat. "And Mr. Kendrick, of course."

"I think you can call me by my first name at this point," Kurt said. "Especially since I'm sure you've called me worse things over the years."

"Whatever do you mean?" Wendy waved her hand, which was clad in an expensive beige leather glove, through the air. "The truth is, I hadn't given you any thought, Kurt, until I moved to Taylorsford and saw that you owned that lovely estate in the mountains."

Kurt crossed his arms over his broad chest. "It's not for sale."

"I assumed as much." Wendy pursed her crimson-tinted lips. "Anyway, since my new development isn't close to your property, I've no interest in acquiring your land."

"But perhaps you'd like to buy some acreage off of Ethan Payne?" Kurt's lips curled back, exposing his large teeth. "Only he isn't enthused about selling either."

I glanced from Wendy to Kurt and back again. There was something unspoken electrifying the air between them. Something as obvious as our breath coiling in the frigid air.

Wendy shot me a sharp look. "Your brother-in-law, I believe? Not one of my favorite people. He's been stirring up trouble, opposing my new development."

I gripped my gloved hands together. "I've heard something about that."

"It's such a self-centered opinion," Wendy said, with a little sniff of disapproval. "Yes, the development will back up on Mr. Payne's land, but it's not like it will be on top of him. There's a good acre or so between his house and the property lines."

"Which I'm sure you're eyeing with ill intent." Kurt's tone was as icy as his eyes.

Wendy pressed her forefinger to her chin as she looked him up and down. "One thing I will say—at least Ethan isn't mixed up with Jaden Perez and his mob of protesters. Environmental activists, they call themselves." She shot a sharp glance at the group gathered near the parking lot. "They have no business messing in Taylorsford's affairs. Out-of-towners, the lot."

"Not all of them." Following Wendy's gaze, I noticed Sunny waving a handful of bright-green flyers over her head. "My friend Sunshine Fields and her family have lived in this area for generations. Ask them how they feel about your proposed development."

Wendy tightened her lips. "I don't have to. I know that bunch supports any form of environmental nonsense."

"It isn't nonsense," I said, meeting her disdainful look with a lift of my chin. "Sunny's convinced that clear-cutting the side of the mountain is a disaster waiting to happen. One strong storm and you'll have a landslide."

"We've designed protections against such things." Wendy stared down her nose at me. "This isn't my first rodeo."

Kurt's nostrils flared. "That's right. You've already mucked up land over near Smithsburg. Leveled a stand of old-growth trees to build that subdivision filled with the ghastly monstrosities you call luxury homes."

"I don't think you should be judging me about anything, considering your past." Wendy huffed and turned on her heel, stalking away without a good-bye.

"Uh-oh, what did you do to tick her off?" I asked, when Wendy disappeared from view.

Kurt shrugged. "Ancient history. And not really my fault. For once." Laying a hand on my shoulder, he looked down at me with a smile.

In the past I might've rolled my shoulders, dislodging his hand, but we'd reached an understanding that made me accept this as a friendly gesture. "I won't ask any questions, then. At least for now."

"Oh dear, I know what that means. I'll get the third degree eventually." Kurt squeezed my shoulder before lifting his hand.

I decided to change the subject. "I need to drop off this bag with Aunt Lydia and Zelda," I said. "Care to tag along?"

"Absolutely. I haven't spoken to Lydia in a few weeks. I should catch up with her." Kurt easily kept pace with me as I headed toward the garden club's booth. "By the way, how are my godchildren these days?"

"You'd know if you ever stopped by." I shifted the bag to my other shoulder.

Kurt made a tutting sound. "Sorry, I've been out of town. And I thought you might be too busy for visitors these days, what with the holidays and Richard's schedule. I know he has rehearsals almost every night."

"It is hectic," I admitted, glancing over at him. "But Nicky and Ella always like to see you." It was true. Defying my expectations, Kurt had turned out to be a splendid grandfather figure for my five-year-old twins. Which almost made up for the fact that Richard's father definitely did not fulfill that role. Of course, my dad, Nick, was a wonderful granddad too, but Jim Muir always seemed to be looking for an exit when confronted with Ella and Nicky.

Kurt pressed his palm to his chest. "I promise to do better. Now, why don't you hand over that tote? It looks heavy."

"It's fine," I said, hoisting the straps of the bag higher up on my shoulder. "Besides, we're already here."

The portion of the facade fronting the garden club's booth was painted to resemble a stone florist shop covered with ivy.

"Reinforcements!" I said, holding up the tote bag. "Hot soup and coffee."

"Bless you, lamb." Zelda Adams straightened the red velvet reindeer-antler headband hugging her crisp blonde curls. Always flamboyant, she'd gone over the top today, wearing a glittering sequin-studded holiday sweater under an emerald-green coat. An extravagant Christmas tree brooch was pinned to one of her lapels. With her round face and rosy cheeks and lips, Zelda looked younger than her seventy-three years. Her full head of hair, dyed blonde, added to the illusion. A short, full-figured woman, she never seemed concerned about anyone's opinions of her fashion choices. *Or anything else*, I thought, offering her a warm smile.

Standing beside her childhood friend, my aunt provided the perfect foil to Zelda's zaftig appearance. Elegant and slender, Aunt Lydia's perfectly coiffed white hair was only a few shades paler than the skin pulled tautly but smoothly over her high cheekbones. Tonight, she wore a tailored black wool coat over a simple burgundy sweater and white turtleneck. Unlike Zelda, her only concession to the holidays was the brightly enameled wreath earrings dangling from her ears.

Well, one earring, I realized. The other appeared to be missing. That was so unlike my fastidious aunt that I remarked on it as I handed over the canvas tote.

"Yes, I know." Aunt Lydia tugged her bare earlobe. "I had both on when I arrived, but apparently one slipped out while I was pulling the wreaths and things out of storage." She cast her commanding gaze to Kurt. "Surprised to see you here. I thought Taylorsford's little festival would be too déclassé for your elevated tastes."

Kurt flashed a wolfish grin. "Not at all. I like to support the town whenever I can. In fact, I think I'll pick up a wreath or two for Highview."

Aunt Lydia's disparaging sniff was clearly audible. "I would've expected you to have hired a decorator to take care of all that."

"I did, but he forgot the front door this year. I need something for that as well as a wreath for the garage." Kurt picked up one of the fresh wreaths, which had been threaded with crimson berries and dried baby's breath and topped off with a large ruby bow. "This will do quite nicely."

As Zelda showed Kurt a couple more wreaths, I turned to my aunt. "I can help look for your other earring if you'll explain how to get back there with you."

"You have to head to the far end and walk along the back aisle to our booth," Aunt Lydia said. "But be careful—remember the steep hill at the edge of the town hall lawn? It's right behind our tables and chairs."

Leaving Kurt examining more of the greenery for sale, I circled around the far end of the facade and made my way along the narrow path formed behind the row of booths. Aunt Lydia was right—the hill behind them fell away sharply, and there wasn't any barrier except a short section of railing near a flight of sturdy wooden steps. The stairs led down to a grassy area bordered by pine trees. In other seasons it was a popular picnic spot, but for the festival the tables had been replaced by a temporary ice-skating rink.

Nicky and Ella will want to try that out if they see it, I thought with a frown. That probably wasn't a great idea. Although they could undoubtedly master the basics of skating fairly quickly, there was always the chance of falling and breaking or spraining something. Not a good choice, especially prior to their debut as part of the *Nutcracker* cast.

Joining Aunt Lydia and Zelda at their table, I gave my aunt's arm a pat. "Where do you think you dropped the earring?"

"Hard to say. I took off my hat when I got here, so perhaps I pulled it out then. Unfortunately, that means it might have flown anywhere." Aunt Lydia motioned toward the stacks of wreaths and swags on the ground. "It could've fallen into any of those piles, which will make it almost impossible to find."

"Is it something you really care about?" I asked, staring dubiously at the greenery.

"Well, they aren't valuable, but Hugh gave them to me last Christmas. Just as a stocking stuffer, but still . . ." Aunt Lydia bent down to brush her fingers through the first stack of wreaths.

I knelt down to check a pile of swags. Hugh Chen was my aunt's partner of many years. While they still maintained separate households, they were devoted to each other and spent as much time together as possible. I knew Aunt Lydia would hate to lose one of Hugh's gifts.

As I helped Aunt Lydia search for the lost earring, Zelda chatted with Kurt about his recent travels. "Buying more artwork for your galleries, I suppose?"

"Gallery," Kurt said. "I sold the place in New York. Now I only have the Georgetown one."

"Really?" Zelda widened her eyes. "Downsizing?"

Kurt shrugged. "I'm not getting any younger. Besides, other than buying trips, I prefer to stay in Taylorsford these days."

"Closer to family," Zelda said, with a swift glance my way. I rolled my eyes at her. "Anyway, I saw you talking to Wendy Blackstone just now. Didn't look to me like a friendly conversation."

I shared a quick glance with Kurt. We both knew that Zelda, a lovely woman in all other ways, was a notorious gossip. "She was simply upset with the protesters gathered over by the parking lot. I guess we didn't offer her the moral support she was looking for, so she stomped off."

Zelda shook her head. "That woman can be so difficult. It's her way or the highway."

"And she'd probably build an interstate right through Taylorsford if it would make her money." Aunt Lydia straightened. "Don't worry about that earring, Amy. I'll look another time."

I stood up, brushing my hands together to dust pine needles from my gloves. "It wouldn't be so bad if I didn't fear Blackstone Properties might renege on their promise to preserve the environment during the building process. I suspect, despite their assurances to the contrary, they'll end up clear-cutting."

Aunt Lydia's pink-tinted lips thinned. "Which is just what we need—more opportunities for runoff into the local streams."

"Exactly." Kurt narrowed his eyes. "Mary is opposed to the project, of course. Even though the development won't impinge upon her property, she's adamant about protecting mountain land from overdevelopment."

Mary Gardener, a local folklore expert, had been a friend of Kurt's ever since she'd worked at the orphanage where he'd spent much of his childhood. She was turning one hundred in a few weeks, an event that had led Kurt, who had grown quite wealthy from his dealings in art and antiques, to become a major sponsor of Winterfest. He'd promised significant funds if the town council dedicated the festival to Mary. Which, of course, they were more than happy to do.

"Well, on a more positive note, I was glad to hear that Mary feels well enough to attend the opening night of the *Nutcracker*," I told Kurt.

"She'll have to be in a wheelchair, but she'll be there," he replied, sliding two wreaths up his long, cashmere-clad arm as he stepped back from the booth. He bent his elbow to hold the wreaths in place. "Well, ladies, since I've bought what I need, I suppose I should get out of the way. I'm sure there are others who'd like to check out your group's wares."

As he turned away, I noticed Wendy Blackstone standing at a booth across the way. It looked like she was staring directly at Kurt, her expression frigid as the winter air.

I shifted my focus to Kurt's craggy face, which had gone still as stone. "Okay now, fess up—is there some sort of bad blood between you and Wendy Blackstone?" I asked, keeping my voice low so Zelda and Aunt Lydia, busy straightening bows on a few pine swags, couldn't hear. "A failed relationship in the past or something?"

He looked down at me, his bushy brows drawn together over his hawklike nose. "Not exactly. It's true that she hates me, but that is her problem, not mine. And, quite frankly, Amy Webber Muir, no business of yours." He turned on his heel and strode away before I could think of a retort.

"Ooo, touched a nerve." Zelda's tea-brown eyes sparkled.

Of course she'd noticed that interaction. "I guess so. I have no idea why, though."

"Do you know, Lydia?" Zelda elbowed my aunt, who gave a final tweak to a bow before looking up.

"No. But then I didn't see Kurt for years and years. We only reconnected around nine years ago. There's a large span of time when I didn't even know that he was still alive, much less what he was up to." A shadow flitted across my aunt's fine-boned face.

"He and Andrew remained good friends, though, even after you got married," Zelda said. Her expression was innocent enough, but I knew she was fishing for information.

"Yes, but I didn't know that, remember?" Aunt Lydia's tone had sharpened to that razor edge she used to warn off anyone probing too deeply into her personal life.

"Right, right." Zelda turned away, busying herself with hanging some of the swags on a display rack.

I laid my hand over my aunt's tensed arm. Andrew Talbot, her late husband, had died young, but I knew time hadn't dimmed her love for him—or her distrust of Kurt, who'd been Andrew's best friend when they were teenagers. *And beyond*, I reminded myself, even though Aunt Lydia hadn't known they'd stayed in touch until much later. Still, she'd always blamed Kurt, who'd been a dealer in the past, for getting Andrew into drugs, an addiction he'd struggled with all of his short life. And, although the blame couldn't be laid entirely at his door, it was true that Kurt hadn't necessarily been the best influence on Andrew. It was something he readily admitted these days, but that didn't totally mollify my aunt.

"I think I'm going to head to the house, if that's okay," I told her. "Richard and the twins will be finished with their rehearsal in a half hour or so, and I'd like to be there when they get home."

"Of course, dear." Aunt Lydia patted my hand. "Thanks for bringing us the soup and coffee. It will help make the next few hours more comfortable, I'm sure."

"No problem." I stepped back, careful to avoid the edge of the hill. "You brought the car, I hope?"

Zelda pulled the coffee thermos out of the tote along with two plastic mugs. "I have mine. Don't worry, lamb, I'll make sure Lydia gets home safely."

"Okay, great. Tell Walt hello for me," I added, before wishing them both a good day. Walter Adams, another one of Aunt Lydia's childhood friends, was now Zelda's husband. They'd loved each other when they were young, but because he was Black and she was white, they hadn't pursued a relationship then, knowing that it wouldn't be accepted by the community at the time. They'd both married others and enjoyed successful relationships before losing their respective spouses. But they'd remained friends, and they'd finally married each other about six years ago.

Walking back across the town hall lawn, I saw someone else I recognized and waved a greeting. "Hi, Ethan. I was just heading home. Sorry I can't stay and chat."

"Neither can I." Ethan, a tall, well-built young man, was thirty-three, six years younger than my brother, Scott. They had married three years ago in an intimate ceremony held at Kurt's estate. "I'm actually on duty."

"Should have realized, since you're in uniform," I said. "Night shift?"

"No, just this afternoon. Although I could've done the overnight shift, because being home doesn't matter so much when Scott is out of town." Ethan pulled down the flaps of his fleece-lined hat. "I got assigned to keep an eye on things here, but I can leave when everything shuts down at eight."

"I'd have thought the sheriff's department would handle security," I said.

Ethan shrugged. "With the lights and propane cooking stoves and grills, we need to make sure no one accidentally starts a fire. Especially with all the wood decorations, cut trees, and other greenery. Could go up pretty quick."

"I can see that." I offered him a sympathetic smile. "Wish I'd known. I just brought Aunt Lydia and Zelda some soup and coffee. I could've brought you something as well."

"Thanks, but our EMT supervisor promised to bring me coffee. The station is close enough to walk."

"That's Hannah Fowler, right?" I asked, remembering Aunt Lydia mentioning something about the young woman, who was part of a family that had lived in Taylorsford for decades.

Ethan shifted from foot to foot. "Yeah. It's nice to have her finally working full-time. She was three-quarter time for a couple of years. We're the only paid members of the squad, you know. Everyone else is a volunteer."

"I remember you mentioning that. It must put a lot of pressure on you." I gazed over Ethan's shoulder. "Uh-oh, speaking of lighting fires, it looks like Wendy Blackstone is marching over to confront those protesters."

Ethan spun around to face the parking lot. "That's not good. I'd better alert the deputy on duty." He raised his walkie-talkie to his lips.

"I think they've already noticed," I said, as a young woman in uniform dashed toward the cluster of protesters.

21

"Okay, good. It's really their jurisdiction." Ethan lowered his walkie-talkie, tapping it against his thigh. "That woman is nothing but trouble," he added. "I wish someone could just . . . well, run her out of Taylorsford, I guess."

"Sadly, I doubt that's going to happen," I said, keeping my tone light. Studying Ethan's face, I was a little unnerved by the tremor in his clenched jaw.

"I don't know. There might be a way, if anyone cared enough to make the effort," Ethan said, his voice thick with anger. "She doesn't care about the town, or the land, or anything, except making money."

"I don't disagree with you, but it's hard to imagine her giving up her plans, even with the protests."

"Maybe she could be made to," Ethan snapped, before striding off in the direction of the confrontation between the protesters and Wendy Blackstone.

Concerned about what might happen, I stood for a few minutes, stamping my boots against the brown, frost-crisped grass to keep up the circulation in my feet. Wendy wheeled around to face off with Ethan as soon as he reached the cluster of protesters and launched into a tirade I couldn't hear clearly. But it was obvious from her furious gesticulations and the raised voices carried on the wind that she was giving him hell.

Ethan stood still as a soldier on guard duty, but I had no doubt that he was equally angry. With his arms crossed over his chest and his chin jutted out, he barked something at Wendy that made her jump back.

Ever the peacemaker, Sunny pushed her way through the crowd of protesters and stepped between them, placing a calming, mittened hand on each of their shoulders.

I turned away, relieved I could leave the situation in Sunny's sensible care. But as I trudged home, a bubble of concern rolled up my esophagus and lodged in my chest. I'd never seen Ethan like that—so angry and aggressive.

If looks could kill, I thought, narrowing my eyes against the stinging wind, *Wendy Blackstone would be dead.*

Chapter Three

The following morning was a Monday, a school and work day, which meant slightly chaotic.

Setting plates of scrambled eggs and toast in front of Nicky and Ella, I noticed that Ella, otherwise fully dressed, wasn't wearing shoes or socks.

"Did you forget something?" I asked Richard, who was sitting at the kitchen table between the twins. Since I'd offered to make breakfast, he'd overseen getting the kids ready for kindergarten.

Richard met my inquiring look with a wry smile. "We had a slight disagreement about the importance of footwear."

"It's wintertime," I said, turning my gaze on Ella. "Far too cold to go out with bare feet. Besides, you know you have to wear shoes to school."

"Hate shoes," Ella said, her mouth full of egg.

I stared into her clear gray eyes, which were disconcertingly similar to Richard's. *And, like her dad, she knows how to use them to good effect*, I thought, stilling a twitch of my lips. "Sorry, but you have to wear them."

Ella's thick black lashes fluttered. "They squish my toes."

I sighed. The twins seemed to grow out of their clothes and shoes on a weekly basis. "You can wear your stretchy summer sneakers then. But you have to wear something."

"I don't like those, they're stupid." Ella rolled her lower lip into a pout.

Nicky, who'd inherited his equally expressive, deep-brown eyes from my side of the family, shot a glance at his sister. He was the quieter, more serious twin, which didn't mean he wasn't up for some mischief from time to time.

"Stupid or not, you can't walk around without shoes in the winter," I said, finally sitting down at the table with my own plate of eggs and toast. Which were, of course, getting cold.

Ella stretched out one bare foot and wiggled her toes, drawing the attention of our ginger tabby, Fosse, who'd been lurking under the table waiting for food spillage. "A lot of times Daddy doesn't wear shoes when he dances."

"No, but Daddy isn't dancing outside in the cold." I grimaced as I took a bite of my tepid eggs.

Fosse pounced, causing Ella to giggle and sweep her fork through the air. A bit of egg sailed to the floor, drawing the cat's attention away from Ella's feet.

Richard, who'd already finished his breakfast, wiped his mouth with a napkin and leaned in closer to Ella. "You don't want your toes to get frostbite and fall off, do you? Then you wouldn't be able to walk, much less dance." He shook his head. "You'd be like that girl in the story I read you—the one about the red shoes."

"Had to have her feet cut off," Nicky said with relish. He made a sharp motion with his hand. "Chop, chop."

Ella leveled him a fierce look. "That's just a story, doo-doo head."

"Elenora Alice Muir, don't talk to your brother like that." I laid down my fork with a clang against my plate.

"Or anyone, really." Richard's typically pleasant expression grew stern.

Ella straightened in her chair, drawing her feet up onto the wooden rungs. Both the children knew that when their dad got that look, they'd better behave. Richard might be a loving father, but he certainly wasn't a pushover.

"Sorry," Ella muttered, staring down at her plate.

"It's okay." Nicky went back to gobbling down his eggs. He rarely lost his temper and never held a grudge, which was strangely appropriate. Named for my dad, he seemed to have also inherited Nick Webber's laid-back personality.

"Okay, head upstairs. Time to brush teeth, both of you, and then put on some shoes, Ella." Richard stood up, collecting the dirty plates and utensils. "We'll let Mommy finish her breakfast in peace," he added with a smile.

"Just sit that stuff in the sink," I said. "I'll throw everything in the dishwasher before I leave."

Richard leaned over to kiss me on the temple, earning squinched faces from both Ella and Nicky. They'd recently decided that our kissing was "kinda gross." Not that their comments affected our behavior. "Upstairs," he told the twins. "Start brushing, and don't just pretend. I'll be right up to check on you."

The children ran down the hall, heading for the stairs, Fosse on their heels. Our other cat, a tortoiseshell named Loie, was perched on one of the wide sills of the windows that looked out over our side yard. The older of our two pets, she merely opened one emerald eye and watched Fosse gallop off before closing her eye again.

Richard placed the plates and utensils in the sink. But instead of immediately turning around, he leaned forward, gripping the edge of the soapstone counter.

"Something you want to tell me?" I asked, observing the tension in his shoulders.

"How did you know?"

"You think I can't read your body language after all this time?" I finished off my eggs and shoved back my chair. "Does this have something to do with that text from your mother you received earlier this morning?"

"I'm afraid so." Richard turned to face me, his expression contrite. "Not quite sure how to tell you this, but she wants to come for a visit next week. Without Dad," he added, holding up his hands. "It would just be her."

I stood and strolled over to him. "Well, that's one small blessing." I reached around him to set my dish and utensils in the sink. "But I thought they were going on a holiday cruise?"

"That's the thing," Richard said, taking a step to the side. "They'll be out of the country for the week of Christmas, so we won't be able to visit with them for the actual holiday. That's why Mom's asked about coming early. She wants to see the kids and give them their gifts and all that before she leaves for the cruise. And attend one of the *Nutcracker* performances, of course."

"I see. She plans to stay here, I guess?" I crossed my arms over my chest. Since we had only three bedrooms, I'd have to bunk the twins together to give Fiona Muir a room. Of course, we'd done it before, but that was part of my concern. I knew what could happen when Ella and Nicky shared a bedroom. There'd be a lot of chattering and playing and not much sleeping.

"I'm afraid so." Richard ran his fingers through his short dark hair, now threaded with a few silver strands. But he was lucky—my own hair had more prominent silver wings streaking the temples. "I know your parents usually stay over at Lydia's, but Mom says she always feels awkward running back and forth between houses."

"It's right next door," I said. *And much larger.* My aunt Lydia owned a historic home that had been in our family since it was built in 1900. It was a three-story Queen Anne Revival with plenty of guest rooms. "But it's okay. We can make it work." I laid a hand on Richard's tensed arm. "Don't worry, it'll be fine. Fiona and I have declared a truce. The only thing is, we should probably get a tree and decorate it before she arrives."

"Because otherwise she'll want to take over the entire process?" Richard asked. "She isn't coming until next Sunday. So we have some time."

"Not much, considering your *Nutcracker* schedule." I patted his arm before lifting my hand. "Speaking of time, hadn't you better dash upstairs and make sure the twins are actually brushing their teeth? I know they've already figured out the *just wet the brush* trick."

"Right. And never fear"—Richard flashed a grin—"I always do a breath test."

"Smart. I knew I married you for more than your looks." I stood on tiptoe to kiss his cheek. "Now, go on. Kid wrangling can't wait."

Richard kissed me back before turning and heading for the hall. "Don't forget I'm picking them up as well as dropping them off today. Have to get them to rehearsal," he said as he headed for the hall.

"So they need their dance bags," I called after him.

He waved a hand over his head in acknowledgment. "Got it under control."

"I'm glad somebody does," I muttered. Turning back to the sink, I rinsed everything and stuck the dishes and utensils in the dishwasher, then checked to make sure the cats had kibble. Heaven forbid I leave the house without ensuring they had food. They were reasonably well behaved but had been known to jump on counters in search of sustenance when we'd forgotten to leave enough kibble in their bowls.

I paused by the window to stroke Loie. "I'm sorry, girl, but you're going to have to put up with that woman who doesn't like cats again." Loie gave me a baleful glare as if she understood.

Leaving the kitchen, I made it to the end of the hall before Ella and Nicky bounced down the stairs, followed more slowly by Richard. The twins were bundled up in winter coats, scarves, and mittens. *Score several points for my husband.*

"We settled on the sneakers," he said, pointing toward Ella's feet.

"Better than nothing." I leaned down to give both kids a hug and a kiss. "Be good—at the rehearsal as well as at school."

"We're always good," Ella replied with a toss of her dark hair.

"You need a hat," I observed.

Richard shook his head. "A bridge too far. She can pull the scarf up over her ears, or so she says."

"Well, you better do that." I bent down to stare Ella in the eyes. "No getting sick before the dance performances. What would Daddy do?"

As I straightened, I caught Richard's wink. "It's true. It would be disastrous for the show." He leaned over the twins to kiss me on the lips.

Nicky and Ella elbowed each other and made faces that I studiously ignored. "Out you go, or you'll be late for school. All of you." Richard was still teaching dance at nearby Clarion University, although in recent years he'd cut back his schedule. This was partially due to the upswing in his contracted choreographic work but mainly in anticipation of a new phase in his career. Over the next twelve months, he and Karla planned to launch a contemporary dance company, developed out of the institute and festival they'd run over the last several summers.

Once the front door closed behind Richard and the twins, I strolled over to the stairs, pausing for a moment on the second step to look out over our unique front room. Comprising the entire width of the house, the room was divided equally between the living room and a space that functioned as Richard's home dance studio. He'd already set that up before we met, when he'd renovated the house he'd inherited from his great-uncle, Paul Dassin. Some of our guests thought it was a slightly peculiar arrangement, but I didn't mind having the studio at the house. It was one way I got to see my husband more often, and it also allowed him to burn off some of Ella and Nicky's energy by teaching them to dance.

After heading upstairs to brush my own teeth and grab my leather purse, I clattered back downstairs, almost tripping over Fosse, who loved to get underfoot. "Something you'd better not do when Fiona's here," I told the cat, who simply plopped down at the foot of the stairs and began nonchalantly grooming his orange-and-brown-striped fur.

"Yeah, yeah, you won't be so calm when she's shrieking at you," I said, as I pulled on my winter coat. Wrapping a scarf around my neck, I pulled on a knitted cap. I wasn't about to follow Ella's lead and rely on the scarf, even if I was driving to work today.

Checking my dashboard clock as I set off, I realized I'd actually left the house earlier than usual. Which meant I could drive the several blocks to the library slowly, admiring the holiday decorations adorning the homes along the main street. Taylorsford, founded in the early eighteenth century, was filled with historic properties that residents decorated in appropriate fashion. Most of the vintage homes, from simple, two-story wood structures with plain black shutters and stoop porches to elegant Victorians festooned with gingerbread trim, sported garlands of greenery, twinkling white lights, and crimson bows. But the oldest homes, built in the style of English cottages from the fieldstone once prevalent in the area, featured only sprays of pine or holly surrounding electric candles placed in each of their deep-silled windows.

I turned onto the narrow driveway that led to the parking lot behind the library. There were no other cars in the lot, which meant I was the first to arrive.

Entering through the staff door on the side of the building, I stepped into the workroom. I stashed my purse on one of the shelves and walked out into the staff area behind the circulation desk, pausing for a moment before turning on the lights. There was something so peaceful about the space when I was the only person in the building. Dust motes danced in the light falling from the tall windows, and the scent of aging paper and book bindings filled the air. The bookshelves stood, tall and straight as hedgerows, separating the entry area from the reading room. With all the historic details of the building lending it an air of antiquity, I could almost envision the space as my own private library at some grand estate.

This illusion was shattered with the click of a light switch. I turned to greet our only paid library assistant, Samantha Green.

She raised her black eyebrows over her dark-brown eyes. "Enjoying the solitude?"

"Well, with the twins . . ." I turned on the desk computer as Samantha switched on more of the lights.

"Say no more." Samantha, who'd raised her daughter, Shay, on her own, understood the challenges of combining children and mornings. Shay was now a senior in high school, but Samantha said that didn't necessarily make things any easier—although Samantha had been able to start working full-time at the library once Shay had started high school, which was definitely beneficial for Sunny and me. Of course, it had meant a battle with the town council to get the proper funding for Samantha's salary, but when most of our patrons supported our request, we'd finally won the day.

"I imagine Nicky and Ella are quite a handful these days," Samantha said while pulling the books returned late on Saturday from the book drop at the desk. "The holidays and the dance production"—she cast me a sympathetic smile—"well, let's say I don't envy you."

I rolled my eyes. "And you shouldn't. Oh, by the way, I wanted to let you know that Richard says Shay is doing a wonderful job with her *Nutcracker* role. He told me she could have a career in dance if she wanted, but he knows she has other plans."

"Just as well." Samantha placed the books on a reshelving cart. "Not that I'd oppose her going into dance, but we all know how tough a career like that can be." She met my nod of agreement with a wry smile. "Anyway, if she ends up becoming an elementary school teacher, as she plans, the dance training will be useful. Something she can do with the kids to burn off excess energy."

"Not a bad idea," I agreed. "Okay, if you'll finish setting up here, I'll go and check over the rest of the building"—I glanced up at the large clock that hung on one wall of the library—"and then unlock the doors."

Walking through the library, I made sure everything was in order, then collected a few books abandoned on a study table and turned on the computer workstations. I paused in the reading room to admire our tree and other decorations again before heading to the vestibule that separated our inner entry from the exterior doors.

Unlocking the front doors, I was surprised by someone bundled in a heavy hooded coat, with a scarf pulled up over their mouth and nose, rushing toward the entrance.

"Oh my goodness, it's the most awful thing!" As she yanked down the scarf, I recognized Zelda. She brushed past me, stomping her boots against the vestibule tile. Her cheeks, rosy from the cold, and the excitement sparking in her eyes belied the tragedy implied by her words. "Have you heard?"

"Heard what?" I closed the door behind Zelda, shutting out another blast of cold air.

"About the body they found at the foot of those stairs at the festival site," Zelda said. When she shoved back her hood, her curls sprang out like a halo around her face. "The steps leading down to the ice rink, I mean. Someone out jogging this morning found a body. Dead from a fall, or the cold, or both, they think."

"Whose body?" I asked, envisioning some unfortunate individual traveling through Taylorsford, lacking the money for a room, trying to find shelter near the town hall.

Zelda followed me into the library and greeted Samantha before dropping her bombshell. "The last person you'd expect," she said, obviously relishing her opportunity to share such news. "Wendy Blackstone."

Chapter Four

"What?" Samantha leaned over the desk, her dark eyes widening. "Ms. Blackstone is dead? Was it an accident?"

Zelda tugged off her gloves. "It isn't clear yet, from what I heard. They think maybe she accidentally fell down the steps and was knocked unconscious and then died from hypothermia. But rumor has it they can't rule out foul play."

"Wait a minute, when would this have happened?" I shoved my hands into my pockets to hide their trembling. *Another person dead in Taylorsford under suspicious circumstances? This can't be good,* I thought, my mind returning to the argument I'd witnessed between Wendy and Ethan.

"Last night, I guess. It must've been after the festival closed down, or people would've noticed." Zelda trailed me around the desk. That wasn't a problem—she'd been a library volunteer for years and was allowed access to staff areas. "I don't know what it means for the festival tonight, come to think of it. The area's swarming with deputies and other investigators right now."

"I guess it would be. They have to figure out what happened." I fiddled with a stack of tourist brochures on the desk. "Did you actually talk to Brad or anyone else who'd really know what was going on?"

Zelda shook her head. "Brad Tucker? I couldn't get near him. I mean, him being sheriff now, he was in the thick of things. No, I just heard stuff from people gathered on the perimeter."

"That's really sad." Samantha tugged her fingers through her short Afro. "I didn't much care for the woman, but losing your life like that is tragic, no matter what." She turned aside and grabbed a cart full of books from behind the desk. "But if you'll excuse me, I think I'll go and reshelve a few books while you two are here at the desk."

"No, that's great, thanks," I told Samantha as she rolled the cart out toward the stacks.

"It is kind of strange, though, Wendy staying until everyone, even the deputy on duty, was gone." Zelda shrugged off her coat and draped it over an empty book cart.

"She might have wanted to make sure everything was shut down properly," I said, talking to myself as much as to Zelda. "Maybe she was checking out the ice rink area and just slipped and fell. If no one else was around at that point . . ."

"That's certainly one theory." Zelda tugged off her bulky gloves. "But you can't rule out someone giving her a little push. I mean, she had words with those protesters and a few other people yesterday."

Including Ethan, I thought, taking a deep breath before speaking aloud again. "What other people? I know she confronted Jaden Perez and his group. I saw that before I left."

Zelda shoved her gloves into the pockets of her emerald wool coat. "Well, there was plenty of animosity brewing between her and Kurt. Surely you remember that."

"Oh, that." I waved one hand through the air. "I can't imagine Kurt shoving someone down a flight of steps. Not that he's an angel," I added, noticing Zelda's lips parting. "But I think if he planned to kill someone, he wouldn't do it quite so publicly."

35

"True." Zelda's curls bounced as she nodded. "I'm sure no one would ever find the body in that case." Her expression sobering, she shot me a questioning glance. "Ethan was arguing with Wendy at one point. Pretty heated, it seemed like."

"I know. I saw it." I gnawed on the inside of one cheek. "But honestly, Ethan? He's all about saving lives, not taking them."

"I agree it seems unlikely. But I imagine he'll be questioned, along with Perez and his followers."

"I suppose so." I drummed my fingers against the pitted surface of our vintage wood circulation desk. "I wonder when they'll announce the cause of death? That will clear up a lot, especially if it was accidental. Wendy could've easily fallen. That whole area along the hill looked dangerous to me."

We both turned toward the front doors as a swoosh signaled the arrival of a patron. I stared at the young man for a moment, not recognizing him as a regular. It was only after he yanked off his toboggan hat, releasing a shoulder-length fall of dark hair, that I realized who he was.

"Hello," he said, striding over to the desk. "Do you have a computer I can use? With internet access, I mean. My laptop is acting flaky, and I really need to look up some stuff."

"We have several." I motioned toward the bank of computer stations across the open space separating the circulation desk from the stacks. "They're set up for public use, so your searches are wiped at the end of the day, but you can save your results if you have a thumb drive, or you can print out pages for a minimal fee."

"That's perfect. Thanks." The young man pulled off one of his tan knit gloves and thrust his bare hand over the desk. "I'm Jaden Perez, by the way. Nice to meet you."

"Good to meet you as well. I'm Amy Muir, one of two library directors here in Taylorsford," I said, giving his hand a quick shake. "You're the leader of the environmental activists, right?"

Jaden lowered his black lashes over his chestnut-brown eyes. "Technically, I'm a coleader. Megan Campbell, who you probably saw standing next to me at the festival, and I are partners."

"The young woman with the curly hair and glasses?" I asked.

"That's her. We actually founded Environmental Advocates together."

"Ah, is that the actual name of your group? I'd heard it was something like that but wasn't sure of the exact wording." Zelda clasped Jaden's proffered hand. "My name is Zelda Shoemaker Adams. I used to run the local post office, but now I'm a library volunteer, among other things. How long are you planning on staying in Taylorsford?"

"I'm not sure," Jaden said, pulling back his hand. "Originally it was until we stopped Blackstone Properties from building their planned development, but now . . ."

Zelda gave Jaden a knowing look. "With the owner dead, it might be a moot point."

"Maybe, and maybe not." Jaden lifted his sharp chin. "Ms. Blackstone has, I mean had, a business partner. Timothy Thompson," he added, wrinkling his nose as if he'd smelled something foul. "He might push ahead regardless. And her daughter Nadia's involved in the business too, and although she's focused on sales and rentals rather than the development side, she appears to be extremely enthusiastic about all of Blackstone's current development projects. We may not be in the clear just yet."

I studied Jaden's face for a moment. If what he said was true, then killing Wendy Blackstone wouldn't have been a surefire way to stop the development. Which gave Jaden and his followers less reason to harm her. *Anyone who knew the details would realize they'd have to take out the business partner and daughter too*, I thought, with a frown. *But did all the protesters know that? More importantly, did Ethan know?*

I hated to consider the possibility that my brother-in-law could harm someone, yet I had to admit that he did have a motive. And there was the anger that had radiated off of him when he'd faced off with Wendy on Sunday . . .

I shook my head. "I'm just sorry that this terrible accident has happened, whatever the cause. I'm sure Wendy's daughter will be devastated, as well as her business partner."

"Her daughter? Possibly, although I understand their relationship has been strained lately. Not so much Tim Thompson." Jaden glanced from Zelda's openly curious expression to my more circumspect one. "There definitely wasn't a whole lot of love lost between Wendy Blackstone and Thompson, as far as I could tell. It was something we were working on—figuring out how to leverage their obvious differences." He slid his other hand free from its glove and bundled the gloves into a ball in his fist. "If you ask me, if anyone killed Wendy, Tim Thompson would be the likeliest suspect. I wouldn't put such a thing past him, anyway."

"Goodness, that's going to be a tangle for the sheriff's department to unravel," Zelda said. "Though I'm afraid they may be looking at your group as well, my dear."

Jaden swept a silky lock of black hair behind one ear. "Let them. We have nothing to hide. We're not the ones looking to destroy lives and property. We're seeking justice."

I stared at him, quirking my eyebrows. *Justice* seemed a strange word to use, but I assumed he meant justice for the earth. *Although*, I thought, *if he truly feels Wendy's death was justified, perhaps I should bump him higher on my list of suspects.* "Speaking of the protests, my friend Sunny joined your cause yesterday. A tall, slender, woman with blonde hair and blue eyes? You must've noticed her."

Jaden, who'd dropped his gaze to his feet, looked up, his eyes brightening. "Oh, yeah. Her family owns an organic farm or something. She was very nice. She even offered to house some of our out-of-town crew if the protests stretched on past the amount we'd budgeted for hotels."

"That sounds like Sunny," I said, my smile fading as I realized that my friend, as well as my brother-in-law, would undoubtedly be questioned by the investigators.

"Well, I won't keep you from your work any longer." Jaden glanced toward the bank of computers. "Do I need a password?"

"Oh, right. Sorry, my thoughts were wandering," I said, handing him a card from a small box next to the desk computer. "We rotate these daily, so you'll need a new card if you come in another time."

Jaden thanked me again and headed for the computers just as Samantha rolled her cart, now empty, back behind the desk. "Who's that?" she asked, keeping her voice low. "I don't think I've seen him here before."

"Not surprising, as he's not a local," Zelda said. "Jaden something, he said his name was."

"Perez," I said. "Jaden Perez."

"Right. Anyway, he just wants to use our computers, since his is on the fritz or something." Zelda pursed her rose-tinted lips. "You might need to troubleshoot the printer later on. It was acting up the last time I was here."

I rolled my eyes. "When isn't it?" We needed a new public printer, but the library budget, always stretched thin, didn't currently allow for such a purchase.

"He's part of the group opposing Wendy Blackstone's new development?" Samantha's dark eyes narrowed as she studied Jaden's seated figure.

"He claims he's the founder of the organization." Zelda slid closer to Samantha. "Which makes him a suspect if the death's declared a murder, doesn't it? He and the rest of the protesters. Although he implied that Wendy Blackstone's business partner might have a motive too. Seems all was not moonlight and roses between those two. Not to mention there were apparently problems in Wendy and Nadia Blackstone's mother-daughter relationship." Zelda bounced up and down on the balls of her feet. "It's all very soap opera–ish, don't you think?"

"I heard there were also issues with her son . . ." Samantha tightened her lips as Zelda's eyes widened. "I really shouldn't say too much. It's just that Cicely Blackstone, Wendy's niece, is Shay's tennis coach."

"Former mayor Bob Blackstone's daughter?" I mentally adjusted my image of Cicely, who'd been a teen when I'd last seen her. "What is she now? In her twenties, I guess."

"Twenty-three, I believe. The same age as her first cousin Dylan, who's Wendy's son." Samantha shot a quick glance at Jaden, who appeared to be totally engrossed in whatever he was viewing on the computer screen. "Anyway, Cicely was talking to Shay about the holidays and family and all that, and she mentioned something about being sad that her cousin was estranged from his mom, because she was hoping she could see him over Christmas."

"Why is Dylan estranged from Wendy?" I asked.

"I think it has something to do with him rejecting any participation in the family business," Samantha said. "He's apparently repeatedly rejected his mom's offer to join the company."

"Interesting," I said, holding up a finger as the doors swung open and two of our regular patrons—Lisa and Damaris, young moms pushing toddlers in strollers—entered the library.

"Well, I should actually do some work, I guess." Zelda shrugged when I cast her a questioning look. "I know it's not my regular volunteer hours, but I don't mind doing something to help out, since I'm already here."

"If you wouldn't mind shelving this other cart of books, that would be great," Samantha said. "Then I can head back to the children's room. Lisa and Damaris might need some help." She caught my eye and smiled. "That leaves you at the desk, where you can assist our visitor on the computer, if necessary."

"Good thinking," I said.

A few minutes later, when Samantha and Zelda had both left, Jaden Perez approached. His expression appeared troubled as he slid the password card across the desk. "Thanks," he said.

"I hope you found the information you wanted."

"Wanted? Maybe not. But I found what I needed," Jaden replied. Slapping his gloves against one palm, he studied my face for a moment, his expression unreadable. "I probably shouldn't ask this, but what do you think of our cause?"

"Stopping the development? I'm all for it," I said without thinking. "I mean, that's my opinion as a private citizen. Don't take it as an endorsement from the library, please."

"I understand. You have to answer to others, I guess."

"The mayor and the town council," I said, offering him a faint smile. "I can't really speak for them, not in my professional capacity."

"That's okay. It's why I'm here. And my compatriots, of course." Jaden turned and strode toward the exit, calling over his shoulder, "To speak for those who can't."

Chapter Five

Knowing it was best to have our tree up and decorated before Fiona's arrival, Richard and I decided to take advantage of a rare span of free time on Tuesday afternoon. I had the day off from the library and Richard didn't have rehearsals until the evening, so after we collected the twins from kindergarten, we headed to Vista View, the organic farm Sunny ran with her grandparents.

The Field family didn't open up their property as a public Christmas tree farm, but for the past few years Sunny had invited a few friends to come out and cut a tree from one of their stands of pines.

"Aunt Lydia and Hugh are meeting us there," I told Richard as we strapped Ella and Nicky into their booster seats. "They thought it best to take two cars, since we need two trees."

"Not much space in here in any case," Richard said as we climbed into the front seats of our silver sedan. Although it was larger than Richard's old compact car, accommodating two children in appropriate booster seats left little room for passengers.

"Are we getting the biggest tree we can find?" Nicky asked, his tone radiating hope.

"No, we are not," Richard replied, with a glance in the rearview mirror. "Our living room has nine-foot ceilings, so how big to you think the tree can really be?"

I turned my head to capture Nicky's serious expression. It was clear he was puzzling out the answer to this question.

"Eight feet!" Ella kicked the heels of her boots against the lower portion of the seat.

"No, 'cause we need room for the star on top," Nicky said. "And the thing that holds the tree up."

"The tree stand." Ella reached across to tap the edge of Nicky's booster seat. "We just bought a new one with Mommy, remember?"

"So maybe seven feet?" Nicky scrunched up his face in concentration. "Or six."

"I think six is best." Richard cast a quick smile toward the back seat. "We don't want to have any problems getting the tree set up, now do we?"

Turning to face the windshield, I gave him a sidelong look. "Please, no. I remember that one year . . ."

"Which is why nothing taller than six feet," Richard said firmly. "Now, what music shall we listen to? Christmas carols?"

"*Nutcracker!*" shouted Ella and Nicky in unison.

I groaned, earning a grin and sympathetic pat on my knee from my husband. I'd listened to Tchaikovsky's *Nutcracker Suite* so many times over the last few months that I swore I could hum the entire score. But, knowing it was useless to complain, I reluctantly pulled up the requested music on the cell phone plugged into the car's stereo system.

We drove out of town enveloped in the soaring score, punctuated by the staccato chatter of the twins explaining every scene represented by the music. Richard shot me a few wry smiles as Ella corrected Nicky's descriptions of specific dance moves.

"You haven't been paying attention," she said, as Richard turned into the gravel driveway marked by a sign Sunny had painted several years back—black text declaring the property to be *Vista View*, accented by a brightly colored graphic of a cornucopia filled with vegetables and fruit. "He hasn't, has he, Daddy?"

"Let's not get too bossy, Ella," Richard said, in the mild tone used to try to defuse our children's bickering. "I think he knows the steps, even if his terminology may not always be exactly right."

Ella humphed and crossed her arms over her chest. "I know the right words."

I glanced back at her. Bundled up in her puffy sapphire coat, with her dark brows drawn in over her clear gray eyes, she resembled a disgruntled bluebird. I stifled a laugh. "Which is something to be proud of," I said, "but not a good reason to pick on your brother."

Turning back around just as Nicky stuck his tongue out at his sister, I focused on the brilliant green of the winter wheat planted in a field on my left and the meadow of sheared orchard grass on my right. Sunny and her grandparents didn't believe in raising animals for meat, so they didn't use much of the hay they baled from their fields. That allowed them to make a profit selling it to area horse farms, supplementing the income they received from sales of eggs and organic fruits and vegetables.

Richard parked our car in a small gravel lot, near a battered farm truck and Sunny's iridescent-blue Volkswagen, the last in a long line of brightly hued Beetles she'd owned over the years. A small, older-model compact car with dings in its silver paint and a four-door heavy-duty truck sat on either side of Sunny's car. The truck looked new, despite the dried mud caked on its wide tires. "I don't recognize the silver car or the larger truck," I said as I climbed out of our sedan. "Sunny never said anything about buying any new vehicles."

"Must be other visitors," Richard replied.

Removing the twins from the car was always an easier task when there were two pairs of hands involved. As we set the children down on a patch of brown grass next to the car, I shaded my eyes and surveyed my friend's family home. The Fieldses' two-story farmhouse was a square box of a house, its simple wooden-siding facade enlivened by vivid yellow paint and delft-blue shutters. Sunny, despite threats of turning the house into a Victorian "painted lady," had ultimately decided to retain the original color scheme when she'd recently had it repainted.

"Don't stomp on my foot," Ella said as Nicky, a little clumsy in his heavy coat, bumped into her.

Nicky leapt to one side, rubbing his mittened hand under his nose. "I'm not, dookie head."

"Yes, you were. And you're a booger boy," Ella tossed back.

"No name-calling," Richard said, his genial expression turning stern. "Look, there's Aunt Lydia and Hugh. Do you want them to catch you quarrelling?"

Ella's eyes widened, and she shook her head so vigorously that her ivory knit hat slipped back. The action created enough static that strands of her dark-brown hair rose up from her head for a moment, like chocolate spun sugar. "Not Aunt Lydia, for sure."

Richard winked at me over the heads of the twins. We both knew that despite my aunt's love for her grand-niece and -nephew, she brooked no nonsense from them.

Or anyone, I thought, as we each held a child's hand and walked across the parking lot to join Aunt Lydia and Hugh at the edge of the farmhouse's lawn.

"Hello there," Hugh said, his dark eyes sparkling in his narrow face. "Ready to pick out a tree?"

He was dressed in a tailored chocolate-brown coat that reached the knees of his sand-colored wool trousers. A flat cap in shades of tan, rust, and brown covered much of his short black hair. Next to him, my aunt was the template of winter-wear elegance in her slim, black wool coat over charcoal slacks and a pearl-gray turtleneck, set off by a vivid ruby scarf, hat, and gloves. "Good heavens, I think I should've made more of an effort," I said, motioning toward my worn blue jeans.

"Don't be silly." Aunt Lydia's eyes glittered like aquamarine gemstones. "We just came from that luncheon I told you about."

I slapped my forehead with my knitted glove. I'd forgotten about the event, which was to honor Hugh's work with the National Gallery. An art expert, he'd often aided their efforts to authenticate works, exposing numerous frauds in the process. *And not just at the National Gallery*, I reminded myself, *but all around the world.*

"We didn't have time to change." Hugh pressed his kidskin-gloved palms together. "We didn't want to miss our outing with you, so we drove straight here from DC."

"Okay, that makes me feel a little better," I said, adjusting the emerald velour scarf I'd tucked into the neck of my well-worn navy peacoat.

Ella tugged on my hand. "Come on, Mommy, let's find our tree. A six-foot tree," she added, gazing up at Aunt Lydia and Hugh. "Daddy says it can't be any bigger."

"Really?" Hugh shared a look with Richard. "Wise man. Lydia is requesting a much taller tree, I'm afraid."

Aunt Lydia lifted her chin. "Because my home has such high ceilings, of course."

"That makes sense, although I don't envy you trying to transport it." Richard looked down at the twins with a grin. "See, you can have your very tall tree. Just at Aunt Lydia's house instead of ours."

Ella bounced on the balls of her feet. "Can we help you decorate it?"

"Please, please, please?" added Nicky, his dark eyes shining.

"Of course," my aunt said, her reserve melting in the face of Ella and Nicky's obvious excitement. "I was counting on it."

"Hello, hello," called out an older woman from the porch of the farmhouse. Sunny's grandmother, Carol, had Sunny's fair complexion, light hair, and blue eyes, but not her height or slender figure. Sunny had inherited those traits from her grandfather, P.J. "Sunny will join you in just a minute. She's out in the big barn, grabbing an axe."

"Am I chopping down the tree?" Hugh's fine black eyebrows rose to the fringe of dark hair brushing his forehead. "I don't think I'm dressed for that."

"Don't worry, I'll take care of the chopping," Richard said, with an exaggerated flex of his arms. "I've got to show off my manly skills sometimes, you know."

Aunt Lydia's golden lashes fluttered. "We don't want you hurting yourself before the upcoming performances," she said, her thin lips quirking into a smile.

A memory surfaced of my husband using a similar tool to help rescue us in a dangerous situation several years before. "Oh, don't worry. Richard definitely can handle an axe."

Richard shot me a grin.

Looking over our group, Carol nudged P.J., who'd joined her on the porch. "Why don't you take Lydia and Hugh to that little grove of pines behind the house, dear. It isn't so hard to get to, and that cluster could use a thinning out. I mean, one tree cut down would be a benefit, don't you think? You can help them tag a tree that Richard or someone else can cut down later."

"All right, all right." Sunny's tall, lanky grandfather, who towered over his wife, bent down to kiss the top of her head.

"And everyone—please come in for some hot chocolate and cookies when you're done," Carol said, before heading into the house.

"Cookies?" Nicky sprang forward.

I grabbed the hood of his coat and pulled him back. "Tree first, cookies later."

P.J. stepped off the porch. "Okay, Lydia and Hugh, follow me," he said, striding toward the side of the house. Hugh and Aunt Lydia followed more slowly, picking their way over rough clumps of frozen grass.

When they'd disappeared from view, Richard cast me a smile. "I guess it's me doing the chopping after all."

"Don't worry," a familiar voice called out from a path leading to one of the farm's barns. "I brought reinforcements."

Sunny walked toward us, looking every inch the farmgirl in her padded denim jacket, worn jeans, and heavy boots. Following her, a man whose short blond hair remained uncovered despite the cold carried an axe in a manner that told me he was more than accustomed to using one.

"So you're providing tree-cutting services now, Brad?" Richard asked. "I didn't know that was part of the sheriff's duties."

The color rose in Bradley Tucker's ruggedly handsome face. *He always was easily embarrassed*, I thought. I'd known Bradley Tucker ever since moving to Taylorsford ten years before, when he'd been the chief deputy in the sheriff's department. We'd become friends, and I'd been happy to help him and his department solve several murders. But now Brad was the newly elected sheriff, and from his troubled expression, I feared that our partnership might not prevail during this particular case. He looked like someone mulling over delivering bad news.

"Not exactly," Brad replied, his pale lashes shadowing his blue-eyed gaze. "Sunny offered us a tree, and I just stopped by to pick one up while Alison and the kids are busy at home, putting up other decorations."

I glanced at Sunny, who gave me a wink. I smiled back at her. It had always impressed me how Sunny could remain casual friends with Brad, whom she'd once seriously dated. Of course, now she was in a long-term relationship with Fred, and Brad was married with children.

Which was one of the reasons Brad and Sunny broke up, I reminded myself. Brad, who was now almost fifty, had wanted kids, sooner rather than later, while Sunny didn't want children at all.

"How are Noah and Zoe?" I asked. "They haven't caught that cold going around, I hope."

"Thankfully, no." Brad shuffled his booted feet through the gravel of the parking area. "I would've brought Noah along if I'd known Ella and Nicky would be here. Zoe, of course, is far too young to be tromping through the woods."

I looked him up and down, observing how he kept fiddling with one of the buttons on his padded flannel jacket. "If you have something you want to share, go ahead and say it. Might as well get bad news out of the way before we swing axes at anything."

"Aren't we going to get the tree?" Ella asked, tugging on the sleeve of Richard's heavy fleece jacket.

Richard cast me a swift glance. "Maybe I should take the kids on out to the lot," he said. "Can you lead the way, Sunny? I don't want to chop down the wrong tree."

"Sure thing." Sunny took the axe from Brad. "You guys thoroughly eviscerate the elephant in the room and then follow us. It's just over that ridge," she added, pointing with the business end of the axe toward a stand of pines poking their shaggy green heads above the rim of a nearby hill.

She strode off, her long blonde braids bouncing against her shoulders. After sharing another knowing look with me, Richard took hold of Ella and Nicky's hands and followed her, leaving me alone with Brad.

"So, as Sunny suggested, maybe we should get the unpleasant stuff out of the way," I said. "Do you have any more information on the Wendy Blackstone case? I mean, anything you can share, of course."

Brad toyed with the button again. "Well, I'm sorry to tell you this, Amy, but we've declared the Wendy Blackstone case a homicide. There's evidence of deliberate action taken by someone other than the victim." He shoved his hands into the pockets of his jacket and rocked back on the heels of his cowboy boots. "This is all coming out at a news conference this evening, so it's not really a secret."

As a deeply inhaled breath of the frosty air burnt my lungs, I coughed and cleared my throat. "And do you have any suspects?" I asked when I could speak.

"A few." The lines bracketing Brad's mouth deepened as he stared down at me. "Including Ethan Payne, of course."

Chapter Six

"You can't really believe Ethan would kill anyone," I said. "I know for a fact that he's risked his life several times to save others. He's not a murderer."

"Saving lives in the context of doing his job isn't any indicator of the capacity to kill in other circumstances." Brad pulled his hands out of his pockets and wagged a finger at me. "After the many times you've helped me with research and informal interviews, you of all people should know that even the least likely person can commit a murder."

I crossed my arms over my chest. "Point taken, but still . . . why is Ethan a top suspect when other people had a grudge against Wendy Blackstone as well?"

"Did I say he was a top suspect?" Mirroring my action, Brad crossed his own arms. "He is being questioned, but so are Jaden Perez and all of the protesters, as well as Ms. Blackstone's family and business associates."

A clang of metal against wood rang out over the nearby field. "I guess they found a tree."

"Seems like it." Brad dropped his arms, shaking the tension from his hands. "But seriously, Amy, I'm not targeting your brother-in-law in particular. It's just that he was seen arguing with the victim on the day she was killed and had some semblance of motive." When I raised my eyebrows, Brad added, "All right, to be perfectly honest, we've discovered he's sent some rather angry emails to Blackstone Properties related to their proposed development's encroachment on his property. Not to mention the fact that it seems he was one of the last people to leave the Winterfest grounds before Ms. Blackstone was killed."

I hadn't known that. "According to whom?"

"Jaden Perez, for one. As well as his partner, Megan Campbell. They apparently hung around until all the visitors and vendors left, gathering up any of their flyers that had been tossed. They say that Ethan was still around while they were clearing up that litter."

My grip tightened on my upper arms. "Of course, they could simply be saying that to cover their own suspicious actions."

"I did think of that," Brad said, his tone sharp as the sound of the axe. "But Ethan confirmed their stories. He said he waited until all the vendors left to double-check that all the propane stoves and grills and so on were completely cool."

"Which is part of his job." The ringing blows of the axe faded away. I knew I should wrap up this discussion. Richard, Sunny, and the children would be back soon.

"Yes, but it means he was on the site later than most. Perez and Campbell and a couple of their followers claim he was still there when they left."

I dropped my arms, shaking them out to relieve the tension. "Which I hope you took with a grain of salt."

"Of course. Despite what you may think, I'm not an idiot." Color had risen in Brad's face again. "Jaden Perez has to be one of our top suspects, if only because I've discovered that he's been involved in a similar altercation before. Apparently, he got in a shoving match with someone during another protest. His opponent injured his knee when he was knocked to the ground by Perez. The only reason it didn't result in an arrest is that the injured man didn't press charges, and numerous bystanders claimed both men were equally culpable in the fight. But of course, that means Perez has past history that will compel my team to look at him very closely. Not to mention we plan to interview everyone who could possibly have been involved—even people who weren't seen in the area that day. It's certainly possible that someone could've entered the picnic area from another direction."

"Because it's backed by a pretty significant stand of trees," I said, more to myself than to Brad.

He nodded. "I've had deputies searching the woods for any clues." Brad's taut face relaxed into a more genial expression. "You have to realize that I'm only telling you all of this because you've helped out the sheriff's office in the past, Amy. Normally, I wouldn't share this much information with a civilian."

Footsteps and the high-pitched voices of excited children filled the air. I glanced over to see Sunny leading the twins, following by Richard dragging a newly cut pine by its trunk. "Thanks, I guess," I muttered, not quite ready to let go of my grievance.

Brad's lips twitched. "It's only natural to be protective of family, but just let us do our job, okay? I promise not to jump to conclusions."

"All right, it's a deal," I said, extending my hand.

Brad's calloused fingers snagged the thick wool of my gloves as he gave my fingers a reassuring squeeze.

"Making a pact to remain friends?" Sunny asked as she approached us.

The twins dashed in front of her. "You missed it, Mommy!" Ella said, flinging her body at my legs. "Daddy did great with the chopping."

Nicky hung back, waving his hand toward the tree, which, while not overly tall, was certainly full and lush. "We got the best one! Even Sunny said so."

"It does look nice," I said, my arm draped around Ella's shoulders to keep her in step with me as I moved away from Brad.

"Well, now that you got the best tree, what's left for me?" Brad asked, his tone light.

"Don't worry, there are plenty more." Richard paused, dropping the tree for a moment to wipe his brow with his gloved hand, freeing the strands of dark hair plastered to his forehead. "You actually might want to choose one with a slightly smaller trunk—unless you enjoy swinging an axe, that is."

Brad offered Richard an understanding smile. "I don't mind it. Although, unlike you, I won't have any help."

"Help? Oh, right." Richard shot me a raised-eyebrow glance over the heads of the twins.

"We saw a spooky building too, didn't we, Daddy?" Ella looked up at him with a wide-eyed gaze.

"It was some sort of old barn," Richard said.

"Part of the old Wire family farm," Sunny said, after I cast her a questioning look. "You remember, Amy—old Mrs. Wire didn't have any family when she passed, so she deeded the farm over to the Nature Conservancy. They haven't had time to do anything with the land yet, but at least it's protected. Anyway, the original barn is right on the edge of our property, so you can see it now that the trees are bare. But no checking it out when you're running around Vista View." Sunny gave first Ella and then Nicky a stern look. "That's a place you want to stay away from. It hasn't been used in years, and who knows what wild creatures are living inside, not to mention how unstable the ceiling and floors might be."

"We just thought it looked cool," Nicky said. "We won't ever go inside, I promise."

"Good. Because I kind of like you guys." Sunny grinned at the twins, who smiled back. "Now, here you go, Brad. Have at it. Anything in the lot just over the hill is fair game," she added, as Brad took the axe from her hand. "Meanwhile, why don't the rest of us head to the house for some of that hot chocolate and cookies?"

The twins didn't have to be asked twice. They took off at a run, turning their dash to the house into a race. "I won!" Ella shouted as they reached the porch.

"No, you didn't. I got here at the same time," Nicky said, elbowing his sister.

Carol, who must've heard the ruckus, opened the front door. "Come on in," she said, ushering my children inside. "P.J. and Lydia and Hugh are already in the kitchen. We can watch them while you get the tree secured," she called out to the rest of us. "And Brad, Lydia's tree is out back, marked with a red ribbon."

Brad lifted the axe in a little salute. "I'll take care of that first," he said, before heading toward the path that led around the house.

"So let's get this done," Sunny said as Richard dragged the tree close to our car. "I could use some of that hot chocolate myself. Honestly, I'm getting awfully tired of working the farm during this cold snap."

"I bet," I said, joining them at the car. "It has been a record-breaking span of days. I can't remember the last time it was so cold in December."

"Years ago, according to the weather reports." Sunny stared at the tree. "You brought rope or bungee cords or something, I hope?"

"In the trunk." Richard fished his keys out of the pocket of his jeans and hit the button that opened the lock. "If you can grab those straps, Amy, I think Sunny and I can lift the tree up onto the roof rack."

"I can help with that too," I said, jogging over to the trunk.

Richard hoisted the trunk end of the tree while Sunny lifted the crown. "You're a little too short, sweetheart," he said.

I opened my mouth but snapped it shut again when I realized he was right. Grabbing the bungee cords, I draped several over Richard's bent arm.

"Thanks," he said, "but it might be better if you took them to Sunny. Tell her to attach the ends on her side and then fling the cords over the tree. I'll pull them tight on this side."

I took back the ties and carried them around the car. "Richard says—"

Sunny took the cords from my hands. "I heard. Maybe step back, Amy. I don't want one of these things to pop loose and fly off. It could hit you."

"What about you and Richard?" I asked, moving out of the way.

Sunny cast me a grin. "We have good reflexes."

"Oh, and I don't?" I made a face at her but didn't step any closer. Her statement might sting my pride, but it wasn't wrong.

The clang of the axe rang out from around the back of the farmhouse, accompanying a few grunts and several strings of swear words as Richard and Sunny wrestled the tree into submission.

When it was finally firmly anchored, Brad appeared, dragging a tall pine tree.

"I suppose we should help him secure that to Lydia's car," Richard said, brushing the needles from his coat.

Sunny tossed her braids over her shoulder. "I'll do that. You go on inside. No, don't protest," she added, as Richard made a disapproving noise. "You don't want to get too worn out before your rehearsal this evening."

"Well, if you put it that way." Richard shot her a grateful smile. "I saw that Lydia has some rope. It's in the back seat. Her car's unlocked, of course."

I grinned. We had a running argument with my aunt about her tendency to leave her vehicle unlocked, even in locations more risky than the parking lot at Vista View.

"We'll take care of it," Brad said, pulling the tree next to Aunt Lydia's car. "Like Sunny said, you don't want to overdo it when you have to direct as well as dance tonight, Richard."

"Well, since I'm playing Drosselmeyer, the dancing isn't too overwhelming. But corralling all the other dancers, especially the children . . ." Richard grinned. "That's another story."

"I bet," Brad said. His six-year-old son, Noah, was participating in the production, so I was sure he'd heard plenty about it.

"Fortunately, I have my stalwart partner by my side, or it truly would be chaos."

"Is Karla performing too?" Sunny asked. "I know you're mostly trying to use dancers from your college and studio classes, but I thought maybe, like you, she'd be doing some smaller part."

"Mother Ginger," Richard said. "It's a slightly different take on the role. I think you'll enjoy it. Of course, the entire production is somewhat different, since we've choreographed it for contemporary rather than ballet dancers."

"Can't wait to see it," Sunny said, glancing toward Brad. He nodded but didn't chime in.

Probably isn't as thrilled, I thought with a smile. But of course, he'd be in the audience, especially with his son onstage for a few scenes.

"All right, let's head inside. The twins will be hyped up on sugar by now. We might need to rescue the older folks."

"A solid plan," Richard said, lifting one foot and then the other to examine the soles of his shoes. "Thought I'd better check for mud before I headed inside, but I guess one advantage to this frigid weather is that even the dirt is frozen."

We wished Sunny and Brad good luck with Aunt Lydia's tree and strolled to the porch. "Funny how well they get along after Sunny basically dumped him," I said.

"You know Sunny. She never holds a grudge and won't allow anyone else to do so either." Richard held the front door open for me. "After you, madame."

"Thank you, kind sir," I replied, leaning back into him for a moment after the door closed behind us. I glanced down the entry hall of the farmhouse, the lower half of which was paneled in pale-yellow beadboard. The walls above the wainscoting were painted sky blue and included a long row of hooks hung with coats, hats, and other outdoor clothing, while the staircase that hugged one wall had a white balustrade and worn wooden treads.

A shriek pierced the rumble of low voices rolling out from the kitchen. I knew that had to be either Ella or Nicky.

Richard wrapped his arms around me and kissed my neck where my scarf had fallen down and exposed my bare skin. "Maybe we should wait a minute or two? Just to give the kids' sugar high time to start to fade."

"Ha-ha, like that will happen until we remove them from the vicinity of cookies." I turned in his arms and looked up into his face. "But if you wanted to kiss me again before we head into the kitchen, I wouldn't complain."

"I should hope not," Richard said, before complying, quite thoroughly, with my request.

"Oh, I'm sorry. Excuse me," said a voice from the stairs.

Richard and I broke apart. We turned in unison to look up at the young woman standing on a middle step.

I immediately recognized her. Her fluffy mane of rose-gold hair and blue glasses were unmistakable. "Hello, Ms. Campbell," I said. "What are you doing here?"

"I'm staying here for a little while." Megan descended the stairs slowly, her gloved hand gripping the rail. She was dressed to go outside in a down coat and winter boots. "Didn't Sunny tell you? She said you're close friends."

"No, she hadn't shared that news yet." I cast Richard a swift glance. "I'm Amy Muir, as you probably already know. This is my husband, Richard."

Megan reached the bottom of the stairs. "Nice to meet you," she said in a tone that made me question the truthfulness of her statement. She pressed her palm against the rounded newel post. "You're the dancer," she added, looking Richard over. "I've seen you on YouTube and TV. But you seem a little older than I expected."

Richard slipped his arm around my waist. "You saw earlier productions, I expect. I don't do a lot of professional performing these days, unless it's for charity. I'm focused on choreography and teaching now."

"Sorry, I didn't mean to be rude." Megan pressed her fingers to her lips for a second. "Sometimes I just blurt out what I'm thinking. It's a bad habit."

"No harm done. We all get older," Richard said, his tone bright.

Glancing up at his face, I noticed that his lips were thinned. While Richard wasn't overly concerned about being over forty, I knew he still mourned the loss of his peak performance ability—not from vanity, but because he enjoyed dancing so much.

"So you're staying here as a guest?" I asked Megan.

"Yeah. Sunny told the out-of-town protesters that she'd be willing to house a few of us at her family farm. I was the only one to take her up on it." Megan shoved her glasses up to the bridge of her nose. "I didn't see the point in paying for a motel room when I had another option."

"Smart," Richard said, just as another squeal of laughter rolled out of the kitchen. "But if you'll excuse us, we need to go and wrangle a couple of overexcited children." He dropped his arm from my waist and motioned toward the end of the hall.

"Those are your kids?" Megan asked, meeting my gaze. "They're cute."

"And now hyped up on sugar," I said, giving her a smile. "Nice to officially meet you, Megan. I saw you the other day at Winterfest, but of course we weren't introduced."

Megan stared down at her feet. "I was working. Environmental Advocates is my job, not just a side gig."

"Yes, I know. Anyway, good luck with everything," I said, before following Richard down the hall.

As we entered the warm, sunny room, I was struck by two things—the fact that Aunt Lydia and Hugh were seated at the yellow Formica-topped table next to the twins, and that each of my children was gripping a large sugar cookie.

"And just how many cookies have you eaten?" I asked them, my lips quirking at the sight of the smears of chocolate and marshmallow streaking their upper lips.

"First one," Ella said, waving the cookie through the air.

"Uh-huh, why don't I believe that?" Richard asked. He turned his gaze onto Aunt Lydia and Hugh. "How many?"

"Three since I've been sitting here," my aunt said. "I don't know how many before that."

"Oh, pishposh, who keeps count? Especially during the holidays." Carol bustled over from the stove, gripping a steaming mug of cocoa in each hand. "Now sit down and warm yourselves up." She set the mugs down on the table across from my aunt, Hugh, and the twins. "P.J., pull up some more chairs."

P.J. muttered something under his breath but dragged a couple of folding metal chairs over to the table. Richard and I thanked him as we sat down.

I shrugged off my coat, hanging it on the back of the chair, and slipped off my gloves before taking a seat. "Now what's this I hear about Vista View being turned into a B and B for a few weeks?" Wrapping my hands around the mug, I enjoyed the warmth seeping into my fingers. "We met Ms. Campbell out in the hall," I added when Aunt Lydia raised her eyebrows at me.

"Oh, Sunny's just trying to do her bit to help keep that horrible company from building a subdivision on the mountain," Carol said, laying a fresh platter of cookies on the table.

Richard grabbed one. "To be polite," he murmured.

Inhaling the spicy scent of cinnamon and the tang of lemon rising from the plate, I picked up a cookie as well. "Why a horrible company? I mean, I don't like what they're doing either, but I don't think they're criminals or anything."

P.J., who was leaning back against the pantry door, his thumbs hooked around the straps of his loose overalls, snorted. "Blackstone Properties? Well, I've heard some tales, let me tell you. Horrible is a perfect word."

"What do you mean?" Aunt Lydia asked, grabbing the back of Nicky's pants and pulling him into his seat as he leaned his entire torso across the table, reaching for the cookies.

"Yes, spill the dirt," I said, pulling the platter closer to my edge of the table. "Quick, before Brad shows up."

"He's not coming in." Sunny appeared in the doorway. Stripping off her coat and gloves, she tossed them on top of a small cabinet.

"We got your tree secured on your car rack," she told Aunt Lydia and Hugh as she crossed to the stove. "And then Brad said he was going to cut his own tree and load it up in his truck and just head home. I think he was worried about taking too much time away from the office."

"I'll have to call and thank him later, then." Aunt Lydia turned to Ella. "If you're done with that cocoa, please wipe your mouth. You too," she added, speaking to Nicky.

Sunny poured herself a mug of hot chocolate. "Anyway, Granddad already told me all about Blackstone Properties. That's one reason I was so eager to help Jaden and Megan and their cause." She turned, leaning back against the edge of the counter, and surveyed us. "The company seems to have no problem overriding the rights of regular people to build their fancy developments, right, Granddad?"

P.J. nodded. "They pay off planning boards and bribe inspectors is what I've heard. I don't have any details, but it's common knowledge in the farming community. And if someone doesn't want to sell their property, they don't hesitate to play hardball."

"I can see where that could make them enemies." I set down my mug and straightened in my chair. "Which means there could be plenty more people out there who'd have wanted Wendy dead."

"Who's dead?" Ella, lifted her drooping head to stare at me. "Somebody died, Mommy?"

Richard nudged my foot under the table. "Yes, but no one you know," I told my daughter, hoping to head off any more questions.

"Did they get shot?" Nicky's brown eyes widened.

"No, they did not. Now, enough talk about people dying," Richard said, sending me a warning look. "It's time we headed home anyway. We need to set up the tree before we go to rehearsal this evening."

"Are we going to decorate it too?" Ella asked, clapping her crumb-covered hands.

At least the topic of dead people had been abandoned. I shook my head. "Not today. We'll just get it in the stand and make sure it's ready to decorate another day."

Ella's lower lip rolled into a pout.

"All right," I said, pushing back my chair and rising to my feet. "Let's get your coats and gloves and all that. And thank Ms. Fields for the goodies."

"Thank you!" the twins called out in unison.

"You're quite welcome," Carol said. "Maybe some cookies to take home?"

I waved my hands. "No, no. They're delicious, but we have enough sweets at home."

This time, both my children pouted. Ignoring this with all the haughtiness she could muster, my aunt joined Hugh in collecting the twins' coats and hats and helped Richard get them ready for the outdoors, while I crossed to Sunny and thanked her for offering up the tree.

"It's nothing," she said. "I mean, why wouldn't I do that for my godchildren? I know I share the honor of godmother with Karla, but I do take it seriously."

"You spoil them rotten," I said as I gave her a quick hug.

"Well, she loves them. No one can doubt that." Carol tapped her finger on her apron, right above her heart. "Sure you don't want some of your own, Sunny girl?"

"Nope." Sunny motioned toward the kids, who were fussing about having to wear scarves and hats. She wrinkled her nose. "These two are perfect. I can spoil them and then give them right back."

Chapter Seven

I was glad I was scheduled to work at the library on Wednesday. I wanted to find out more about Wendy Blackstone and her development company and knew I'd probably have time to do a little sleuthing through digital resources while covering the circulation desk.

After an influx of patrons returning and checking out books earlier in the day, there was a lull in the early afternoon. While Samantha took her lunch break and our volunteer Denise shelved books, I took the opportunity to commandeer the desk computer.

I'd already spent the morning thinking through the problem. I knew that was a necessary first step, because there were so many resources available and numerous ways to tackle any specific research question. If I didn't want to waste time, I had to narrow down my research path before I began.

My initial search pulled up the website for Blackstone Properties. Not only would that give me a better sense of the company, it would probably also list past and current projects.

The website was slick and dynamic, the kind that cost a good chunk of change to develop and maintain. There were biographies—glowing, of course—of all the principal players, including Wendy,

Timothy Thompson, and Wendy's daughter, Nadia. Reading through background information, I realized that the company had actually been founded by Wendy's husband, Roger, who'd been the older brother of Taylorsford's former mayor, Bob Blackstone. But he seemed to have died young.

Leaving the website open, I clicked on another tab to search out more details on Roger Blackstone's death. "That's really tragic," I said aloud.

Samantha, returning from her lunch break, peeked over my shoulder. "What's that?"

"Just a little personal research."

"You're doing some digging to help Ethan?" Samantha met my wide-eyed gaze with a smile. "Not too hard to figure out. I've worked with you for a while now. I expected you to use your research skills to figure out more details about Wendy and determine who else could possibly be a suspect in the case."

"I haven't gotten quite that far," I replied, sliding over so Samantha could stand next to me. "Just looking at some background info now. On the company, mainly. One thing I've discovered is that Wendy experienced a tragic loss when her children were pretty young. Apparently Wendy's husband, Roger, was an amateur pilot. He died at thirty-nine when he crashed his Cessna while flying solo over the Blue Ridge Mountains."

"That is sad." Samantha peered at the digitized article still filling the screen. "His daughter was ten and his son only four at the time."

"Yeah." I closed that tab, revealing the Blackstone Properties website. "Now the daughter, Nadia, is twenty-nine. And, like you mentioned before, she works for the family business." I clicked on her biography. "She doesn't resemble Wendy at all, does she?"

"No, she must take after her dad. The Blackstones do tend to have dark hair and eyes. I wonder if the son looks more like his mom. He isn't listed on the website, of course."

I studied Nadia Blackstone's photo. She possessed the coiffed hair and blindingly white, perfectly straight teeth all real estate professionals seemed to have. Staring into her dark eyes, I wondered if her conflict with her mother could've led to murder. *It wouldn't be the first time family issues caused such a tragedy*, I thought, before looking up at Samantha. "You said Dylan was estranged from the family and rejected joining the business. Do you know what career he pursued instead?"

Samantha shook her head. "I think he just graduated from college a year or so ago. He's still in his early twenties. Cicely said something about him living in Maryland, but she didn't mention what he was doing now."

"I guess the sheriff's department will talk with him. At least," I said, clicking another link on the website, "I hope so."

"Being estranged doesn't mean you'd kill a parent." Samantha slid her forefinger along the top of the desk as she stepped away from the computer. "I haven't spoken to my dad in years, but I don't have any desire to harm him."

"I know, I know. I'm not saying he should be a suspect," I said, although I was still keeping him on my personal list. "But he might know some of the family secrets. Things others wouldn't want to share." Staring at the screen again, I examined the list of past projects. There were several subdivisions closer to DC but also one resort community in the mountains. It was still in Virginia, but farther south. I tapped the link.

The before and after photos of the project were quite startling. Apparently, Blackstone Properties had acquired a large piece of property, including a sparsely populated valley, in the mountains. They'd subsequently flooded the valley to create a lake. Luxury homes, cabins, and condos had been built on the hills rising above the lake, giving homeowners gorgeous views of the water. There was also a clubhouse and several other amenities.

I whistled. "Wow, I bet that cost a pretty penny. Crystal Lake," I added, when Samantha shot me a raised-eyebrow glance.

"I've been there. Shay and I stayed at a rental cabin with some friends a few years back. It's nice but very pricey. The restaurants and general store on-site overcharge for everything."

"Why doesn't that surprise me?" I said as I clicked through the glossy photos. "I wonder what happened to the people who lived there? I mean, those who had homes in the valley before it was flooded. It says the area was sparsely populated, but that doesn't mean no one lived there."

"I guess they were probably paid very well for their property and moved out," Samantha said, as the entry doors swung open and a bevy of moms and dads entered, toddlers in tow. "Looks like we'll have a good crowd for story hour. I was going to read *The Polar Express*. Is that okay?"

"Sure, sounds great," I said. Samantha, Sunny, and I took turns reading books for our weekday story times. I was glad today was Samantha's turn. It gave me a little more time for research.

Which isn't actually your job, I reminded myself with a twinge of guilt. I knew I sometimes gave my own personal research priority over what should've been my actual focus. *But only for a truly good cause*, I thought. *Only for friends or family.*

That wasn't absolutely true, if I was being totally honest. I crossed my fingers behind my back and promised to do better in the future.

But not today. Not with Ethan under suspicion. I scrolled through some of the other projects listed on the Blackstone Properties website, jotting down the names of each. Once I had a page of notes, I began searching for any references to conflict or protests involving Wendy's other developments. Given the well-organized protest over the proposed development near Taylorsford, I suspected it might not have been Wendy's only troublesome project.

I wasn't wrong in that assumption. I soon uncovered news articles documenting resistance to Crystal Lake, as well as opposition to the conversion of a large tract of land—a historic farm near Roanoke, Virginia—into a subdivision called Mountainside Farms. This had displaced numerous colonies of wild bees and destroyed the habitat of several local bird species. Glancing through the articles related to this project, I noticed that Jaden Perez had been one of the leaders of the protest efforts. However, his current organization, Environmental Advocates, wasn't mentioned, which led me to assume the group hadn't yet been founded.

One other name jumped out at me—Daniella Jensen. While it wasn't that unusual a surname, it still made me question whether the woman, whose family had once owned the farm, was any relation to Candy Jensen, the costume designer for *The Nutcracker*. Candy had been one of the protesters gathered at Winterfest the day Wendy was killed. If her family had a long-standing feud with Blackstone Properties . . .

A subtle cough made me look up from the computer screen.

"Sorry to interrupt," Kurt said. "But I wanted to check in with you while I was in Taylorsford."

"And what brings you to town today? Are you planning to enjoy more of the Winterfest activities?"

"Nothing so pleasant, I'm afraid. I was asked to stop by the sheriff's department to answer a few questions." Kurt offered me an uncharacteristically closed-lip smile. "It seems that rumors of my less-than-chummy relationship with Wendy Blackstone have been widely circulated over the last few days. And, as with your books, I suspect that circulation originated here in the library."

I lifted my chin and met his intent stare without faltering. "You mean you think it came from Zelda."

Kurt's eyes narrowed. "She was in the vicinity when Wendy was casting some rather icy glances my way. I don't doubt, knowing her ability to ferret out gossip, that she might have extracted some information from a few people."

"You make her sound like an inquisitor," I said. "Besides, figuring out that there was some animosity between you and Wendy Blackstone didn't require any special techniques, torturous or otherwise. It was blatantly obvious."

"Ah, and there I was, congratulating myself on my self-control." Kurt pressed his gloved hand to the lapel of his gray cashmere coat. "I thought I'd masked my true feelings quite well. It is one of my skills, after all."

"I'm afraid it failed you in this instance," I said, tightening my lips to keep them from twitching into a smile.

"Hubris strikes us all at some point, I suppose." Kurt shrugged his broad shoulders. "At any rate, word got around. Thus my forced visit to the sheriff's department this morning."

"And how did that go?" I stood on tiptoe to glance around him to make sure there weren't any other patrons lining up for assistance.

"Fine." Kurt flicked a fleck of lint off his coat sleeve. "It was a typical session with the authorities, which quite frankly means answering all their wrong questions with facts that won't help their case."

"Wrong questions?" I dropped back down on my heels. "Why do you say that?"

"Because nine times out of ten they don't craft queries that will actually supply them with the information they need. It's usually like someone using a crowbar when what they want is a jeweler's pick."

"Not subtle enough for your brilliance, you mean." I arched my eyebrows. "I suppose they didn't really get much out of you."

69

"Nothing I didn't want to share." Kurt flashed a toothy grin. "But enough, I hope, to put their suspicions of me having any involvement in Ms. Blackstone's death to rest."

"If only we could do the same for Ethan," I said.

Kurt's smile faded. "Are they really looking at him as a major suspect?"

"It seems so. I ran into Brad Tucker yesterday, and he certainly gave me that impression."

"Just because he and Wendy tossed a few barbs back and forth?" Kurt asked, his blue eyes clouding. He seemed lost in thought for a moment, which was probably why he hadn't noticed that he'd used Wendy Blackstone's first name.

But I noticed, I thought, examining his craggy face with interest. *And how it was spoken in a quite familiar tone too. There's more history there than he's letting on.* "It seems it wasn't the first time they'd argued, and unfortunately, Ethan sent Blackstone Properties some rather . . . angry emails."

"That is unfortunate. Have you spoken to Scott? Given his skill set, he'd seem to be an advantageous ally in your quest to clear Ethan of any suspicion in the case."

"No. I'm sure he and Ethan have talked, despite the circumstances, but I wasn't certain . . ." I cleared my throat. "Well, I knew Scott was in the field on some mission he couldn't talk about, and I didn't want to compromise him."

"That's commendable, I suppose, but I think he would want to know. Even if they have spoken, Ethan may not be telling him how dire the situation is. I know how that can happen and the problems it can cause." Kurt's expression had grown pensive. I wondered if he was thinking about Aunt Lydia's husband, Andrew Talbot, who'd died over forty-five years ago. Kurt and my uncle had been extremely close as teens and young men. *Best friends, and possibly more, at least*

70

on Kurt's side, I reminded myself. But I also knew from previous conversations that Andrew hadn't shared all of his own difficulties with Kurt—troubles with drugs and money that might have contributed to his death in a tragic car accident. *I'm sure Kurt doesn't want to see that sort of thing happen again*, I thought, with a little pang of sorrow.

"I'll contact Scott tonight," I said. "Not sure if my call will go through, but I'll try."

"Good. I'd want to know all the details, good or bad, if I were him." Kurt turned his head as the children's room doors screeched open. "You need some WD-40 for those," he observed, as a chattering horde of children and parents spilled out into the main portion of the library.

"Thanks for the tip. I'll take care of that in all my spare time," I replied, squinching up my face at him. "But for now, you'd better move, unless you want to be swept up in the torrent. They'll all be heading in this direction with books to check out, I bet."

"A wise choice," Kurt said, backing away. He caught my eye over the sea of adults and children who'd lined up in a haphazard knot in front of the desk. "Let's talk again soon," he called out, before heading for the exit.

Too busy checking out books and wishing everyone a happy holiday, I didn't bother to reply.

Chapter Eight

S ince Aunt Lydia had volunteered to pick up the twins from kindergarten so they could help her decorate her tree, I decided to stop by the Taylorsford Fire and Rescue Squad after work. I didn't know if Ethan would be on duty but figured it was worth a little of my time to see if I could talk to him face-to-face.

One of the large garage bay doors stood open, displaying the town's newly acquired state-of-the-art firetruck. It had taken considerable fund-raising efforts to buy the new vehicle, a project spearheaded by former mayor Walt Adams, who was on the squad's board of directors.

Taylorsford was fortunate to have a dedicated group of volunteers who manned fire and rescue services for the town. Ethan and Hannah Fowler, the only salaried members of the squad, oversaw the recruitment and training of the volunteers, most of whom had taken coursework to become certified in fire and rescue services. It required a significant commitment, making all the squad members heroes in my eyes.

Crossing the parking lot, I waved to a few local residents, including Bill Clayton, who also volunteered at the library. Before I reached the side door leading into the administrative offices, a young woman stepped outside to greet me.

"Hello, Amy. If you're looking for Ethan, I'm afraid he isn't here today. He has to pull the overnight shift later, so I'm currently holding down the fort." Hannah, who was at least half a foot taller than me, had brown hair trimmed into a pixie cut that hugged her head and highlighted her broad face and wide chestnut eyes.

"That's too bad. I was hoping to speak with him," I said. "Should've called first, I guess."

Hannah looked me over. "Would you like to step into the office? To get out of the cold, I mean."

The intensity of her gaze made me think there was an ulterior motive driving this invitation. "Thanks, that would be great."

I followed Hannah into the building and down a short, tiled hallway decorated with photos of squad members and commendations from the town and the state. As soon as she led me into the main office, she closed the door firmly behind us.

"Please, have a seat," Hannah said, gesturing to one of the armchairs placed beside a small table. "Would you like anything to drink? We always have coffee on tap, but there's also hot water for tea."

I sat down. "No thanks, that isn't necessary."

Hannah remained on her feet. "You might be wondering why I brought you in here rather than talking outside. Well, the truth is—"

"You wanted to tell me something that you didn't want the volunteers to hear?" I settled back in my chair. "That's my assumption, anyway."

"A correct one, as it turns out." Hannah settled in the other armchair. "There is something I want to share, but I don't want to start any rumors. Which could happen if anyone overheard what I'm about to say." She pressed the fingers of one hand against the

Victoria Gilbert

tabletop. "Not that our volunteers are gossips or anything, but you know how it is—people start discussing things and expressing opinions, and before you know it, stories are circulating throughout the entire town."

"I have experienced that phenomenon," I said, offering her a wry smile.

"Anyway"—Hannah drew in a deep, audible breath—"the truth is, Ethan was quite late returning to the station after his shift at the winter festival the day Wendy Blackstone was killed. I didn't think anything of it at first. I thought maybe he'd stopped to grab a bite to eat before he came back. He'd volunteered to stay that night, you see. I wasn't feeling too great as the day went on. Some little virus, I guess. Anyway, when I took him some coffee earlier in the evening, he noticed and said he'd take my overnight shift. We often switch around like that." Hannah lowered her eyes, staring down at her tightly clasped hands.

I stirred uncomfortably on the hard cushions of my chair. "So he was planning to go back to the station and stay all night? After working at Winterfest that afternoon?"

"Yeah. It wasn't the original plan. As I said, when I took him coffee, he offered to cover my overnight shift because he could tell I wasn't feeling my best." Hannah shrugged. "He said he didn't really care, since Scott was out of town. Said he just had to run home and feed the dog and let her out for a minute, but then he'd head right back to the station to relieve me."

"So you expected him, when? Around eight thirty or nine that evening?"

"That's right." Hannah lifted her hand and examined her short, blunt nails. "Like I said, when he didn't show up by nine, I figured he might have taken a little extra time to pick up some dinner. But then"—Hannah dropped her hand into her lap—"he didn't show up until around ten thirty."

74

"Did he say anything about why he was delayed?"

"Honestly, he didn't say much of anything. Mumbled an apology and told me to head on home. It was odd, because Ethan's usually so thoughtful about stuff like that. He didn't have any takeout with him either." Hannah pursed her lips. "So I thought, okay, he stopped and ate somewhere instead, but then after I packed up my gear and was leaving, I saw him in the kitchen, scrambling some eggs."

I slid to the edge of my chair, leaning forward. "You told the deputies all this, I guess?"

"Well, not exactly." Hannah cast me a wary glance. "I mean, they asked about his movements that day, and I told them about us switching schedules and all. And that he arrived here around ten thirty. But I didn't say anything about expecting him before that. I mentioned him going to his house because of the dog, and that he might've gotten something to eat in the interim. I didn't say anything about my uneasy feelings because he was so much later than I initially expected. And I didn't mention fixing food when he got here."

"Maybe he was just hungry again," I said.

Hannah frowned. "Maybe. But Ethan generally doesn't eat anything after dinner. It's part of his health regimen. That's why I thought it was odd. I mean, if he took the extra time to either fix something to eat at home or grab something out somewhere . . ." Hannah leapt to her feet and paced over to the large metal desk filling one end of the office. "The thing is, the more I think about it, the more confused I feel." She turned, leaning back, her fingers gripping the rolled edge of the desk. "What do you think? Should I mention my concerns to the detectives or just leave it alone? I don't want to exacerbate the scrutiny focused on Ethan if I don't have to."

"Why tell me?" I asked, rising to face her.

"Well, I know you've helped the sheriff's department with some cases in the past. I thought you might have a better sense of whether these feelings of mine are really valuable as evidence or not."

"As evidence, maybe not," I said, my mind racing with the implication of her words. "But I appreciate you mentioning it to me. I think what might be best is if I talk to Ethan and try to get him to clarify his exact movements that evening with the authorities. There may be a perfectly innocent reason why he arrived here much later than he originally told you, but . . ."

"If I voice my concerns first, it might not look so innocent?" Hannah clasped her hands tightly at her waist. "That's what I thought. It's better if Ethan is the one to explain things, rather than me stirring up questions."

"Of course, you could talk to Ethan directly, if you prefer," I said, not wanting to force Hannah to accept me as a go-between.

"No, no, it will be better coming from you. I mean, maybe if I had said something right away"—Hannah twisted her hands until her knuckles blanched—"but at this point I'm afraid it would look like I was falling into the suspicious-minded camp, and I don't want that. If you could just say something about me mentioning the timing and *you* finding it odd . . ."

"So I can be the bad cop?" I lifted my hands at Hannah's stricken look. "No, it's okay. I get your point. I've played amateur detective in the past enough times that Ethan won't be taken aback about me quizzing him on the details."

"That was kinda my thought," Hannah said, her expression brightening.

"And I don't have to work with him, which I'm sure is another benefit." I flipped the trailing end of my scarf over my shoulder. "All right, don't worry. I was planning to talk to my brother later anyway.

I'll see if I can find out when he'll be back in town. Soon, I expect, given the circumstances. Once I know for sure, I'll set up a time to meet with him and Ethan at their house."

"Thanks. That makes me feel much better." Hannah flashed a warm smile as she strode past me to open the office door. "I know the authorities are looking closely at Ethan, but I just don't believe he's capable of harming anyone."

"Neither do I." Thanking Hannah for her consideration, I added, "But if you do find out anything you feel is solid evidence, please go ahead and share that with the sheriff's office. I don't want you to get in trouble."

Leave that to me, I thought, my smile turning a little grim as I exited the station.

*   *   *

By the time I arrived at Aunt Lydia's house, Ella and Nicky were snuggled up under a blanket on the sofa in the sitting room, watching cartoons on the large-screen television. My aunt was slumped in her favorite suede-upholstered armchair, her feet propped up on a matching hassock.

"Wore you out that much, huh?" I asked, my lips curving into a smile.

"It wasn't all them," Aunt Lydia said. "I'd been running errands all morning, so I started out a little weary."

"Mommy!" Ella jumped off the sofa and bounded over to me, followed closely by her brother. "We helped decorate the tree. Well, the bottom part, 'cause Aunt Lydia said she didn't want us to climb up on the step stool."

"A wise choice," I said, sharing a look with my aunt.

Nicky tugged on my hand. "It looks really pretty. Want to see?"

"Of course. Lead the way," I said.

The twins galloped out of the room and into the more formal parlor across the hall.

The parlor, with its heavy mahogany furniture and damask and velvet upholstery and drapes, was rarely used, but I had to admit it was the perfect spot for a Christmas tree. The turret that rose on this side of the house formed a half circle that enclosed the tree, whose lights could be seen from outside, framed by the tall, arched windows.

I followed Ella and Nicky across the rose-patterned wool rug that covered most of the hardwood floor, sparing a glance for a curio cabinet that sat next to a chair my great-grandmother, Rose Baker Litton, had imported from England.

Ella climbed up onto the chair, which I'd always thought supremely ugly. The horsehair-stuffed velvet seat had faded from black to a coppery brown, and its dark-wood back was carved into a fantastical motif of vines and roses that managed to look threatening as well as uncomfortable. Ella perched on the edge of the chair, her legs dangling.

"Now I'm the queen," she said, stretching her arm out as if holding a scepter. "And you have to do what I say."

Nicky dropped down onto the thick rug, his legs crossed in an unconscious yoga pose. "You aren't the boss of me," he said, meeting his sister's imperious gaze with a snort of laughter.

"Okay, now, enough nonsense." Aunt Lydia stepped up beside me. "Show your mother what we did this afternoon."

Ella gestured toward the tree. "We put on the bows and those dangly crystal things," she said. "Aunt Lydia hung the ornaments 'cause they're glass."

"They break easily," Nicky said, looking up at me. His dark-brown hair and eyes were a perfect match to mine, but his face was more angular than mine had ever been.

"Yes, we had to have a little discussion about that." Aunt Lydia placed a hand on my shoulder as we surveyed the tree, which was quite lovely. Tiny white lights were threaded through the branches, while crimson velvet bows glowed against the emerald needles. The crystals that Ella had mentioned—actually faceted clear acrylic—hung amid the greenery like icicles. Aunt Lydia's collection of antique glass ornaments completed the vintage look of the design, which was topped off by a gigantic red-and-green plaid velvet bow whose trailing ends spilled down over the full branches like a waterfall.

"It's quite splendid," I said, giving both Ella and Nicky nods of approval. "I'm sure Aunt Lydia appreciated your help too."

My aunt's fingers tightened on my shoulder. "Of course. Most helpful," she said cheerfully, before adding in a softer voice, "Once we laid down some strict ground rules."

A chuckle escaped my lips. "I'm sure."

Nicky jumped up from his cross-legged position with a grace that reminded me of his dad. "Can we go back and watch our show now?"

"Yes, yes, go on. I need to tell your mother something anyway," Aunt Lydia said, lifting her hand and swishing it through the air in an autocratic wave.

Ella slid off the chair and followed Nicky, who'd already dashed out of the room.

"What's this you need to tell me?" I asked, turning to face my aunt.

"Nothing bad. I just wanted to let you know that I spoke to your mother this morning, and she said she'd heard from Scott." Aunt Lydia patted down a flyaway strand of her silver hair.

"So he's no longer incommunicado? That's good. I'll phone him later. I need to talk to him about . . . well, something to do with Ethan's situation."

Aunt Lydia's blue eyes focused on me, cool as spring water. "You needn't bother trying to call tonight. Debbie told me that Scott is on his way, but given his travel itinerary, he won't be easy to reach. She said he should be home around midnight on Thursday. So I'd suggest waiting and checking in with him on Friday."

"Okay, good to know," I said. Turning back to the tree, I admired it for a moment before adding, "It really is gorgeous. We still need to decorate ours. Not exactly in this style, though. We have to incorporate some handmade ornaments from the kids and things like that."

"I'm sure it will be quite festive." Aunt Lydia's rose-tinted lips twitched. "I assume you plan to take care of that before Fiona arrives?"

"Heavens, yes. We certainly don't want her to offer her decorating advice," I said, rolling my eyes. "You know how opinionated she can be. Richard thinks it's best if we have all the decorations up so she can't interfere. I mean, of course she'll probably put in her two cents about everything . . ."

"Undoubtedly," Aunt Lydia said dryly.

"But once it's all done, she probably won't feel the urge to change anything. Probably," I emphasized, as my aunt lifted her golden eyebrows.

"Shall we place bets?" she asked.

"No," I replied with a sigh. "I don't have that much money to spare."

Chapter Nine

I worked at the library again on Thursday, having switched days with Sunny so I could have both Friday and Saturday off.

"I really need a couple of days free in a row. For one thing, I must clean the house before Fiona arrives on Sunday," I'd told Sunny when asking for the schedule change.

"You don't want to fail the white-glove test?" Sunny had replied with a sly grin.

"I probably will anyway, since it's impossible to keep a house perfectly clean when you have young children, but I do want to try to get it in the best shape possible. Richard will do some last-minute vacuuming on Sunday morning, I'm sure, but I need to tackle the dusting and the bathrooms and kitchen on Friday. And of course, Richard and the twins have rehearsals mixed in there too."

"Sounds terribly exhausting," Sunny had said, giving me a pat on the back. "Better you than me. I'd much rather run a farm and the library."

So, in preparation for several days filled with cleaning, decorating, and helping to ferry Ella and Nicky to their *Nutcracker* rehearsals, I called in some orders to my friend Hani Abdi's catering business. Despite not wanting to spend time cooking, I needed to have a few tasty and healthy food options on hand for lunches and dinners over the next three days.

At lunchtime on Thursday, I drove the short distance to Hani's, planning to store the food in coolers I'd loaded into the trunk of the car. I needed to complete the task on my lunch break, because I had to get home as soon as possible that afternoon. Richard, who was picking up the twins from kindergarten, had suggested that we decorate the tree before he left for an evening rehearsal with the principal dancers.

I parked in the small lot behind Hani Abdi's historic foursquare fieldstone home and circled around on foot to enter the smaller, wood-framed addition that housed her catering company.

A bell attached to the heavy wooden door jangled as I entered the shop, drawing Hani from the workroom located behind the plain wooden counter. Hani, whose ebony hair hugged her scalp, accentuating her wide black eyes and elegant bone structure, greeted me with a bright smile.

"Hello, Amy," she said, slipping off a pair of disposable plastic gloves and laying them on the white quartz countertop. "Are you parked out back? Why don't you slip behind the counter, and I can help carry everything out to your car."

"That sounds good. But let me settle up with you first," I said, handing over my debit card.

"Thanks, that makes sense." Hani rang up my order, consulting the invoice, which I'd already confirmed over the phone. "So your mother-in-law arrives on Sunday?"

"Yeah. You might get another order from me next week, if I run out of ideas, and time, to make dinners that will suit her."

"I won't complain about that," Hani said, handing back my card. "I hope the visit goes well," she added with another smile.

As I studied her for a moment, the thought of her possible knowledge of town history crossed my mind. Hani had lived in Taylorsford ever since her parents had immigrated to the area when she was only two, which made her tenure here much longer than mine. "I guess you've heard about the murder?"

"Of course. It's almost all anyone is talking about." Hani shook her head. "Such a shame. I know Wendy Blackstone wasn't everyone's favorite person, but she was always nice to me."

"You did some catering work for her?"

"Quite a bit, actually. Mostly business lunches and that sort of thing."

I slipped my debit card back into my wallet. "I know she moved back to Taylorsford a few years ago, but she also lived here when her husband was alive, didn't she?"

"Yes." Hani tucked the plastic gloves into the pocket of her apron. "As a matter of fact, my mother and father used to do some work for her and Mr. Blackstone. Gardening, mostly, though Mom created some flower arrangements for the house as well. That was when I was still in college, so I wasn't asked to help. But I remember Mom saying the Blackstones were always polite, not to mention they paid quite well."

"Didn't Wendy move away right after her husband died?" I asked, as Hani lifted up a wooden, hinged portion of the counter, allowing me to join her.

"She did. And it was very fast. Wendy bundled up the kids and moved out of their house within a month of Roger's death." Hani led the way into her commercial kitchen, which provided a vivid contrast to the vintage feel of the front of the shop. White tiled walls, metal shelving and worktables, and industrial mixers, ovens, and other equipment filled the space. "My parents heard that Bob Blackstone had to hire people to sell off most of the furniture and other household items and that he was the one who actually listed the house." Hani opened the double doors of a large refrigerator. "Here we are.

Your items are all marked, so if you want to grab a couple, I'll get the rest."

"It seems like Wendy was pretty traumatized by her husband's death," I said, pulling out two of the smaller sealed foil containers marked *Muir*.

"Well, there was some talk . . ." Hani cast me a sidelong look as she balanced two larger casseroles in her arms and opened the back door. "Not to spread rumors, but some folks thought Roger's death was not an accident."

"You mean they suspected that he deliberately crashed his plane?" I asked, clutching the foil containers to my chest with one arm as I fumbled for my car keys.

Hani waited until I popped my trunk, then set her casserole containers inside the coolers before answering. "It was just a rumor. But I think that was why Wendy fled Taylorsford—because people could even think such a thing. I mean, that would sour you on a place, wouldn't it?"

"That does put a different spin on it," I said, looking up at the sound of a vehicle barreling down the alley. "I hope he doesn't block me in," I added as a sports car pulled into the parking lot. Hani and I stepped around the side of my car and waited until the cherry-red vehicle parked.

"Well, that's everything," Hani said. "I suppose I should go in to greet my next customer. Anyway, I hope you enjoy."

"I'm sure we will," I said, wishing her a good day as she headed back inside.

Closing the trunk of my car, I studied the driver of the sports car as he climbed out of his vehicle. He was a slender man of medium height who looked no older than forty-five. He was wearing a finely tailored navy suit and a brightly patterned silk tie. Although I knew many of Taylorsford's residents from my work in the library and my family connections, I didn't recall meeting this man before, even though for some reason he did look vaguely familiar.

"Hi," I said as the man glanced over in my direction.

The man brushed his fingers through the silver hair at his temples. The rest of his carefully coiffed hair was walnut brown, as were his eyes, which were so narrow he appeared to be squinting when he smiled. "Hello. I suppose you're availing yourself of Ms. Abdi's delicious concoctions too? Good move."

"She's a fantastic cook and baker," I said.

"Indeed." The man sauntered over to me, extending his slender hand. "I don't believe we've met. I'm Timothy Thompson, but please, call me Tim."

"Amy Muir," I replied, giving his hand a quick shake. *Ah, that was it*, I realized. I'd recently seen his photo when researching. "You're with Blackstone Properties, right?"

"Yes, one of the partners." Tim's bright expression dimmed. "The only one now, I'm afraid."

I shuffled my loafers in the gravel of the lot. "I'm very sorry for your loss."

"Thank you, thank you," Tim said, pressing his forefinger under one eye as if to brush away a tear. "It was quite a shock."

"I'm sure," I said, noticing no trace of actual moisture under his eye.

He looked me up and down. "Muir? I've heard that name. Is your husband the fellow producing the dance thing for Winterfest?"

"Yes, he and his partner, Karla Tansen, are in charge of the *Nutcracker* performance this year." I noticed that Tim Thompson's pocket square was a perfect match for his tie. "And I'm also the director of the town's public library. Well, one of them. I codirect with Sunshine Fields."

"Ah, of course," Tim said in a jovial tone that did nothing to convince me that he'd heard anything about the local library, much less me or Sunny.

"Well, since you obviously need to pick up something from Hani's shop, I should let you go."

"Just dinner for me and a few friends." Tim straightened the lapel of his sleek suit. "Wait a minute—Muir. Aren't you connected to that Kurt Kendrick fellow somehow?"

I squared my shoulders and gazed up into Tim's rather vulpine face. "He was the foster son of my husband's great-uncle, Paul Dassin," I said, not wanting to bring Aunt Lydia or my late uncle into the conversation.

"Right, right." Tim tapped the toe of one of his expensive leather shoes against the gravel. "And if I've heard right, you live in Paul Dassin's old house, next door to that glorious Queen Anne Revival mansion."

"Not exactly a mansion," I said, fighting to keep my tone pleasant. "Although it is large, as were many houses of the time. It was built by the Baker family back in 1900." I wanted to add *and it's not for sale* but thought better of it.

"Hmmm, yes. I know Wendy admired it immensely, although she did say it needed a bit of renovation." Tim flashed a brilliant but insincere smile. "Anyway, since you know Kurt Kendrick, perhaps you can satisfy my curiosity."

I instinctively took two steps back. "About what?"

"Whether he ever mentioned his feelings about Wendy, that's all."

"The subject hasn't come up," I said. That was a lie, but something about this man made me disinclined to share the truth.

"Really? How interesting. Wendy certainly had plenty to say about him."

I thrust my hands into my coat pockets. "Such as?"

"Oh, heavens, she hated the man. Claimed he ruined her father, Steven Barclay. Kendrick's never mentioned that name?"

"Not to me," I said, glad to be able to speak honestly this time.

"Apparently"—Tim pressed his hand to his chest—"they were quite close friends. Perhaps more than friends, if you get my meaning."

My lips tightened. "What does that have to do with anything?"

Tim shrugged. "It's just that Wendy thought her dad was obsessed with this Kendrick fellow, to the point where he lost all common sense. Wendy said her dad got involved in buying art just because Kendrick was a collector and dealer and that's what ruined him. Steven Barclay, I mean, not Kendrick."

"Ruined him how?" I asked, curious in spite of myself.

"He started chasing rare items, things that required dealing with some disreputable sorts. Criminals, really." Tim's eyes narrowed into slits. "Wendy thought Steven did it to impress Kendrick and that Kendrick probably even introduced him to several seedy dealers. Sadly, it was one of those deals that enticed Steven Barclay into a back room in a run-down warehouse, where he ended up dead."

I blinked rapidly. This was news I hadn't seen in the old reports. "He was murdered?"

"Unfortunately. The killer was never found, and it was written off as some sort of organized crime hit. Well, not by the Barclay family. They obviously didn't want people to think Steven was mixed up with the mob, so they made up some story about a random killing, like Steven was just an innocent bystander, caught in the cross fire." Tim pressed his finger to his narrow nose. "Wendy was obsessed with the situation, I'm afraid. She was always bugging the cops to reopen the case, but without new evidence"—Tim lifted his hands in a *What can you do?* gesture—"there was no point."

"So she blamed Kurt, not for the murder, but for getting her dad involved with the wrong people?"

"Exactly. And to be honest, I think she did eventually wonder if Kendrick had anything to do with her dad's murder. She was always trying to dig up dirt on him. Who knows? Maybe she did, in the end. And perhaps Kendrick decided to silence her before she shared that evidence with the cops."

I sucked in a deep breath. "So now you're accusing Mr. Kendrick of murdering Wendy?"

"No, no, of course not." Tim stared up and over my head. "I'd never do such a thing. Although," he added, lowering his gaze to look me in the eye, "I might've mentioned some of this to the detectives who kept pestering me with questions concerning the business and my relationship with Wendy and all that. Just to make sure all bases were covered, you understand."

I drew myself up to my full, if still unimpressive, height. I did understand. Tim Thompson was throwing Kurt into the snake pit of suspicion for some reason. *Perhaps*, I thought, *to deflect from his own guilt?* Whatever the reason, the man standing before me had now rocketed to the top of my own personal list of suspects.

"Well, it was nice to meet you, Tim," I said, hoping my anger wasn't too evident in my voice. "But I must get home now, and I'm sure you want to collect your dinner and be on your way too." I marched past him without waiting for a reply and threw open my car door. Sliding into the driver's seat, I slammed the door with a little too much force.

Tim Thompson stepped away as I backed up my car. I couldn't tell for certain, but it almost looked like he was smiling.

Chapter Ten

I left work a little early, reassured by volunteers Zelda and Denise that they could handle the rest of the day. Carrying one of the coolers up onto our front porch, I opened the door and walked in on a truly adorable sight. Richard was seated on the sofa, holding a children's book, while Ella and Nicky snuggled up on either side of him. Not to mention Fosse was sprawled across Ella's thighs and Loie was curled up in Nicky's lap.

I paused for a moment, a wave of emotion flooding my chest. It was a feeling of love so overwhelming that tears welled in my eyes. In that moment, I knew I would do anything to protect my family. *I'd even kill,* I realized, a thought that reinforced the concept that anyone could commit murder, given the proper motivation.

"Oh, hi there," Richard said, looking up from the book to meet my emotional gaze. "Everything okay?"

"Yes, yes, it's fine," I replied, using my gloved finger to sweep away a tear. "But I could use a hand with a couple of coolers when you have a minute."

Richard closed the book and leapt up from the sofa. "Of course. Just set that down." He turned to look down at Ella and Nicky.

"Sorry, kids, story time is over. I need to help your mom. We'll read the rest another time, okay?"

The twins bobbed their heads in unison. "We can read some of the words, Mommy," Ella said. "At least I can."

"Me too!" Nicky bounced off the sofa, dislodging Loie, who meowed her disapproval and rolled over to rest against the pillow pressed against the sofa arm. Nicky turned to face us, his hands on his hips and his knobby elbows akimbo. "Ella doesn't read any better than me."

Richard, reaching me, quirked his dark eyebrows. "They both were picking up a lot of words," he said. "I bet they'll be reading by themselves in a month or two."

"I don't doubt it." I lifted my face for a quick kiss. "There's a cooler on the porch and another in the trunk."

"Our dinner, I take it?" Richard asked as Nicky ran over, arms up, looking for a hug.

"Dinners, actually. I got enough for a couple of days." I picked up Nicky and gave him a hug and kiss on the cheek. "Are you ready to decorate the tree?"

A lock of his dark hair fell into his eyes as he vigorously nodded his head.

"Me too!" Ella, who'd been soothing the cats' disdain at being dumped from laps, slid off the sofa and dashed over to join us just as Richard headed outside.

I set Nicky down and picked her up for her own hug and kiss. "As soon as Daddy brings in the coolers, we'll get started. What do you say?"

"Yes!" Ella wriggled in my arms.

Setting her down beside her brother, I pointed toward the tree, which had been set up in one corner of the living room. "Okay, let me take off my coat and stuff, and I'll help open the ornament boxes."

Both children turned and dashed to the tree. "I want my nut-cracker to go in the very front," Ella said, referencing the duplicate ornament she'd made when we created our contributions for the library tree.

"No, my mouse king!" Nicky faced off with his sister. Standing together, their resemblance was more striking.

Especially when both of them are giving off those familial stubborn vibes, I thought with a little smile.

"Plenty of room on the tree for both to be front and center," Richard said, kicking open the door so he could use both hands to carry in one of the coolers.

I grabbed the edge of the front door and closed it behind him. "You guys did pick out a full tree. Lots of branches to fill."

"You know that's how I like things, nicely rounded but not too tall," Richard said, giving me a wink as he walked past me.

I swung my right foot at him. He just laughed and headed for the kitchen.

Ella stared at me, her gray eyes widening. "Why'd you try to kick Daddy?"

"I didn't—I wouldn't. Just shaking out my foot," I said, as heat flushed my cheeks. "Now, let's start hanging some of the ornaments, shall we?"

* * *

Later, after the children were in bed and Richard had returned from his rehearsal, he and I settled on the sofa, enjoying a glass of wine and admiring our decorated tree. Fosse and Loie, curled up like a yin-yang symbol on the seat of an adjacent armchair, paid the tree no attention, which was a pattern I hoped would continue.

Our tree didn't exude the elegance of Aunt Lydia's, and some of the ornaments—like the paper cutouts heavily doused in glitter that the twins had made at kindergarten—were a little tattered, but it was still beautiful in my eyes. We'd used small multicolored LED lights that could be set to twinkle on and off. Of course, Ella and Nicky preferred that option, and even though I would've chosen a steady glow, I'd acquiesced to their request.

"Because Christmas, you know? It should be magical for kids," I said as I rested my head against Richard's shoulder.

"Only for kids?" Richard leaned over and kissed my temple. "I don't know. I think it can be rather enchanting for adults as well."

"Well, you would, wouldn't you, with your magical growing tree and nutcrackers turning into princes and all that," I said, laying my hand on the taut muscles of his upper thigh.

"Please don't mention the tree," Richard said, pressing his hand over mine. "We've been having some troubles with that. Blasted thing wants to get stuck every other time we test it."

"I'm sure you'll figure it out." I leaned forward to grab my wine-glass from the coffee table.

"I do have an idea. It would be a drastic change, but it might be fun, and a little more innovative too," Richard said.

I took a long swallow of wine. "Oh, what would that be?"

"I think I'll keep that as a surprise," Richard said, squeezing my hand before releasing it and picking up his own wineglass. "Something you can look forward to when you see the full production for the first time."

"All right, that sounds like fun. I've seen *The Nutcracker* more times than I can count, so something different would be nice."

"You haven't seen this version." Richard sipped his wine for a moment. "I hope people will understand how we had to change things to make it work with contemporary dancers. We do have a few ballet dancers in the mix, but most of it is quite different, even though the music remains the same."

I set down my glass and swiveled so I could look him directly in the face. "It will be brilliant, of course. With you and Karla in charge, what else could it be?"

"A disaster?" Richard drank a gulp of the wine.

"That's just your perfectionism talking." I gently took the glass from his hand and set it on the coffee table, then leaned in to give him a proper kiss. "Now listen, you—no doubting your genius."

"Or what?" he asked, placing his hands on my shoulders and holding me at arm's length. "If you mean you'll have to kiss me into confidence, I might have to become swamped with doubt."

"That's not what I mean, and you know it." I slid away and slumped back against the sofa cushions.

"Pity." Richard slid his arm around my shoulders and hugged me to his side. "Oh, by the way, speaking of *Nutcracker*, you need to take the kids in for a final costume fitting either tomorrow morning or Saturday."

"Really?" I sighed. "I guess I'll do it tomorrow, although I do need to clean this house before your mother gets here."

"I'll help with that."

"When will you have time? With the production going into tech week on Sunday, you'll barely be around. Not that it's your fault," I added, snuggling closer to him. "Anyway, I'm just going to do the best I can. If Fiona isn't happy with that, well, she can get a hotel room."

Richard looked down at me, amusement sparkling in his gray eyes. "That would be a conversation I wouldn't mind missing." He brushed my hair back from my forehead with his free hand. "But seriously, you don't have to kill yourself getting the place ready for Mom. She'll have to take it or leave it. Anyway, she'll mainly be focused on the kids."

"I know." I stared up at the ceiling fan, whose still blades cast long shadows across our white beadboard ceilings. "Speaking of killing, I had the most uncomfortable conversation with someone today, concerning Wendy Blackstone and her connection to Kurt."

As I filled Richard in on all the details of my encounter with Tim Thompson, his expression grew increasingly troubled.

"I can't picture Kurt pushing someone down a flight of stairs and leaving them lying there, can you?" he asked when I finished talking.

"Not really. But if what Tim Thompson says is true, Kurt did have a close relationship with Wendy's father and she apparently blamed him for getting her dad killed, so there was a connection between them, and an antagonistic one at that."

"*If* what Thompson said is true. From your impression of him, I can easily imagine that he was lying to cover his own tracks," Richard said.

"Which means he's someone who needs a closer look." I slid to the edge of the sofa cushion. "I wonder if there are any reports of conflicts he might've had with Wendy. Sure, they were partners, but that doesn't mean they always got along. In fact, when I spoke with Jaden Perez, who stopped by the library recently, he said they were often at odds."

"I'm certain you'll be digging into that possibility as soon as you can." Richard stood, gazing down at me with concern. "Just be careful, Amy. Thompson sounds like someone who could have a shady side."

"Don't worry, I won't confront him directly. Just do a little research," I said, motioning toward the empty wineglasses as I rose to my feet. "Can you turn off the tree lights as well as the lamps? I'm going to take these glasses into the kitchen and then head upstairs. I'm ready for some sleep."

"Okay, but . . ." Richard pulled me close and kissed me with a passion that told me he was thinking of something besides sleep.

"Are you trying to seduce me, Mr. Muir?" I asked when he released me.

"Definitely." Richard flashed a brilliant smile. "Is it working?"

I looked up at him from under my lowered lashes. "Most definitely."

Chapter Eleven

Friday morning I drove Ella and Nicky to the theater, which was located in Smithsburg, a town about a thirty-minute drive from Taylorsford. The twins were bouncing in their booster seats, excited to see the actual performance space. Since the theater had been booked for other events before the *Nutcracker* load-in, which wasn't happening until later in the day, all of their rehearsals had taken place at Karla's dance studio. Only Richard, Karla, and the other lead dancers had been working at the theater, and then only in its two basement studios.

Parking in the lot behind the Art Deco cinema that had been transformed into a community performance venue, I told the twins to settle down. "If you behave during your fittings," I said as I took their hands to guide them into the building, "I'll walk you out on the stage so you can see how it will feel."

The costume shop had been set up in an former office space on an upper floor of the theater building, so we took the elevator up to that level. As soon as the doors slid open, the twins bounded forward, heading for the one open door at the end of the hall.

"Hey, I said you need to behave," I called out, picking up my pace to catch up with them.

"It's fine, I've got them corralled," said the young woman who stood at the edge of a large table covered with bolts of fabric and rolls of trim. She had one of her arms, which was covered in tattoos, stretched out to block entrance to the area of the shop where metal racks held a festive display of costumes.

"Hi, Candy, how's it going?" I asked as I latched on to Ella's and Nicky's hands.

Candace Jensen had been an MFA student in Clarion University's theatre department when Richard and Karla had first hired her to work on one of their major productions. Now she was the head costumer for their summer institute and also designed pieces for many of Richard's other choreographic works. Her ability to allow dancers free and unfettered movement while still providing evocative visuals was, according to both Richard and Karla, a unique skill.

Candy dropped her am. "Now let's see," she said, looking Ella and Nicky up and down. "I bet you're in the party scene, is that right?"

The twins nodded, both apparently fascinated by Candy's short-cropped strawberry-blonde hair, whose spiky tips were dyed a vivid purple. "Is your hair real?" Ella asked.

"Yep. It's all mine." Candy tugged on a short strand. "Just colored a little different. For fun, you know?"

Ella turned her gaze on me. "Can we color my hair, Mommy?"

Candy, squatting down so that she could look at Ella directly, pressed a finger under her own kohl-rimmed eyes. "Your hair is so pretty, I'd really hate to see you change it. And anyway, it's a lot harder when you have very dark brown hair, like yours. Besides"—Candy straightened—"we need to keep your hair like it is for the show."

"I'm a party guest," Ella said. "I get to dance around with a toy. I think mine is going to be a stuffed rabbit."

Nicky puffed out his chest. "Me too, but my toy is a sword. A fake one, though."

"I know. I work with all the other designers, you see," Candy said. "Maybe your dad told you how we all get together and discuss the production, so our designs will mesh together?"

The twins bobbed their heads, totally enthralled. Having been raised watching dance and theater, they were fascinated with anything to do with the stage, especially the more magical aspects of performances.

"Okay, so Deke is going to take you back to the dressing rooms," Candy said, motioning for a slender young man standing in the corner to step forward. Looking up at me, she added, "A couple of the dance moms are in the back. They'll help the kids get into costume."

"I can help too, if needed," I said.

"Nah, have a seat." Candy patted the top of a stool pulled up to the cutting table. "I'll have the kids come out to give you a proper fashion show."

Deke, who I assumed was one of the Clarion MFA students Candy had hired as assistants, shepherded Ella and Nicky down a short hallway that led to a set of dressing rooms. I cast Candy a sympathetic smile. "You look a little tired, but I guess that's to be expected. It's a big show."

"It is that. Just a minute." Candy hurried down the hall and gave instructions to whoever was working in the back. Reappearing, she flashed me an apologetic smile and plopped down on a stool across the table from me. "Sorry, I wanted to make sure they'd pulled the right pieces."

"You didn't make everything, did you? I mean, I know you had a little help, with the assistants and some volunteers, but that seems like it would be totally overwhelming."

"I wish. But no." Candy rested her elbows on the table, showing off her tattoo sleeves, which were intricate and vivid depictions of flora and fauna done in the style of Celtic illustrated manuscripts. "I'd love to have the staff to design and build everything from scratch, but it just isn't practical. You know how it is—we always have to count our pennies."

Having observed Richard and Karla wrestling with tight budgets plenty of times, I nodded. "So you make some pieces and buy and rent the rest?"

"Pretty much. I mean, I do tend to add my own touches, even with the rental items," Candy said with a smile. "Just to try to make things look cohesive."

"Capture the vision," I said.

"Yeah, that's it." Candy swiveled on her stool at the sound of feet pattering against the shop's wooden plank floors. "Ah, there they are, Mom. Don't they look splendid?"

I examined the twins, who'd been transformed into slightly abstract versions of well-to-do nineteenth-century children. I knew from conversations between Richard and Karla that they weren't going with absolute verisimilitude in the design. Because they were reworking the *Nutcracker* to feature contemporary rather than ballet dancers, they'd also wanted to create a different feel for the design— less realistic, with an emphasis on evocative lighting and impressionistic sets. The costume designs appeared to be in keeping with that style. Ella's dress, while maintaining a Victorian silhouette, was made of a diaphanous material layered over sheer lace petticoats rather than heavy velvet and starched cottons.

"It's floaty!" As Ella spun around, the light layers lifted, displaying her legs, which were clad in ivory-colored tights.

"It is certainly that, and very pretty too," I said. "What do you think, Nicky?"

My son tugged down his jacket, which was also a softer material than those used in most *Nutcracker* productions I'd seen. Worn with matching breeches and cream-colored tights, the indigo-blue outfit had the lines of a Victorian boy's outfit without the stiffness of that style. Even the high collar didn't appear constrictive.

"I like the buttons," he said, giving one a tug. "They're like silver coins."

"Very nice," I said. "Now, let's see a step or two."

My children didn't have to be asked twice. They both did a simple pirouette, then struck a pose, pointing their feet with the elegance they'd learned from watching and practicing with Richard.

"Well, you're certainly going to steal the show," Candy said. "Now, since everything seems to fit, go back and change while I talk to your mom about what we're looking for in terms of makeup and hair."

Obviously inspired by the costumes, Ella and Nicky sailed back toward the dressing rooms, leaping like dancers.

Candy cast me a grin. "Oh my, those two are naturals. You're going to have to join the dance-mom brigade now."

I held up my hands, palms out. "Nope. They have a dance dad. And a dance godmother in Karla. I think that's quite sufficient. Not that I won't support them if that's what they want, but . . ."

"You aren't going to push them? Smart." Candy slid off her stool and stretched her arms over her head.

"It's a challenging life," I said.

"No question. Your husband works harder than anyone I know, and I can see it wears on him sometimes."

"Well, as he'd be the first to tell you, he's not getting any younger. Although, of course, he's still more talented and energetic than most people half his age." I picked up a length of rose-tinted satin ribbon and wrapped it around one of my hands. "Changing topics—I noticed you in that group of protesters at Winterfest the night Wendy Blackstone was killed. I assume you're a supporter of Environmental Advocates?"

Candy's expression grew wary. "I am. Especially when they're fighting against Blackstone Properties, because . . . well, that's a bunch of ruthless users and takers if ever there was one."

"They seem to have made a good number of enemies," I said, keeping my tone light. "I was doing a little research on them, in light of Wendy Blackstone's unfortunate death, and ran across mentions of protests at some of their other projects too."

Candy sat back, crossing her arms over her chest. "I guess you saw the one connected to me?"

"I wasn't sure it was connected, but I did notice there was a development built on a farm once owned by a Jensen family."

"My grandparents," Candy said, her eyes narrowing. "When they died, the farm was in debt. My family worked with some people, including Jaden—although that was before he created Environmental Advocates—to raise the money to buy the land. But we ran out of time, and the bank sold it to Blackstone Properties."

"Who razed everything and turned it into a subdivision." I slipped the coil of ribbon off my hand. "I can understand why that would rankle."

"We had a group of people fighting for us. They wanted to take over the property and turn it into a communal organic farm—a place where area residents could also rent garden plots. They even had plans to set up a training program for disadvantaged youth. But despite us raising enough funds to counter any offers, the bank sold to Blackstone. We figured Wendy and her team twisted the arms of some local politicians." Candy's lips curled into a sneer. "More taxes would be generated by a bunch of homeowners than they could squeeze out of a farm, you see."

"So you've worked with Jaden Perez before."

"And Megan Campbell. Now, don't get any wrong ideas." Candy dropped her arms and leaned over the table. "No one in the group advocates violence. We wouldn't be the ones shoving Wendy Blackstone down a flight of stairs, no matter how much we were tempted."

Remembering Brad's comments about Jaden injuring a man in another shoving incident, I wasn't convinced her assurances could be trusted. It seemed Jaden had enough of a temper to lose control from time to time. What if one of those times was when he'd confronted Wendy at the top of a flight of stairs?

But there was no point in antagonizing Candy with my suspicions. "I wasn't accusing anyone . . ." I closed my mouth when Ella and Nicky dashed back in the room.

"You said you'd take us out on the stage if we were good." Ella tugged on the sleeve of my jacket.

"And we were, so can we go?" Nicky, standing behind Ella, waved one hand over his head.

"Okay, okay. As long we're done here," I said, glancing over at Candy.

"Sure. I'll just give you this." Candy plucked a single sheet off a stack of papers and slid it across the table to me. "It has suggestions and instructions so the parents can take care of the kids' hair and makeup. We're trying to keep it simple, to allow you to do it at home." She lifted her hands. "We don't have a ton of dressers, so having the children ready to simply slip on their costumes when they arrive will help a lot."

"That's fine," I said, folding the paper and tucking it into one of my pockets. "All right, kids, let's allow Ms. Jensen and her team to get back to work. Say thank-you for the lovely costumes, please."

The twins enthusiastically thanked Candy as I stood up. "I wasn't asking questions because I suspect you," I told her while grabbing Ella's and Nicky's coats.

"You just want to try to find a way to take the focus off of your brother-in-law?" Candy cast a swift glance at Deke, who scuttled back down the hall. "I get it, but you should be careful, Amy. The only person I saw lay hands on Wendy that day was Ethan Payne."

"What?" I thrust their coats at the twins, giving them a quick instruction to put them on. "I saw them arguing, but that was all."

"This was later, when the festival was closing down," Candy said, raising her voice to be heard over Ella and Nicky's loud chatter. "Right as our group was heading for our cars."

"You saw Ethan attack Wendy?" I asked, my voice squeaking on the last word.

"Not attack, but he grabbed her arm. It looked like she was trying to yank it away, but he apparently had a tight grip." Candy swept her hands through her short hair. "Sorry, Amy, but that's what I saw. I didn't think anything of it at first, but when the deputies questioned me a second time, it all came back to me and I felt I had to tell them."

"Okay, well, we should be going," I said, rounding up the twins and herding them out the door.

"Something wrong, Mommy?" Nicky asked, his brown eyes filled with concern.

"No, no. Everything is fine. Come on, let's see that stage." I took hold of his hand, then Ella's, and led them to the elevator.

They were thrilled when we slipped past the black curtains that hid the backstage area, then stepped out onto the wide stage. I allowed them to explore for a few minutes, keeping my eye on them as I turned Candy's words over in my mind.

She'd claimed that Ethan had not simply argued with Wendy on the day she was killed, he'd also physically assaulted her. Between that and Hannah telling me that Ethan hadn't returned to the station at the time she'd expected, it certainly looked suspicious.

But in Candy's case, I thought, as Ella and Nicky bowed for a nonexistent audience, *is she simply trying to divert attention away from anyone associated with Environmental Advocates? Because she, along with Jaden Perez and Megan Campbell and maybe others, had history with Wendy Blackstone too. And who knows if that history was even more volatile than it first appears?*

I puzzled over this the entire drive home, so absorbed in thoughts of all the individuals who had legitimate beefs with Wendy Blackstone that I didn't even notice the extra car parked in Aunt Lydia's driveway.

It was the twins who alerted me to the visitor standing on our front porch.

"Uncle Scott!" they shouted as they raced to be the first to reach him.

I followed more slowly, my gaze fixed on my brother's face. Although he smiled as he bent down and wrapped Nicky and Ella in a bear hug, I spied something in his expression that made me catch my breath.

"What is it?" I asked, opening the door to allow the twins to run inside before I turned back to face him.

Scott took hold of my hands and stared at me. His eyes, shadowed by the lenses of his glasses, appeared damp.

"Ethan is missing," he said.

Chapter Twelve

"What? Wait, come into the house where we can talk properly." I shoved open the front door and followed Scott inside. After Scott spent several minutes chatting with the twins and reassuring them that he'd be around for Christmas, I sent them upstairs to play in one of their bedrooms.

"Nicky's room," I reminded them as they clattered up the steps. "We need to keep Ella's room clean for Grandmother Fiona, remember?"

Scott, sitting down in one of the armchairs in the living room area, cast me a questioning look. "Fiona's visiting?"

"Starting Sunday, for about a week," I replied, dropping down onto the sofa with an eye roll that coaxed the faintest of smiles from my brother. "Now, what's this about Ethan being missing?"

"He's not at home, nor at the station, his truck is gone, and his cell phone appears to be switched off," Scott said, his lips tightening into a straight line.

"That's odd. What about Cassie?" I asked, knowing how attached Ethan was to his dog.

"She was at home when I got in late last night. She had plenty of kibble and water and had obviously been walked earlier in the evening, because she wasn't desperate to go out." Scott yanked off his tortoiseshell-framed glasses and rubbed at his red-rimmed eyes. "Sorry, I didn't get any sleep."

I leaned forward, gripping my knees with both hands. "I'm sure you didn't. So what do you think is going on?"

Scott grimaced as he slipped his glasses back on. "I don't know. It's so unlike Ethan. He's usually great about keeping in touch, but this time he didn't even leave a note."

"And you got in around midnight? That's what Aunt Lydia said your plan was."

"Yeah. A little after, honestly. It was basically the middle of the night." Scott tugged down the sleeves of his cream fisherman's-knit sweater. "So I was immediately concerned."

"Because the truck was gone?"

"Right. But then I thought he might've switched with Hannah again and taken on another overnight shift at the station. He knew I wouldn't be home until late, and he'd told me Hannah had been feeling a little off lately." Scott's dark lashes fluttered over his deep-brown eyes. "It was when I called the station and Hannah answered that I got really worried."

"And he isn't answering his phone? That is strange." I sat back, slumping into the sofa cushions. "Hannah had no idea where he might've gone?"

"None whatsoever." Scott stretched out his legs. Although of average height, he was taller than me and had a slender build I'd always envied. In truth, I'd always considered him more attractive than me, but Scott tended to downplay his good looks. He'd perfected the image of a stereotypical computer nerd or a reclusive professor, but this was simply a carefully crafted persona. As a field agent for one of the more classified government agencies, he'd chosen to appear introverted and nonthreatening so he could hide in plain sight. "The most damning thing is that Ethan's backpack is also missing. It's the one he fitted up as a go bag, in case he got called to a significant fire or other emergency." Scott rubbed his temple, as if doing so could erase his worries. "He was on the list to be called in for anything major in surrounding counties, so he liked to have a basic survival kit ready to go."

"Which means he may have wanted to disappear," I said, talking to myself as much as my brother.

Scott leapt to his feet and strode over to the Christmas tree. "That's what has my stomach in knots." He turned to face me, his hands thrust into the pockets of his corduroy pants. "Don't get me wrong—of course I don't suspect him of trying to flee because he's under suspicion in Wendy Blackstone's death."

"But you're afraid the authorities might." I stood and crossed to Scott. Laying a hand on his shoulder, I gazed up into his face. "I know it doesn't look good, but I'm sure there's some logical reason why he's incommunicado right now. Maybe he decided to go for a late-night drive to clear his head and somehow broke his phone or forgot to charge it or something."

"Okay, but why would he stay away so long, in that case?"

"I don't know," I said, giving his shoulder a gentle squeeze before lowering my hand. "Perhaps the truck broke down? And maybe, if so, he had to hike back from some remote location."

Scott inhaled a deep breath. "I suppose all those things are possible, but let's face it, Amy—they are also highly unlikely."

"Still, it's worth waiting to see." I tipped my head to give him a questioning look. "You haven't reported this to the sheriff's office yet, have you?"

"Absolutely not. As you said, it won't look good, given Ethan's status as a suspect in a murder case. No, I want to wait, and keep searching for him." Scott slid his hands out of his pockets and gripped my lower arm. "Can you think of anyplace he might've gone if he was, as you suggest, driving to a remote locale? Or perhaps heading to someplace to go hiking? I've accompanied him on numerous hikes, but I'm still not as familiar with the area as I'd like to be."

"Maybe the Twin Falls trail? I know he liked to hike that one, because I ran into him on that path a few times several years ago."

"Could you show me where that is? I'll drive, but I don't want to waste time going around in circles," Scott said, dropping his hand.

"Sure. I'll have to see if Aunt Lydia can watch the kids, though." Thumping overhead drew my gaze upward. "Not to mention, I probably should go and see what they're doing right now."

Scott shook his head. "Don't you remember us getting rowdy when we were sent to play in our rooms? There was never any real harm done."

"Except for that time we set up a toy dump truck as a trebuchet and launched several of your action figures out the window—with the screen still in place. As I recall, we had to pay for a new screen out of our allowances." The memory of this incident washed over me, making me recall other parts of our shared childhood.

I squared my shoulders. I had to help Scott any way I could. We were family. Even though we might not have spent as much time together after we became adults, Scott would always be the younger brother I felt I had to look out for.

"Yes, we did get in a few scrapes. But kids have to be kids, don't you think?" Scott glanced toward the stairs as a loud bang resonated through the ceiling. "Tell you what—I'll go and see what Ella and Nicky are up to if you'll check with Aunt Lydia about babysitting them this afternoon."

"Deal." I gave him a brief hug. "Don't worry. We're going to figure this out, and before Brad Tucker and his team are any the wiser."

"I certainly hope so," Scott said, hugging me back.

* * *

Aunt Lydia agreed to watch the twins, but only if she could do so at my house. "It will be easier. They have all their toys and books and things there," she said.

Once she'd settled in, with Nicky and Ella playing with a few of their favorite toys in the living room and the television tuned to a public broadcasting children's program, Scott and I headed out to search for Ethan.

As we drove outside of town, I texted Richard to let him know what was going on. We soon reached the head of the Twin Falls trail, but not seeing Ethan's truck in the small parking lot or anywhere along the nearby road, we turned around and explored some other options.

"This seems to be a hopeless quest," Scott said, as we left yet another trailhead. "If Ethan did decide to go hiking in the middle of the night, he had to have parked the truck somewhere, and we've yet to see a grille or bumper of anything that even faintly resembles it."

"Maybe we're approaching this all wrong." I stared out the passenger's side window of Scott's car, frowning as we drove past rows of skeleton-branched hardwood trees and scraggly pines. "Where else might Ethan go if he needed to get away for a bit? Any favorite shops or other businesses come to mind?"

"Not really. What would be open in the middle of the night, anyway? Unless . . ." Scott maneuvered his car around a rough cul-de-sac at the end of a dirt road and headed back down the mountain. "He does like that diner halfway between Taylorsford and Smithsburg. The one that's open twenty-four seven. I mean, he might not still be there, but maybe they remember seeing him earlier."

"Good idea." I leaned back in my leather-upholstered seat and shot a glance at my brother. "You know, there is someone else who might be willing to help us. Someone who wouldn't be inclined to immediately report the situation to the police, I mean."

Scott side-eyed me. "You're talking about Kurt, I suppose."

"He does have his little network of spies and lots of connections in the area," I said. "He might be able to leverage some of those in our favor."

"Maybe." Scott gnawed on his lower lip as he kept his eyes on the road. "But I think at this point I should take you home and continue the search by myself. It's getting late, and I doubt you want to force Aunt Lydia to give the kids supper."

I glanced at my watch. "Oh, shoot, it is late. Yeah, take me home. Ella and Nicky don't have rehearsal today, thank goodness, since it's load-in day for the sets and lights and all that, but I don't want to impose on Aunt Lydia. And Richard won't be home until late, so dinner and all is up to me."

"Richard's overseeing the load-in, I assume?" Scott turned onto the paved road that led back into Taylorsford.

"Correct. Also conferring with all the technicians and designers, which means he probably won't be home until after the twins and I are in bed."

"Okay, here's what I think we should do. I'll get you home so you can relieve Aunt Lydia and take care of your family stuff while I continue to check out a few other places, like that diner I mentioned." Scott's knuckles blanched as he tightened his grip on the steering wheel. "But if you could call Kurt to let him know what's going on and see what he might be able to do to help, that would be great."

"Sure, no problem," I said.

We both fell silent as we drove down Main Street, each preoccupied with our own thoughts. When we drew closer to my house, I sat up ramrod straight in my seat. "Problem."

Scott swore as we pulled into the driveway next to a sheriff's department vehicle. "Let me do the talking," he said as we climbed out of the car.

"Hello, Scott, and Amy, of course," Brad Tucker said from his position next to the porch steps. "I'm glad I caught you. I just have a few questions . . ."

"Concerning what?" Scott asked, strolling forward with a nonchalance I was sure he didn't actually feel.

"The whereabouts of your husband, for one thing." Brad, who'd been leaning against the railing post, straightened. Considerably taller than Scott, he stared down at my brother, his blue eyes hard as glass.

"Funny, I was just wondering the same thing," Scott said. "I suspect he may have decided to go on one of his extended hikes. He likes to do that sort of thing when he gets stressed."

Brad's eyebrows lifted. "So you haven't hear from him lately? That seems odd, especially since I know you just arrived home from one of your out-of-town work projects."

I pressed my fist to my mouth. Brad, like most people, thought Scott was a computer security specialist who worked with various US government agencies on special projects. He was aware of the classified nature of some of Scott's work but didn't really know the truth. Which was something I wasn't about to reveal.

"We texted yesterday," Scott said mildly. "But sometimes my husband likes to abandon technology and get back to nature. I think, considering the stress of his work, that's understandable."

Brad adjusted his hat, pulling it down a little lower on his forehead. "So have you heard from him *today?*"

Scott examined Brad, who I admitted could appear rather intimidating in his sheriff's uniform, complete with a gun belt. "No. But then, we aren't attached at the hip. I'm not too worried about it."

I knew this was a lie, but Scott's stoic expression gave nothing away. "My brother and I have been having a little sibling bonding time while my aunt watches the twins," I said. "With Scott's work and my crazy schedule, we don't get together as much as we'd like."

"I'm sure that's true, but that's not really the focus of my enquiries today." Brad cast me a speculative look. "Have you seen or heard from Ethan Payne lately, Amy?"

"No," I said, lifting my hands. "But again, our schedules don't really mesh very often."

"Right. Well, we've been trying to track down Mr. Payne today, just to ask a couple more questions, and it seems he's nowhere to be found." Brad tapped his metal-toed boot against the concrete of our walkway. He turned his steely gaze on Scott. "He didn't happen to leave a note or send a text or anything saying where he was going today, did he?"

Scott casually brushed back a lock of dark hair that had fallen over his forehead. "I'm afraid not. But if I hear something, you'll be the first to know."

"I'd better be." Brad strode past my brother and me, pausing at the edge of the driveway. "I'm pretty sure you both understand what *obstruction of justice* means. Please keep that in mind. I'd hate to see you have to deal with any consequences arising from a misguided sense of loyalty."

"Not sure loyalty can be misguided in this case," Scott muttered, too low for Brad, who was getting into his car, to hear.

"I'm afraid he's already decided that Ethan is guilty," I said as Brad fired up his vehicle's engine and backed out of the driveway.

"I know. Which means there must be more evidence than I'm aware of, or at least"— Scott's expression darkened—"more people willing to offer testimony, true or not, that links Ethan to the case."

I thought of Candy Jensen's comments about seeing Ethan man-handle Wendy on the evening she was killed. "That does seem possible. The question is—are those reports being provided to authorities because the witnesses want to see justice done, or because they're looking to protect themselves?"

Scott linked his arm with mine. "Excellent point. Ethan might simply be the easiest person to scapegoat."

When we'd climbed the steps to the front porch, I slid my arm free and turned to face him. "Before we go inside, tell me one thing—do you think there's any possibility that Ethan could've hurt Wendy? Not deliberately, but accidentally, like shoving her during an argument or something?"

Scott lifted his chin and stared up at the porch ceiling for a moment. "It's possible," he said at last. Lowering his head, he gazed into my eyes, his expression racked with sorrow. "He does have a temper. He would never do anything premeditated, but in the heat of the moment . . . who knows?"

"And if he had made that mistake—in the heat of the moment, as you say—is it also possible that he might make a run for it? I mean, he's an outdoorsman. He knows how to navigate the woods and survive in the wilderness. Would he try to escape and disappear?"

Scott's eyes welled with unshed tears. "Leaving me?" he said, his voice cracking on the final word. "Maybe. Because he could never bear to live in a cell, closed off from nature, with no views of the earth and sky. That would kill him, I think."

I pressed his hands between mine for a moment. "I just wondered. I thought that might be true. So that scenario is one we do have to consider."

"Yes, I know." Scott lifted his glasses and dabbed the dampness from his lashes with the tip of one finger. "Regardless, I still need you to fill me in with anything you know, Amy, no matter how irrelevant you may think it to be."

"I will," I said, unlocking the door. "But let's do that while I'm heating up some dinner. And over a glass of wine."

"I'm honestly not hungry," Scott said. "And I'd better skip the wine if I want to keep searching for Ethan this evening. However," he added, as I began to protest, "I will come in and hear what you've learned about the case from your research."

"And spend a few minutes with Ella and Nicky," I said firmly.

"That too. As a matter of fact, I'll keep them entertained while you call Kurt. Deal?"

"Deal," I said, and led him into the house.

Chapter Thirteen

S cott didn't stay for more than thirty minutes Friday afternoon. He lingered long enough to speak briefly with Aunt Lydia before she headed back to her house and to hear what I'd learned about others who could've had a reason to harm Wendy. But when my first attempt to call Kurt resulted in reaching his voice mail, Scott said he had to go.

"I'll keep trying," I reassured Scott as he left to continue his search for Ethan.

The remainder of the evening I focused on Ella and Nicky, who were both a little upset that Scott had departed so quickly.

"Don't worry, he'll be back. And he said he'd be here for Christmas," I told them as they sulked at dinner. "Now, come on and eat. Remember what Daddy always says about needing good fuel for dancing. You have a lot of rehearsals starting tomorrow, so you want to have plenty of energy."

Not that they'd ever lack energy, I thought with a wry smile. But my encouragement did seem to have the right effect. The twins cleaned their plates, making a game of it to see who could finish first.

After dinner, I supervised their baths before we settled down on the couch to read more of *The Hobbit*, which Richard and I had been reading to them—in short sections—every evening over the last few months. The readings were interrupted by many questions, which was fine with me. It was a way for us to bond as well as for them to learn new words and concepts.

Once the twins were safely tucked up in bed, I returned to the sofa with my laptop to do more research. I hadn't really investigated Tim Thompson since our run-in yesterday and wanted to see what I could find out about Wendy Blackstone's business partner.

At first, all I discovered were the usual puff pieces discussing Blackstone Properties and its development projects, but a little more digging turned up Thompson's recent, contentious divorce from his wife of twenty years and an older lawsuit that had been filed against him for "misleading business practices." I noted that this was before he'd partnered with Wendy. He also appeared to be one of those people who liked to join service organizations like the Rotary Club, but when I searched for any evidence that he was actually active in his club's projects, I came up short. It seemed to me that he had only joined these organizations so he could list them on his résumé.

But it was in perusing the photos from a charity gala held by one of the clubs that I discovered an extremely interesting photograph. It featured Tim Thompson standing in front of an elaborate floral display. He had his arm around the waist of a younger, dark-haired woman I thought I recognized but couldn't name. Reading through the accompanying article, I realized the woman was Wendy's daughter, Nadia Blackstone.

Don't jump to conclusions, I told myself, although of course I was wondering how they might be connected. Doing a little mental calculation, I realized that Nadia would be around twenty-nine now, while Tim had to be at least forty-five. Perhaps she had simply accompanied Tim to the gala because they worked together at Blackstone Properties.

Or perhaps there's more to it than that, I thought as my cell phone buzzed.

I picked it up off the coffee table and checked the number before answering. "Hello, Kurt."

"Hi, Amy. Sorry I didn't ring you back earlier, but I was haggling with someone over a painting for what seemed like hours," he replied.

"Did you win?"

"Naturally." Kurt's voice brimmed with humor. "But enough of my successes. I actually called to see what I could do to help Ethan, and by extension, Scott."

"Convince the new sheriff that Ethan isn't the number-one suspect?" I sighed. "The truth is, I called earlier at Scott's request. He thought you might be able to help, what with all your spies and connections in the area."

"I wouldn't say *spies*, but go on—what do you need?"

I took a deep breath before replying. "Ethan has disappeared. You wouldn't have heard anything about that, would you?"

"Other than the all-points bulletin put out on him that was announced on the news tonight? No, I'm afraid not."

I let loose a swear word that probably, coming from me, shocked Kurt. Or then again, maybe not. "I was busy with the twins and didn't watch the news tonight. The sheriff's department has really put out an APB on Ethan?"

"I'm afraid so. The news report made it sound like he was the sheriff's number-one suspect and was now on the run. They asked anyone who had seen him to call the department."

"Just because he's missing? What if he's the one in trouble? Maybe he saw the killer or something. They don't seem to be considering that."

"Well, he did have history with the victim and was seen arguing with her and even laying hands on her the night she was killed.

So I suppose I can understand Brad Tucker's line of reasoning. However"—Kurt cleared his throat—"I agree with you that there could be many other suspects."

"You, for example," I said, throwing caution to the winds. If Kurt had anything to do with Wendy's death, I knew I'd just thrown down the gauntlet.

"I definitely should be on their list. Although, for your information, I didn't kill the woman, much as I disliked her. Honestly, if I murdered everyone I disliked, I'd be a serial killer," Kurt said with a bark of laughter.

"Okay, but there's also people from her past, like the Jensen family. Despite the family's desire to sell to an organic cooperative, Blackstone Properties manipulated things and turned their farm into a cookie-cutter subdivision."

"Very true. I know that the development company has made many enemies," Kurt said. "Then there's Wendy's business partner."

I traced the edges of the photo still up on my laptop screen with my finger. "Tim Thompson. I had an encounter with him recently and then was doing a little online digging, and . . . well, let's just say I wouldn't put it past him. Murder, I mean. Not if it benefited him, I mean."

"He does have a rather questionable reputation." Kurt paused for a moment. "There are also the children."

"Wendy's kids? How would her death benefit them?" I asked.

"Nadia would inherit her mother's portion of the business, I expect."

"Yes, but she was already a part of the company. It's the younger brother, Dylan, who seems to be left out."

"Part of a company and running it are two very different things," Kurt said. "Perhaps Nadia wanted more control?"

I thought of the photo resting under my fingers. "There's this picture floating around online of Nadia and Tim Thompson at a gala. They looked rather chummy. Could they have been in a plot to get rid of Wendy and take over?"

"Always a possibility, I suppose. Perhaps we should ask Nadia's brother that question."

I slumped back against the sofa cushions. "What do you mean?"

"That was the other reason for my call. I recently received a message from Dylan Blackstone. He wants to meet with me to talk about what I remember about his grandfather, Steven Barclay. Apparently, his mother refused to discuss any details about her father, although she was quite happy to tarnish my name by suggesting all sorts of outlandish things. Dylan wants to know the truth, which I said I was more than happy to share."

"He's agreed to meet with you?"

"And you, once I suggested that it might be best to have an impartial observer at our little tête-à-tête. So—can you come to Highview tomorrow around two? I wasn't sure, knowing your busy schedule . . ."

"I can come," I swiftly replied, mentally adjusting the house-cleaning schedule I'd set up for Saturday. "Richard and the twins will be busy with *Nutcracker* rehearsals all afternoon, so I can slip away easily enough."

"Good. I didn't really want to meet with the young man alone. One never knows what to expect when people are dredging up the past."

"I'm sure you could handle it, whatever happened," I said dryly. "But I would like to hear what he has to say. I doubt the authorities have done more than a cursory interview with him."

"Wonderful. I'll see you a little before two, then. And Amy, please don't worry too much about Ethan. I'm sure he just took off somewhere to clear his head. A foolish choice, but understandable."

"Yes, I hope so," I said, before wishing Kurt a good evening and ending the call.

Tapping the phone against my palm, I briefly considered my options. I could wait until tomorrow to do any more digging into the case. Perhaps I should enjoy a glass of wine and watch something light on the television and simply relax.

Of course I didn't do that. I returned to my laptop and began searching for more information on Blackstone Properties and the family that had founded it. I didn't find anything particularly useful, except for one interview with Nadia where she spoke of her interest in branching out into coastal developments.

Ambitious, I thought as I scrolled through the article. *Perhaps she felt her position in the company was holding her back? Or maybe her mother refused to support Nadia's efforts to expand Blackstone Properties, resulting in a feud that led to Wendy's death?*

These were certainly the sorts of questions I intended to ask her brother the following day.

Chapter Fourteen

S aturday morning passed in a blur of housecleaning. Fortunately, Richard took charge of Ella and Nicky, making sure they had a nutritious breakfast and lunch before the three of them left for the theater.

"I'll bring them back after their portion of the rehearsals," Richard said. "I know your plan is to continue cleaning as well as visit Kurt. Although, sweetheart, please don't exhaust yourself trying to please Mom." He arched his dark eyebrows. "You realize that's an impossibility, no matter what you do."

"I know, I know. Anyway, I'll make sure to be home by five thirty, since you have to head back to the theater after you drop off the kids."

"That's fine. It'll probably be closer to six, anyway." Richard gave me a kiss and ushered Ella and Nicky out the door.

Left alone with the cats, who vanished the moment I rolled the vacuum out of the hall closet, I used my cleaning time to work through all the theories and questions I had about Wendy's death.

Ethan disappearing is the real mystery, I thought. *I just can't picture him fleeing without any attempt to clear his name. Unless, of course, he is guilty.*

That was the real sticking point. As I showered after completing my whirlwind housecleaning, I recalled Scott's words about Ethan fearing any sort of physical confinement. My brother knew Ethan better than anyone, so I couldn't dismiss his fears that his husband might become a fugitive rather than face prison time.

But he left Cassie behind, I thought as I dried my hair. *Would he really abandon his dog?* Slipping on a pair of jeans and a loose sweatshirt, I had to admit that Ethan might've made that choice *because* he loved his pet. Cassie was getting older. She'd be safer at home, where she'd have Scott to look after her, than roughing it in the wilderness.

I also had to remember that there were other viable suspects. That was the point I had to keep emphasizing to Brad and his deputies. As I drove out of town, I reminded myself of all the reasons the killer could be someone like Tim Thompson, or even Nadia Blackstone. Not to mention the many people, like Candy Jensen, whose families had been impacted by Wendy's business practices. And then there was Jaden Perez, a man with a temper that had led him to shove and injure someone before. It certainly wouldn't be totally out of character for him to have hit and shoved Wendy during an angry encounter at the festival grounds.

Kurt's historic estate, Highview, was located up in the mountains just outside Taylorsford. The gravel road that led to the entrance of the estate was riddled with potholes and ridged like an old washboard, but all that changed as soon as I turned onto the driveway. Stone pillars topped with urns sat at either side of a metal gate. I lowered my window and leaned out to press the buzzer on the intercom embedded in one of the pillars. As soon as I gave my name, the gate swung open.

The driveway was paved, its blacktop surface smooth as a satin ribbon. Surrounding the trunks of the bare-branched hardwood trees that lined the driveway, azaleas and rhododendrons, their glossy leaves still clinging to their interlaced limbs, provided a pop of midnight green amid the brown-and-gray winter landscape.

Sunlight flooded through the windshield as I rounded a corner, making me slow the car. Set in the middle of a large clearing, Kurt's home was old enough to look like it had sprung up as a natural part of the landscape. The three-story central section was constructed from variegated fieldstone that had once been prevalent in the local fields. Tall windows with wavy antique glass punctuated the expanse of mottled gray stones. The two-story wood-framed wings were painted a pale jade green and extended from either side of the central structure like welcoming arms. Square windows framed by black shutters gleamed against the wood siding, and a lacy veil of ivy draped the stone chimneys.

As I parked in the circle of blacktop at the end of the driveway, I noticed another car—an older-model compact sedan with an angry scratch marring the navy-blue paint of its passenger side door. Dylan Blackstone must've already arrived, and judging by his vehicle, he was definitely not taking advantage of his family's money.

I crossed to the small roofed porch with its Grecian-style pillars. One of the wreaths Kurt had purchased from the garden club hung on the forest-green front door. The only other decorations visible from outside the house were the sprays of evergreens and holly berries surrounding stout pillar candles—undoubtedly electric, given Kurt's valuable art collection—filling each deep windowsill.

Kurt greeted me, opening the door before I even pressed the doorbell. "Heard your car," he said as he led me into the wide hall that ran from the front to the back of the house.

Unlike the understated exterior, the hall had been lavishly decorated. Fresh pine garlands hung from the wide white moldings and draped each doorway. The garlands were festooned with crimson berries, ruby velvet bows, and pinecones and laced with tiny white lights. This decorative style continued into the large living room, at least in terms of the tables and sideboards as well as the stone fireplace that dominated the outside wall.

But there were no decorations placed anywhere near the numerous paintings that hung on the ivory plaster walls. *Of course not*, I thought. *Kurt would never allow any vegetation or other decorations anywhere near his valuable original artworks.*

Looking around the room, I caught the eye of a young man seated in a wood-framed chair I knew to be from William Morris's nineteenth-century Arts and Crafts studio.

Dylan Blackstone's resemblance to his mother was uncanny—he had the same slender build, large eyes, and angular face. But there was a softness in his hazel eyes and a wariness in his expression that Wendy had never displayed. At least, not in my presence.

"Please don't get up," I told him as I crossed to one of the room's leather sofas. "Hello, I'm Amy Muir." I sat down and stretched my arm across the sofa's buttery-soft armrest.

"Dylan Blackstone." He clasped my hand for only a second and then immediately sat back. "Mr. Kendrick told me that you're related somehow?"

Settling onto the sofa across from me, Kurt flashed a wolfish grin. "In a roundabout way."

"Kurt was the foster son of my husband's great-uncle, Paul Dassin," I said, shooting Kurt a questioning look.

He leaned back, stretching his long legs out across the Persian rug that covered the hardwood floor between the sofas. "That's one connection. I also knew Amy's aunt, Lydia Talbot, or Lydia Litton as she was known then, when we were young. As a matter of fact, I was good friends with her husband, Andrew Talbot."

"The artist?" Dylan gripped the wide wooden arms of his chair. "I saw an exhibition of his paintings in the lobby of the Smithsburg theater not long ago."

Kurt stared over my head, avoiding my direct gaze. "Ah, yes. To be honest, I actually set up that particular show. I like to keep Andrew's work alive in the public consciousness when I can."

"Because you were good friends?" Dylan's knuckles blanched as his grip tightened. "Like you were good friends with my grandfather?"

"Not exactly." Kurt turned his icy gaze on Dylan, who slid back in his chair. "Steven Barclay and I were friends, but it was hardly a lifelong relationship."

"My mother would never provide any details about that, although she was always bitching about how you ruined her father's life. And, by association, hers." Releasing his hold on the chair arms, Dylan dropped his hands into his lap. "That's one reason I wanted to talk to you, Mr. Kendrick. I've heard so many half-finished sentences and vague accusations related to you over the years. To be honest, I've always wondered what Mom was hiding."

"I'm not sure if she had anything to hide. I certainly don't." Kurt's laconic tone didn't fool me. I could sense the intensity behind his words.

"You never knew your grandfather?" I asked Dylan.

"No, Granddad Barclay died when my mother was only thirteen." Dylan glanced at me. "He was killed in some random shootout. Wrong place, wrong time. But you probably already know that. Mr. Kendrick said you were a librarian and obsessed with research."

I nodded. "I'd heard something about it. It was connected to an art deal gone wrong."

"Yeah. That's the story the family always told, anyway." Dylan toyed with the zipper pull on his hooded sweatshirt. "But privately, Mom used to say that you"—he turned to face Kurt—"set him up."

"Really? How extraordinary." Kurt leaned forward, his large hands resting on his thighs. "I can assure you I did not."

Dylan lifted his sharp chin. "She also said you were a drug dealer. Is that true?"

"Eons ago, yes. But not when I knew Steven Barclay," Kurt replied, his tone razor sharp.

To his credit, Dylan's gaze didn't falter. "But that was Mom's argument—that my grandfather ran afoul of some of your criminal pals. Cheated them, or at least they thought so. Which led them to murder him. And, according to Mom, you did nothing to stop it."

"Your mother was quite mistaken." Kurt sat back, crossing his arms over his broad chest. "In point of fact, I actually warned Steven to stay away from certain people, but he refused to listen to me. He was too eager to prove . . . something."

Dylan sniffed. "You got him into dealing art, though."

"I won't deny that. But only because he desperately wanted to get involved. I didn't think it was a good idea, but Steven and I were friends, so"—Kurt shrugged—"I overruled my own better judgment and agreed to help him start buying and selling a few pieces. I admit that was a mistake. He was too eager to make a big score, too easily and too soon." Kurt examined Dylan with a quizzical expression. "What else did your mother tell you about the situation?"

Dylan's eyes narrowed. "Nothing, really. But I always thought there was more to it. And it's made me wonder . . ."

"If she had some dirt on me and I killed her to keep her quiet?" Kurt bared his teeth in a humorless grin. "That's what's this is really all about, isn't it? You wanted to try to get me to implicate myself in Wendy's death, and you wanted a witness so you'd have someone to back up your accusations." Kurt shot me a raised-eyebrow look. "Sorry, Amy, it looks like Dylan has been trying to play us both."

Dylan leapt to his feet. "That isn't it! I never planned to turn you in."

"You wanted Kurt to confess and then you'd just do nothing?" I asked, as Dylan paced back and forth across the rug. "That doesn't make sense."

"Actually, it does." Kurt stood and halted Dylan by gently placing a hand on his shoulder. "You're afraid someone else killed her, aren't you? You were hoping to hear me say I was at fault so you could set your mind at ease."

Dylan jerked his shoulder free. "I don't know what you're talking about."

"Is it your sister? I've heard a few rumors that she and your mother were recently at odds. A lot of shouting was mentioned." Kurt looked down at Dylan with a sympathetic smile. "Families can have serious issues, and when money is involved . . ."

"Nadia had nothing to do with Mom's death," Dylan spoke forcefully, but the tremor in his lips told me he wasn't entirely sure this was true.

"Wait—was your sister even around on the night your mom died?" I rose to my feet and cast Kurt a warning look. "I mean, if she has a solid alibi, it doesn't matter how many arguments they'd had. To be a viable suspect, she'd need opportunity as well as motive."

Dylan took a step back and swept his shaggy dark-blond hair away from his face with both hands. "I don't know. I was at work." He sent me a sidelong look. "I work at the county humane society and do a lot of overnight shifts. That's where I was the evening my mom died. So I have no idea where Nadia was. Or Tim Thompson, for that matter."

"They were an item, weren't they? Nadia and Thompson, I mean," I said, earning a swift, surprised glance from Kurt.

"Yeah. I thought it was gross. I mean, Thompson's so much older. And he's such a snake. I didn't understand what she saw in him." Dylan shook his head. "I think it was just that he had all these ideas on how to expand the company and make even more money and that's what attracted her. That's what Nadia really loves, you know. Money. She can never seem to make enough of it to satisfy her."

"While I'm assuming you aren't that interested in it, judging by your choice of job," I said.

"That's right." Dylan cast Kurt a derisive sneer. "I bet you can't understand that. Just like Mom never could. I'm not money hungry. I want to make a positive difference in the world. My current job has shown me the changes that are needed. I plan to go back to school for an advanced degree—learn enough to work with an organization that's trying to stop species extinctions and save animals. My mom thought that was nonsense."

"Hence the estrangement," Kurt said. "And despite my wealth, son, I do understand."

"Really?" Dylan's gaze swept the room, taking in the expensive furnishings and priceless artwork. "I doubt that. But anyway, I didn't want anything to do with the family business, which drove Mom nuts. Sure, she had Nadia on board, but she was still old-fashioned enough to want her *son* to eventually take over." He cast me a sardonic smile. "Trust me, that drove Nadia up the wall. She hated the fact that Mom preferred me as an heir apparent. But even if I was interested in real estate, which I'm not, there are things about my family's business practices that I don't like . . ."

"Such as?" I asked.

Dylan must've caught something overeager in my expression. He shook his head. "I won't go into that right now. I don't have all the facts yet."

So much for extracting more information about Nadia or her plans for expanding the business from him, I thought. "What about Tim Thompson?" I asked, sitting back down on the sofa. "Didn't he want to be in charge?"

Dylan strolled over to the fireplace. "He did, or at least that was my impression. I think that's why he went after Nadia. He got a divorce not that long ago, so now he's free to marry her." He turned to face Kurt and me. "So yeah, maybe I'm worried that Thompson convinced my sister to do something crazy, like shove Mom down a flight of stairs. I wouldn't put it past him."

"Or maybe Tim Thompson was the one to give Wendy that push," Kurt said. "I think that might be more likely."

"But if Nadia is covering for him"—Dylan looked from me to Kurt—"she'll still get in trouble, won't she? Aiding and abetting and all that." He lifted his hands. "There's six years between us, and we don't always get along, but she's the only family I have left."

Kurt's expression softened. "Look, son, I wouldn't worry too much. Personally, I doubt your sister was involved. At least, not knowingly or willingly. But as Amy said earlier, I have some sources who might be able to provide more helpful information. I don't mind using them to look into the matter." He thrust his hands into the pockets of his tweed trousers. "And while I can assure you that I had nothing to do with Wendy's death, I don't mind remaining under suspicion if it helps widen the investigation. If they aren't focused on just one individual, they may come across more pertinent information."

I caught Kurt's eye and offered a wan smile. "Let's hope so, anyway."

"Okay." Dylan took a deep breath and crossed over to stand in front of Kurt. "I really just wanted to meet you to see if you were the ogre my mom always said you were. I thought if I talked to you, I could make up my own mind."

"And have you?" Kurt asked.

"Yes." Dylan thrust out his hand. "She got it wrong somehow. I don't believe you had anything to do with the death of my mother, much less my grandfather. I think that was all in her head."

Kurt gave Dylan's hand a firm shake. "Good to hear. Now, if that's all, let me show you out. Apologies, but I do have some other business to take care of this afternoon."

Dylan told me good-bye and followed Kurt out into the hallway. After I heard the front door open and close, Kurt returned and sat down on the sofa across from me.

"I know that speculative look. You have questions," he said, relaxing against the cushions.

I scooted to the edge of my seat. "Wendy thought you and her father were having an affair, didn't she?"

Kurt's stoic expression confirmed my suspicions. "Wendy was only twelve or thirteen when Steven and I met and became friends. Friends," he reiterated, holding up a finger. "That's all it was, at least on my part."

"But Wendy thought otherwise."

"Yes. Probably because her father had finally allowed feelings he'd buried all his life to rise to the surface. It drove him to leave his family in the end."

"So he came out as gay, and Wendy blamed you. Did she think you'd seduced him or something?"

"I suppose she did." Resting his elbow on the arm of the sofa, Kurt cradled his chin in his hand. "It wasn't true. Steven developed romantic feelings for me, but they weren't reciprocated. I liked him, but only as a friend. Sadly, he thought he could convince me otherwise."

"So he was pursuing you? I guess Wendy didn't see it that way."

"No, she thought I was the big, bad wolf"—Kurt flashed a toothy grin—"who'd lured her dad away from his family and led him down a disreputable path." Pausing for a moment, Kurt stared up at the elaborate plaster medallion encircling the overhead light fixture. "The truth is, because I've had relationships with both men and women, people like Wendy think I'm some sex-crazed predator who wants to seduce everyone I meet. Which is far from the truth, believe me." He lowered his eyes, meeting my questioning gaze. "I'm actually quite discriminating. I prefer my independence and only embark on a relationship if I meet an individual who I can connect with on a deeper level."

"Steven Barclay was not such an individual, I take it?"

"Hardly. He was an enjoyable companion, as a friend. But I had no interest in having a romantic relationship with him. Which, unfortunately, made him rather reckless."

"You said he wanted to prove something. Was that to you?"

"He was determined to score a big art deal—something that would show me he could be a useful partner in the business. I suppose he thought that was step one to becoming partners in other ways." Kurt drummed his fingers against the sofa arm. "Unfortunately, he knew about some of my less-than-legal connections in the art world. I warned him not to make any deals with them, but . . ."

"He did it anyway." I pressed my knuckles against my jaw. "I bet he thought if he showed you that he could negotiate deals with such a dangerous crew, you'd respect him more. See him as tough and dynamic. He probably thought that would make you desire him or something."

"Undoubtedly true." Kurt's sigh filled the air between us. "It wouldn't have changed anything, of course."

"So he brokered a deal with criminals and got killed when something went wrong. That is sad, but not your fault," I said.

"No. Anyway, it's certainly not one of the things that have weighed heavily on my heart over the years." Kurt cast me a rueful smile. "Yes, there are many others that do, but not Steven Barclay's death. That was his choice, and I can rest easy knowing I did everything I could to dissuade him."

I glanced at my watch. "Oh dear, look at the time. I'd better go. I need to be home when Richard brings the twins back from rehearsal."

Kurt stood as I rose to my feet. "Thank you for coming over today, Amy. I really didn't want to meet with Dylan Blackstone alone." He quirked a bushy eyebrow. "I wasn't sure what Wendy had told him, you see."

"Were you afraid he'd come armed with a gun?" I asked as we walked to the front door.

"The thought did cross my mind," Kurt said, opening the front door.

I looked up at him from under my black eyelashes. "Loaded with a silver bullet?"

Kurt laughed and threw an arm around my shoulders. "Oh, my dear, what a pity we aren't closer in age. If I hadn't been so old when we met, I would've given Richard a run for his money."

I offered him a smile, but as I walked out onto the porch, I called over my shoulder, "You would've lost."

Another peal of laughter followed me to my car.

Chapter Fifteen

M y mother-in-law, Fiona Muir, arrived early Sunday afternoon. As Richard dragged her overly large suitcase up to Ella's bedroom, Fiona greeted Nicky and Ella, displaying a level of affection she'd never shown me. *Or her son, come to think of it.*

I stood back, amused by Fiona's willingness to be pulled to the Christmas tree, one twin clutching each hand. As Ella and Nicky chattered about the ornaments they'd created, Fiona made appreciative noises.

Richard stepped up behind me. "Is this the same woman who never attended any of my dance performances until just a few years ago?" he whispered in my ear.

"I guess it's true what they say—being a grandparent is a completely different thing than being a parent," I replied, keeping my voice low.

As Fiona bent over with her head close to Ella's and Nicky's, her dark locks, pulled back into a smooth chignon, blended with the twins'. I was sure she dyed her hair to remove any traces of gray, especially since she was always telling me that I'd look much younger if I colored mine.

Richard placed his hands on either side of my waist. "It doesn't hurt that they resemble her. I think she enjoys having little mini-me's."

I leaned back against his chest. "You look just like her. That didn't seem to help in your case."

"No. But the years have obviously mellowed her." Richard hugged me against him for a second before dropping his hands to his sides. "And she doesn't have to worry about other people's opinions so much. If the twins don't turn out *perfect*, she can always blame us."

"As I'm sure she will," I said, turning to face him. "Now, don't you need to get to the theater? I know you have a major technical rehearsal this afternoon."

"Into the evening, I'm afraid." Richard tipped up my chin with his forefinger. "Sorry to leave you to deal with everything, but you're right—I do need to go." He leaned in and brushed my lips with a kiss. "Try not to murder her before I get back."

I wrinkled my nose at him. "I won't. I'll wait for you to return so you can provide an alibi."

Richard laughed, which made Fiona straighten and turn to face us. "You have rehearsals today, I suppose, Richard?"

"As always," he replied, stepping around me and strolling over to the coat-tree near the front door. "Fortunately, the kids aren't needed today, so you can spend some quality time with them."

"We're going to make cookies!" Nicky said.

"That's nice." I caught Fiona's eye. "I may or may not have all the ingredients you need. But since you'll be here with Ella and Nicky, I can always run out to the grocery store to pick up supplies."

Fiona pointed to a plastic bag she'd set on one of our side tables. "Oh, don't worry. I thought that might be the case, so I brought my own ingredients."

"Hey, Ella and Nicky, get over here," Richard said as he tugged on his coat. "I'll probably be late getting home, so give me a hug and a kiss now in case you're already asleep when I get back."

"You can wake us up," Ella said as she and her brother crossed the room at a gallop.

Richard shot me a look over their heads. "Uh, no. I don't think Mommy would like that very much." Bending down to hug both of them, he added, "Besides, you need a full night of rest. We have dress rehearsals on the stage this week, remember?"

"And opening night is Friday!" Ella spun around after getting a kiss on the cheek from Richard. "You're coming, right, Grandmother?"

"I certainly am," Fiona said. She adjusted the collar of her sleek navy dress. "Wouldn't miss it."

I shared another look with Richard, who simply widened his eyes as he fastened the buttons on his coat. Slinging his dance bag over one shoulder, he offered a cheery "See you later" before heading out the door.

"He's always flitting off somewhere, isn't he? I thought he might slow down once he stopped taking those professional dance jobs, but he's just filled it in with other related stuff." Fiona tucked a loose strand of her silky hair behind one ear. "I'm sorry you have to put up with that, Amy, but I suppose you knew what you were getting into when you married him."

"I did, and I really don't mind," I said, keeping my tone mild. "Now, if we're going to make cookies, would you like to change into something less dressy? The twins tend to be a little messy when we bake together."

"Just an apron will be fine." Fiona unbuttoned the crisp white cuffs of her dress and rolled back her sleeves. "You do have an apron somewhere, I suppose? I know I gave you one a few years back, but I've never seen you wear it."

"I do," I said, after relaxing my gritted teeth. "It's hanging on the back of the pantry door."

"Well, come along, children. Nicky, please carry that bag for me." Fiona set off down the hall that led to the kitchen. "Of course, we must wash our hands before we start making anything," she said, motioning toward the hall bathroom. "I'll use the kitchen sink, but you two can use the powder room."

She took the bag from Nicky as the twins obediently dashed into the bathroom.

Sounds of splashing water and jostling followed. "I'll use the powder room too, I guess," I said. "That will give me a chance to clean up any messes in there once the twins are done."

"Oh, you don't need to worry, Amy." Fiona swept her free hand through the air in a graceful but dismissive arc. "The children and I can handle the cookies. No need for you to get involved. I know where all your pans and utensils and things are from when I've helped out before."

"Okay then." I moved out of the way as Ella and Nicky dashed out of the hall bath, water droplets flying from their fingers. "Stop. Towel." Grabbing one of the guest towels from the rack next to the sink, I tossed it to Ella, who barely swiped it across her palms before handing it to Nicky. "How many times do I have to tell you two to thoroughly dry your hands?" I asked as Nicky passed the towel back to me.

Fiona made a tutting noise. "Now, now, Amy, they're still learning."

I twisted the towel between my fingers, fighting the urge to throw it in her face. "Well, if you're going to be in charge, Fiona, I think I'll take the opportunity to sit on the sofa and read. It's been a while since I had time to do that."

Fiona widened her clear gray eyes. "But you're a librarian. Surely you have plenty of time to read at work."

I counted to five before trusting myself to speak. "Anyway, have fun." As I turned away and marched into the living room, my lips formed a word I'd never speak aloud. At least, not in Fiona's presence.

Realizing I was still clutching the towel, I tossed it onto the coffee table next to the book I was currently reading and slumped down onto the sofa. I sat for several minutes, simply staring up at the ceiling, before I leaned forward to grab my book.

I tried to concentrate on reading, but noises from the kitchen kept distracting me. Bursts of high-pitched laughter and the constant buzz of my children's chatter sailed down the hall, reminding me that while my relationship with Fiona was fraught with tension, Ella and Nicky had no such problems.

Which is good, I told myself as I flipped back and forth between two pages whose text appeared to swim before my eyes. Loie and Fosse, who'd huddled under the coffee table upon Fiona's arrival, slunk out and leapt up on the sofa to sit on either side of me.

"It really is a good thing," I told the cats while stroking their soft fur. "The kids need to have a close relationship with their grandparents, and while I know they'll never make much headway with Jim Muir, at least they can make warm memories with their paternal grandmother."

The fact that Fiona had never really created a loving bond with Richard, much less me, was something I needed to let go. Or so I told myself as I slammed my book shut and laid it back on the coffee table.

Rising to my feet over the protests of the cats, I strode down the hall into the kitchen, the delectable aroma of baking cookies drawing me forward.

The scene that met my eyes resembled an indoor snowstorm. Flour and powdered sugar covered the top of the kitchen island, Ella and Nicky, and even the upper portion of Fiona's sleeves. The apron had protected the front of her navy dress but not all of it.

I surveyed the three faces beaming at me. All three radiated joy. Even Fiona's, which was a first, at least in my experience. I placed my hands on my hips. "Well, well," I said. "So who's going to clean up before it's time to fix dinner?"

Fiona and the twins shared secretive smiles.

"You?" suggested Ella, her gray eyes widening.

I shook my head. "Think again."

Fiona waved me off. "Go on back to your reading. We'll take care of this mess. Right, children?"

As Ella and Nicky bobbed their heads, white puffs of flour and sugar filled the air.

I fixed my gaze on Fiona. "Okay, but while I make dinner, I know a couple of bakers who are going to need baths."

She looks happy, I thought as she volunteered to supervise the twins' bath time. *Maybe it's being around the kids, although she's spent time with them before. But*—I narrowed my eyes as I watched Fiona direct Ella and Nicky in some cleaning efforts—*not without Jim. So maybe it's her husband who makes her so tense and reserved. Knowing him, I could see how that could happen.*

As if in confirmation of my thoughts, I earned a faint smile when I thanked Fiona for offering to take care of the cleanup—of the twins as well as the kitchen.

* * *

Later, after Ella and Nicky had gone to bed—with Fosse and Loie snuggled up beside them, much to Fiona's dismay—I asked my mother-in-law if she would like to join me in a glass of wine.

"I don't mind if I do," she said, settling into one of the living room armchairs. "I prefer red, if you have that."

"Merlot? Cabernet Sauvignon? Pinot Noir?" I asked, smiling when Fiona arched her feathery dark brows. "These days we have quite a collection of wine. You should know that your son has become something of an aficionado over the last few years, and I . . . well, I don't mind a glass or two in the evening either."

Fiona looked me up and down. "A Cabernet Sauvignon, then."

I brought back two glasses of the wine from the kitchen and handed one to Fiona. Sitting down on the sofa, I took a long swallow from my glass. "It's been a day," I said when Fiona cast me a questioning glance.

"I suppose it has." Fiona delicately sipped her wine for a moment before adding, "Have you heard anything from your brother-in-law? I know you're all anxious about him."

"No, not yet." I took another gulp of wine. "Thanks for asking."

"No problem. I can't imagine what I'd do if someone in my family went missing." Fiona kicked off her leather pumps and wiggled her toes inside her stockings.

"It's hardest on my brother, of course. Especially with all the rumors floating around. I imagine you may have already heard that Ethan is one of the suspects in Wendy Blackstone's death? I mean, it's nonsense, but now people are saying he must be guilty because he's made a run for it."

"I have heard some people say that. But honestly"—Fiona held up her still-full wineglass—"I'd be much more inclined to suspect Wendy's business partner or even one of her children."

"Oh, what makes you say that?" I asked, sitting up straighter.

"Even though Wendy has been living just outside of Taylorsford recently, Blackstone Properties' home office is still based in my hometown, so I've heard things from friends. Gossip, of course, but I do believe there's a kernel of truth behind it."

I set my glass on the coffee table. "You're talking about Tim Thompson when you say business partner, I assume."

"Yes. Not one of my favorite people." Fiona pursed her lips. "We don't actually know one another, but I've encountered him at a few charity functions. One of my old friends throws a gala each year to support the local children's hospital. She's always invited Wendy Blackstone and Tim Thompson because they were good for a check."

Fiona took another sip. "A rather small check, considering their profits, but it was something, I suppose."

"That doesn't surprise me. I recently met Tim Thompson and was not impressed," I said. "He seems very . . . slimy or something."

"I always called him the used-car salesman, which Jim told me was rude." Fiona stared into the depths of her wine. "But Thompson did give off that vibe. And then there was that time he showed up with Nadia Blackstone instead of Wendy. Well, I was appalled with the way he was hanging all over her, to be honest." Fiona set her glass on the side table next to her chair.

"I saw a photo from that event when I was doing research on the company," I said. "Or at least, from some event where Tim Thompson and Nadia Blackstone looked like a couple."

Fiona sniffed. "Disgraceful. The man is almost old enough to be her father, and for him to carry on like that with his partner's daughter just left a bad taste in my mouth. But then again, I've heard rumors that Nadia and Wendy didn't have a very good relationship. From what people have told me, it seems Nadia was desperate to gain more power in the company."

"You said *children*. But Wendy's son isn't really involved in the business."

"No, but that's another story." Fiona crossed her ankles and tucked her feet up close to the chair skirt. "Dylan Blackstone had serious issues when he was a teenager. He even had to go live with a friend's family for a while."

"Why?" I asked, leaning forward.

Fiona picked up her glass. "He publicly accused his mother of driving his dad to suicide," she said, before taking a sip of wine. "I don't know that there's any truth to that, but it was common knowledge in my hometown. A lot of my old friends shared the drama with me while it was happening."

"So Dylan does have a reason, right or wrong, to hate his mom," I said, talking more to myself than Fiona.

"I'd say that was a possibility." Fiona held up her empty wineglass. "I wouldn't mind another."

"Sure." I grabbed my own glass as I stood up and crossed to Fiona. Gripping the stems of both glasses in one hand, I hurried into the kitchen, pondering Fiona's words. They confirmed some of the information I'd already collected, which made me even more convinced that Brad and his team should be looking more closely at Tim Thompson as well as Wendy's children.

"You know," Fiona said when I handed back the wineglass, "I'd be happy to find out more about Blackstone Properties, as well as all of the people involved with Wendy and the company. I do have solid connections who may be able to offer some insight."

I looked down at her, clutching my wineglass with both hands. "Really? That would be great. I'd definitely appreciate anything you can find out—anything I can share with the sheriff's department that will encourage them to broaden their focus."

She must've read the astonishment in my face. "I know we haven't always seen eye to eye, Amy, but I do want to help. Ethan is family, after all. Ella and Nicky would undoubtedly be upset if anything bad were to happen to him."

"Very true." I held out my wineglass. "Okay, you're on. I welcome whatever you can find out concerning Wendy or her associates and family."

Fiona raised her glass and clinked it against mine. "Here's to a partnership, then. Perhaps we can solve this unfortunate issue before Christmas."

"I'll drink to that," I said. And I did.

Chapter Sixteen

I reaped one benefit of Fiona's visit on Monday. I had to work at the library and Richard needed to spend the entire day at the theater, and since school was out for the holidays, having Fiona available to stay with Nicky and Ella was a boon. It meant I didn't need to ask Aunt Lydia to babysit. Not that she minded watching the twins, but she'd already done so much after-school care over the last few months that I was happy she could take a break. Besides, I knew my aunt. She'd revel in the time to bake all the items she liked to give away as holiday gifts.

We received similar gifts at the library late Monday morning. One of our regular patrons, Mrs. Dinterman, brought in lemon pies as holiday gifts for me, Samantha, and Sunny. Sunny was off, and although I knew she was working at the library on Tuesday, our small break room refrigerator couldn't accommodate a pie on top of everything else. Since I didn't want a custard pie to sit out overnight, I decided to deliver it to Vista View over my lunch break.

I threw on a fleece jacket before heading out to my car. The weather had warmed to temperatures more typical of northern Virginia in December, so I didn't have to bundle up in a hat or scarf, although I'd still pulled on some thin gloves. Setting the pie on the seat beside me, I drove out to the farm, taking care not to hit too many bumps and dips in Vista View's gravel driveway.

I parked between Sunny's iridescent Beetle and the battered silver compact car that I assumed belonged to Megan Campbell. Carrying the pie with both hands, I called out a loud "Hello" as I reached the front door.

Carol appeared, wiping her hands on her apron. "Hi, Amy. What have you got there?"

"A gift for Sunny from Mrs. Dinterman," I said, striding into the house as Carol held the door open. "I didn't want to leave it out all night, so I thought I'd better make a delivery over my lunch hour."

"Thank you, dear. How sweet." Carol took the pie out of my hands so I could peel off my gloves and jacket. I shoved the gloves into the pockets and draped the jacket over my arm. "But that probably means you're not going to have time for lunch, so let me fix you a sandwich or something before you leave," she called over her shoulder as I followed her into the kitchen.

Megan Campbell was standing over the chrome-edged yellow Formica table that filled the center of the room, packing plastic-wrapped sandwiches into a large brown paper bag. Worry lines fanned out from her taut lips as she looked up when we entered the room.

"Ms. Muir, whatever brings you here?" Megan's tone was sharp as a stiletto. She stared at me with a wary expression.

"Just delivering a patron's holiday gift to Sunny," I said, hanging my jacket across the back of a kitchen chair. "Is she around?"

"She's out checking on the chickens. We heard some squawking and were afraid something had gotten into the coop," Carol replied before Megan could open her mouth. "She should be back any minute."

"Are you having a picnic?" I asked Megan, figuring that if she could question me so abruptly, I could return the favor. "That's brave of you. I know it's gotten a little warmer, but I still don't think I'd want to eat outside right now."

"What? Oh, no, nothing like that." She brushed back a coiled tendril of red-gold hair that had fallen across her brow. "I'm just getting some food together for a meeting EA is holding later today."

It took me a moment to realize she was referencing Environmental Advocates. "Ah, I see. Some snacks for the group."

"And water," Megan said, shoving a few bottles into another bag. "It won't be cold, but it will have to do."

Carol slid the lemon pie into her white enameled refrigerator. "I'm sure no one will mind. As long as it's wet, right?"

"That's what I figured. Besides, our group isn't picky about things like that." Megan's eyelids were lowered, making her eyes impossible to read, especially behind the round lenses of her glasses. "This will be fine, believe me." She folded the top of each bag down and then snatched them both off the table, gripping one in each hand. "Thank you for the sandwich makings and all, Carol," she said. "I probably won't be back until late, so don't wait dinner on me."

She practically ran out of the room, giving me a barely perceptible head bob as acknowledgment as she dashed past me.

When the front door slammed, Carol placed her hands on her hips and shook her head. "That's one peculiar young woman, I must say."

"In what way?" I asked, after a quick glance at my watch. I didn't want to be late returning to the library, but I was too curious to cut Carol short.

Carol opened the bread box on the counter and extracted two slices of marble rye. "I don't know. She seems very nervy. I keep thinkin' she's going to flap her arms and squawk, like my chickens when a critter is circling the henhouse."

Picturing this image, I laughed. "Maybe it's her work. She appears to be extremely devoted to her organization. Things like Wendy Blackstone's death throwing everything into question might be making her anxious."

"Could be." Carol pursed her lips. "But you'd think that would help her cause. It'll be a while before everything is sorted out. Blackstone Properties isn't going to be able to bring in their bulldozers anytime soon."

"True." I shifted my weight from foot to foot. "Do you have any other thoughts about Megan, Carol?"

"Other than the fact that she holes up in the guest room like a scared rabbit when she isn't out meeting with her environmental group?" Carol pulled a plastic storage container from the refrigerator. "Egg salad okay?"

"Sounds good," I said. "No, actually great. Your food is always delicious."

Carol flashed me a smile. As she spread some of the egg salad on the bread, her expression grew less cheerful. "As for Megan, well, I don't know. She just seems awfully anxious, which I wouldn't expect from someone who's trying to, you know, *fight the power*. Why do you ask?"

"I'm just trying to figure out if anyone associated with Environmental Advocates could've had a reason to harm Wendy Blackstone."

"Like me?" Sunny waltzed into the room, pulling off her work gloves and tossing them onto the table.

"No, not like you," I said with an exaggerated roll of my eyes. "This may come as a surprise, but not everything is about you, Sunshine Fields."

Sunny responded to my teasing with her usual good humor. "Really? I had no idea. I thought the world revolved around my fine—"

"Sunny!" Carol interjected, before my friend could complete her comment.

"Anyway, what brings you here today, Amy? I thought you were working at the library all day."

"I am," I said, with another glance at my watch. "I need to leave soon so I can be back on time, but I wanted to bring you a gift that was dropped off at the library this morning."

"Lemon pie," Carol said, motioning toward the refrigerator. "Amy very kindly drove over here on her lunch hour so it wouldn't be left sitting out overnight."

Sunny pulled off her denim jacket. "From Mrs. Dinterman, I bet. She loves bringing us pies."

"You're correct," I said. "Anyway, it was no problem to run it over here."

Carol held up the sandwich she'd covered in plastic wrap. "I made Amy something she can eat in the car on the way back. Figured she might miss out on lunch otherwise."

"Always worried about people going hungry." Sunny draped her jacket over the back of a chair and crossed to Carol. She threw her arm around her grandmother's shoulder. "Heaven forbid anyone leave this house without something to eat," she added, giving me a wink.

"That's country hospitality," Carol said with an audible sniff. "And don't you forget that, missy. When I'm long gone, it'll be up to you to continue that tradition."

Sunny's golden eyelashes fluttered. I knew she hated any reminder of her grandparents' mortality. They were all the family she'd ever had. *Other than her found family that includes all of my relatives, Richard, and many other friends*, I reminded myself. "I was asking Carol what she thought of your houseguest. Maybe I should ask you the same thing."

"Still trying to get Brad to focus on someone other than Ethan?" Sunny slid her arm away from Carol's shoulders and strolled over to the counter that held an electric kettle. "Have you heard anything from him yet?" she asked, flicking the switch to heat up the water already in the kettle.

"Unfortunately not. Scott is beside himself with worry."

"I bet." Sunny rummaged around in a basket that held a variety of tea bags. "I think something's wrong there, to tell you the truth. Ethan would get in touch with Scott if he could. I'd put money on that."

"I know. It has me worried too." I gnawed the inside of my cheek for a second. "I'm actually worried that his cell phone broke or died or something and he's stuck somewhere, needing our help."

"I guess it's good that the sheriff's department is searching for him, then." Carol plucked a mug from the dish drainer and slid it down the counter to Sunny. "I know you don't want him arrested, Amy, but if he's hurt or otherwise in trouble, it's best that he be found."

"I suppose," I said, picking up the sandwich Carol had laid on the table. "I guess I should be running along. Thanks for this, Carol." I slipped on my jacket and dropped the sandwich into one of its deep pockets.

"Thanks for bringing that pie," Sunny said as she poured hot water into the mug. She appeared lost in thought as she dropped in a tea bag. "Before you go, Amy, there is one other thing. Maybe it's nothing, but . . ."

I paused, my coat zipper halfway closed. "If it has any relevance to the Blackstone case, I want to hear it."

"Maybe. It does involve a member of that family," Sunny said.

Carol, who'd been looking puzzled, snapped her fingers. "Oh, you're talking about that young man that stopped by to talk to Megan."

"Dylan?" My watch warned that I was going to be late, but I decided I'd just have to send Samantha an apologetic text and make up the time another day. "Wendy's son?"

"That's the fellow," Carol said. "Seemed like a nice young man. Polite."

"What did he want with Megan?" I asked, directing my words toward Sunny.

She tossed her head, flinging her long blonde braid behind one shoulder. "I didn't catch all the details. They were talking in the living room, so I could only hear so much." She flashed me a grin. "No matter how hard I tried to eavesdrop."

"I couldn't hear much either," Carol said with a sly smile. "But when I took them in some mugs of coffee, well, I did pick up a few things. Mostly it seemed like the young man was sharing information about a few Blackstone Properties projects with Megan. She did seem very interested, for what that's worth."

"He mentioned two in particular," Sunny said, plucking out the tea bag and tossing it into the sink. "Something called Mountainside Farms and another called Crystal Lake."

"Two cases where the company ran into serious opposition or had other issues building out the developments." Noting both Carol's and Sunny's interest, I added, "I came across that information when I was doing some research recently." I didn't mention Candy Jensen's connection to Mountainside Farms, thinking that was something I needed to dig into a bit more before I shared any suspicions.

"So there may be any number of people with a grudge against Blackstone Properties?" Carol tugged up the drooping strap of the white cotton apron she wore over her tie-dyed T-shirt and jeans. "Seems to me that Brad Tucker and his crew ought to be looking into that, not just trying to pin the crime on Ethan."

"Now, Grandma, I don't think Brad is trying to pin anything on anyone." Sunny's spoon clanged against the sides of the mug as she vigorously stirred her tea.

"Humph. You know how these cops are," Carol said, turning away to put the egg salad container back into the refrigerator.

I caught Sunny's eye and raised my eyebrows. Carol and P.J. hadn't totally lost the aversion to authority figures they'd developed back in their flower-children days. It was one reason they hadn't been upset when Brad and Sunny broke up.

Although now she's dating a private investigator, I thought. But that seemed to carry fewer negative connotations for the Fieldses, who'd said Fred wasn't really part of the establishment. "He isn't operating strictly by the rule book all the time," was how P.J. had put it.

"Okay, I really must go," I said. "But thanks for that info. It might come in handy."

"Always happy to help." Sunny raised her mug in a mock salute. "All for one and one for all and so on."

"I'll let you know if I ever need your good sword arm," I said with a smile.

"Don't laugh. I bet I could handle a sword pretty darn well," Sunny replied.

"I bet you could too," I called out as I left the room.

Chapter Seventeen

When I got back to the library, one of our loyal volunteers, Bill Clayton, was staffing the circulation desk.

"I got here a little early today," he said. "I thought I'd just cover the desk until you got back so Samantha could go to lunch."

"Good thinking." I looked out over the library. "Has it been busy?"

"Not really. There was a rush right around noon. You know, when people dash in to grab a book or two during their lunch hour. But it's slowed down again."

I noticed a full cart of books behind us. "I thought Denise reshelved everything this morning. Have there been that many returns since then?"

Bill shook his head. "That's just what she collected before she left." He quirked his bushy gray eyebrows. "The Nightingale has been here."

"Oh dear, she's really been busy today, hasn't she?" I said with a deep sigh. The Nightingale, whom we'd jokingly named in honor of the famous nurse, was a regular patron whose attempts to be helpful included reshelving books. But since she had no concept of the cataloging system, she always returned things to the wrong places, like shoving car repair manuals in with the history books.

"Since you're here now, I'm happy to go shelve these in the proper locations," Bill said. "Denise already scanned them with the bar code reader to make sure none were checked out and put them in call number order, so all I have to do is get them back on the shelves."

"That would be great, thanks." I studied his craggy face for a moment. "But first—would you mind giving me your impressions of Ethan Payne? I know you volunteer at the fire and rescue station as well as here, and I just wondered . . ."

"If I thought your brother-in-law was capable of murdering someone?" Bill ran his fingers through his shaggy mane of gray hair. "My answer is no. I've never seen any indication that Ethan is violent. Oh, he has a temper, but don't we all. It's never directed at people, though. He tends to get angry when equipment doesn't work or something breaks down at the worst possible time, but I've never seen him even yell at the volunteers. And believe me, a few of them do some really stupid stuff."

I tapped my finger against the surface of the desk. "That's good to know. What about Hannah Fowler?"

"Is she a suspect in the murder of Wendy Blackstone too? Can't imagine why." The lines bracketing Bill's mouth deepened. "I like Hannah. She's always been nice to me, even when I've made mistakes. One of my volunteer tasks is to pack up the medical kits, you see. I used to forget an item from time to time, but Hannah didn't cuss me out like the guy we had before her used to do. She just had me print out a list that we taped to the inside cover of the kits so I could check off what was needed. Smart girl, with a cool head in an emergency."

"And honest, you think?" I asked, thinking of her comments about Ethan's movements the night Wendy was killed.

Bill took a step back. "Sure. Why? Is someone calling her a liar?"

"No, no," I said. "I just wondered what you thought."

"Well, I think she's great." Bill turned away and grabbed the book cart. "I'll go shelve these now, if that's okay."

"It's fine. Thanks again," I replied as he rolled the cart out from behind the desk and headed for the stacks.

I didn't have any patrons approach the desk for several minutes, even though I'd anticipated some questions from a group of home-schooled students who visited the library every Monday to work on research projects. But they seemed to be finding what they needed on their own. Of course, Sunny and I had worked extensively with them in the past, so they understood how to use both our print and online resources quite well.

I was leafing through a new catalog sent to us from one of our book vendors when the door from the vestibule swung open and a tall, dark-haired young woman entered the library. Although I knew she wasn't one of our regular patrons, she looked familiar. Then it hit me. I'd seen photos of her recently. It was Nadia Blackstone.

She strode up to the desk, her black cape swinging like a flag in the wind. She wasn't a traditional beauty, but she was an attractive woman, with a square jaw and strongly defined features. Her shiny cocoa-brown hair brushed her shoulders, and her carefully applied makeup enhanced her dark-brown eyes.

"Hello," she said, unfastening the clasp of her cloak. She swept off the cloak and draped it over one arm, exposing her fawn-colored cable-knit dress. "I'm Nadia Blackstone. Are you the library director?"

"One of them," I said cautiously. Unsure why Wendy's daughter had decided to visit the library, I remained on guard. "I'm Amy Muir."

"Then you're the one I want." Nadia lifted her chin and looked down her nose at me. "Your brother is married to Ethan Payne, from what I hear."

"That's true." I thrust my hands into the pockets of my beige slacks. "How may I help?"

"You can tell the authorities where that brother-in-law of yours is hiding, for one thing."

"I'm sorry," I said, rocking back on my heels. "I'm afraid I have no idea where Ethan is."

"And you expect me to believe that?"

"Since it's true, yes," I said, tightening my lips.

This assertion seemed to take some of the starch out of Nadia. She relaxed her shoulders and lowered her chin. "That seems highly unlikely, but I suppose there's no way to prove you're lying."

I yanked my hands from my pockets and pressed them against the desk. "I don't lie."

"Nonsense. Everyone does." Nadia cast me a withering look. "Especially when there's a lot at stake."

"That may be your experience, but I can assure you it isn't mine." I lifted my palms off the desk. "Sorry for getting a little angry, but I don't enjoy being called a liar."

"It doesn't matter. I should've known I wouldn't gain any satisfaction from this little expedition." Nadia slung the cape back around her shoulders. "Just tell your brother that the Blackstone family is not about to let his husband get away with murder. We'll be pursuing justice, no matter how long it takes. So unless he wants to stay on the run forever, Ethan Payne might as well go ahead and turn himself in."

She wheeled around and strode out of the building, nearly running into Zelda.

"Good heavens, what bee got up in her bonnet?" Zelda asked when she reached the front of the desk.

"Oh, nothing," I said, not sure I wanted to share Nadia's words with someone who loved gossip almost as much as chocolate. I also wasn't convinced that Nadia's grand display wasn't just a way to divert suspicion off someone else. *Like herself,* I thought, deciding that was another thing I shouldn't share with Zelda. No matter what my suspicions were concerning Nadia Blackstone, I had no proof, and I certainly didn't want Zelda sharing unsubstantiated rumors. "What are you doing here? I thought only Denise and Bill were on the volunteer roster for today."

Zelda tugged off her cobalt-blue knit gloves. "I didn't actually come to work. I just wanted to see how you were doing. And maybe share a little information you might find interesting." Puffing out her chest in her ruby-red down jacket, Zelda reminded me of an indignant robin.

"Gossip, you mean," I said, my smile meant to take any sting out of my words.

"Call it what you will, lamb. It's still something that might prove useful." She shook one of the gloves at me. "Lydia told me you've been doing a little research on Blackstone Properties and other things that might help Ethan's case."

"That's true." I looked her over, amused by the high color in her cheeks and sparkle in her light-brown eyes. I knew she was dying to share her news. "So what is it you want me to know?"

Zelda, who admittedly had helped some of my amateur sleuthing efforts in the past, squared her shoulders. "Believe it or not, is has to do with the young woman who just stormed out of here."

"Nadia Blackstone? What about her?" I asked.

Zelda balled up her gloves in one fist. "Oh, nothing. Just that she and her mother were not on the best of terms lately, according to some of the rumors I've heard. In fact, they had a very noisy fight in the middle of the Heapin' Plate the other day."

"Really?" I frowned. If Wendy and Nadia had openly argued in the diner where most of Taylorsford's business owners ate lunch, they certainly hadn't been trying to hide their animosity toward one another. "What was the fight about?"

"Something to do with Wendy not allowing Nadia to make any decisions on her own." Zelda shook her head. "Apparently, it got so heated that Bethany Virts had to tell them to leave."

"That certainly paints a picture of family disfunction," I said.

"And if they argued like that in public, surrounded by people, who's to say they didn't argue the night Wendy died?" Zelda tipped her head to the side.

"The only thing is, no one saw Nadia there the night Wendy was killed," I said.

"No one who's mentioned it, anyway," Zelda countered. "Also, there are woods near the area where Wendy fell. Nadia could've been hiding until the time was right."

She was right, of course, but I wanted to temper my response. Even if I thought Nadia could be the killer, I didn't want Zelda to tell anyone else that. "I don't know . . ." I twirled a pencil between my fingers. "I guess I can imagine Nadia shoving her mom in anger, but planning to kill her is an entirely different thing."

Zelda's smile faded. "Still, if she and Wendy were at odds over the business, that does give Nadia a motive. She's undoubtedly set to inherit Blackstone Properties."

"Part of it, anyway," I said. "There's also her brother, Dylan, and Tim Thompson."

"Heavens, that wouldn't matter much. From what I hear, Nadia and that Thompson fellow are an item. Everyone expects they'll end up marrying and running the business together. As for Dylan Blackstone"—Zelda widened her eyes—"a little bird told me that you've already spoken to him. Did he seem like a killer to you?"

"No," I said, wondering who had found out about my meeting at Highview with Kurt and Dylan. "And he claims he isn't interested in the business. Although, as Nadia just informed me, sometimes people lie."

"Indeed they do. Quite frequently, in my experience." Zelda tugged her gloves back on. "Well, that was my news. I thought you'd like to know, just in case you're trying to steer Brad Tucker and his team toward a few additional suspects."

"Did you hear that from some little bird as well?" I asked.

"Oh no, dear. No need." Zelda strolled out from behind the desk. Pausing to look me in the eye before she sauntered away, she added, "Thinking of you and what you've done in the past, I was sure that's what you'd be up to these days."

Chapter Eighteen

Since Nicky and Ella had a special rehearsal on Tuesday morning, Richard took them to the theater so he could troubleshoot some technical issues while the children in the production worked with Karla in one of the basement studios.

"I'll bring them back around lunchtime," he told me. "They aren't in the run-through tonight, as we're focusing on the second act. We wanted to give the kids a break, especially as they'll have to stay for the entire dress rehearsals tomorrow evening and Thursday night."

"Was it the kids you wanted to give a break, or you and Karla?" I asked as I double-checked the twins' dance bags to ensure they had the proper shoes and other necessary items.

Richard didn't answer that question. He simply gave me a wink and leaned in to kiss my cheek. "I'll go make sure the kids are ready to head out," he said, taking the zipped-up bags off the bed. "Oh, by the way, did I hear something about you walking into town with Mom this morning? What brought that on?"

I shrugged. "We're actually getting along better these days. I thought I'd show her around the few shops we have downtown. She said she still has a little holiday shopping to do."

"Will wonders never cease?" Richard flashed a broad smile. "Okay, have fun. As much as possible, that is."

After we bundled up Nicky and Ella and got them strapped into their booster seats, Richard drove off, mouthing, "Good luck," as he waved good-bye.

Back in the house, I immediately headed into the kitchen for another cup of coffee. Fiona was at the sink, rinsing off the breakfast dishes.

"Do you want these washed, or should I just load them into the dishwasher?" she asked without turning around.

"Dishwasher is fine." I poured myself a mug full of coffee but set it down on the counter when Loie and Fosse barreled through the cat door from our screened-in back porch. "Uh-oh, it looks like a couple of others want their breakfast."

Fiona audibly sniffed. "I don't know why you want those creatures running all over the house. Sleeping with the children, no less. It's hardly sanitary."

Since her back was still turned, I pulled a comical face at the cats, who sat at my feet, staring up at me expectantly. "Okay, guys, don't trip me. I have to get your food before I can pour it into the bowls."

But Fiona wouldn't take a hint. Turning around as she dried her hands with a kitchen towel, she shot the two cats a disdainful glance. "I understand that you don't want to leave them outside in cold weather, but couldn't they stay on the porch?"

"It isn't heated," I said mildly. "And they never go outside, cold weather or not. Too many wild critters in the woods behind the house that might see them as a tasty snack."

Fiona's expression indicated that she didn't consider this a problem. "Well, it's your house. I just wouldn't want cat hair all over my furniture. And, I'm afraid to say, I have found them on the counters."

I made a noncommittal noise as I poured kibble into the cat bowls. "So, concerning our excursion this morning—we'll have to wait until the shops open, so I'd suggest heading out a little before ten. Does that work for you?"

"That's fine," Fiona said, draping the hand towel over the dishwasher handle. "I need to call Jim this morning, so I'll do that before we leave."

"Tell him hello from Richard and me." I placed the cat food bag in the pantry. When I closed the pantry door and turned to face Fiona again, I noticed the quizzical quirk of her eyebrows.

"I'll do that, although"—Fiona's lips thinned—"he probably won't pay any attention. He sent me a text last night asking me to call today. I think all he's thinking about is our trip. That's what he'll be focused on, I'm afraid."

I nodded, aware of my father-in-law's tendency to obsess over things. *Well, things important to him, anyway.* I offered Fiona a sympathetic smile. "I get the feeling you aren't totally enthusiastic about this cruise."

"Heavens, no." Fiona crossed to the kitchen island. "It was all Jim's idea. He's never been one for celebrating Christmas and always looks for a way to circumvent holiday events or celebrations."

Retrieving my mug, I contemplated this information. *One more thing that probably made Richard's childhood less than magical,* I thought, sipping my coffee.

"I'd prefer to stay home, to be honest." Fiona pressed her palms flat against the soapstone surface of the island. "I was actually looking forward to decorating the house and having Nicky and Ella visit on Christmas day. Later in the day, of course," she added, meeting my gaze. "I know you usually celebrate here with your parents and aunt in the morning."

I finished off my coffee, remembering the past few Christmases, when we'd visited Richard's parents a day or two later. "That would've been nice. We usually have brunch at Aunt Lydia's, but we certainly could've gone to your home for dinner."

"That was my plan. But then Jim up and bought cruise tickets." Fiona tapped her manicured fingernails against the countertop. "I'm afraid he's always been like that—making decisions without consulting me, I mean."

I could tell by the downward curve of her lips that Fiona was not happy with this state of affairs. *But she's stayed with him all these years,* I thought as I carried my mug to the sink. *There must be some reason for that, although I can't really figure out what it is. Perhaps it's just the financial security.*

"I need to do some laundry," I said as I turned away from the sink. "But I'll plan to be ready so we can head out later."

"That works for me." Fiona straightened and tugged down the sleeves of her gray sweater. "I'll be upstairs for a bit but will be down by quarter of ten." Casting a sharp look at the cats, who'd finished eating and were now perched on the chairs at the kitchen table, she left the room.

I spent the next hour trying to deplete the pile of laundry our family seemed to generate on a daily basis, then changed into a pair of brown wool slacks and a cream sweater over a rust-red blouse—clothes that seemed more appropriate for a shopping trip. Or at least a shopping trip with my mother-in-law.

Fiona was quiet when we left the house and walked the few blocks to the edge of Taylorsford's small business district. When I asked about her phone call with her husband, she brushed me off with a snippy "Everything's fine."

But I had the feeling everything was not so great. There was a faint red tinge to Fiona's eyes that made me wonder if she'd been crying. Of course, I didn't say anything. I knew how proud she was.

"Oh, look, it's the temporary local office for Blackstone Properties," I said when we reached one of the brick storefronts that lined one block of Main Street. These structures, built in the 1940s, were less picturesque than the older stone and wood-framed buildings that made up most of the town, but they did have the large plate-glass windows that many businesses preferred.

Fiona paused in front of the building. "Shall we go in?" she asked. "To express our condolences, and perhaps pick up a few clues to help your brother-in-law." She adjusted the pewter-gray silk scarf she'd tucked into the neckline of her charcoal wool coat. "I have met Tim Thompson and Nadia Blackstone before, so I feel I can say something without it seeming too odd."

I cast her a sidelong glance, noting the color that had risen in her pale cheeks. She seemed eager to engage in a little amateur sleuthing with me. *It's probably a good distraction from whatever's bothering her*, I thought. *And it might actually be helpful.* "Why not? I've met Tim Thompson, and Nadia too, although only briefly. But I wouldn't mind speaking with both of them again."

"Very well, then." Fiona pushed open the door to the office and marched inside.

The space was obviously not meant to be permanent. Movable partitions created a couple of offices in the back, while the front area was a large reception area, complete with seating and small occasional tables as well as a desk. But the furniture and rugs looked expensive, and large, professional-quality photos of the firm's various projects hung on the side walls.

An attractive young woman who'd been seated behind the desk rose to her feet as we crossed the room. "Hello, welcome to Blackstone Properties. How may I help you?" she asked in a carefully cultivated voice.

"We'd like to speak to Mr. Thompson and Ms. Nadia Blackstone, if they're available," Fiona replied in an equally formal tone.

"Do you have an appointment?" The receptionist's simple cranberry wool sheath dress was probably more expensive than anything in my wardrobe.

"We do not, but I know Mr. Thompson and Ms. Blackstone through my friend Emma Stanley, and I just thought I should personally offer my condolences on the loss of their partner and mother." Fiona, standing ramrod straight, matched the receptionist's superior expression with a haughty gaze of her own.

Before the young woman could say anything else, two people hurried out of the back offices. One was Tim Thompson. The other was Nadia Blackstone.

"It's fine, Audrey," Tim Thompson said. "I've met Ms. Muir before. Both of them, actually."

Nadia's disdainful stare swept over me. "And I've recently met the younger version."

I hung back as Fiona stepped forward to clasp Tim's hand. "I was so sorry to hear about Wendy," she said, dropping Tim's hand and turning to Nadia. "Your mother was such a pillar of the community."

I fought the urge to roll my eyes.

Nadia was wearing a black wool jersey dress that managed to show off her lovely figure while still looking appropriately professional. A luxurious scarlet cashmere wrap was draped over one of her arms. "Thank you, Ms. Muir. I do remember meeting you at a few of those hospital galas," she said, giving Fiona's hand a quick shake. Her crimson lips twitched as she turned to me. "Hello. Didn't expect you to show your face around here."

I offered her a sympathetic smile. "I just wanted to express my condolences again as well."

"That's rich, considering that your brother is married to Ethan Payne." Nadia's black eyebrows drew together over her aquiline nose.

"Yes, but let me assure you, Ethan had nothing to do with Wendy's death," I said, feeling my palms grow damp inside my gloves.

"Oh dear, we didn't want to upset you," Fiona said. "We simply wanted to express our sympathy for your loss."

"Fine, but maybe don't bring along the killer's sister-in-law next time." Nadia tossed her chocolate-brown hair. "Now, if you'll excuse me, I have an errand I must run." She shot Tim a knife-edged look and, throwing her wrap around her shoulders, stalked past us. The front door slammed as she left the office.

"So sorry," Tim said, motioning for Audrey to sit back down. "I'm sure you can understand how difficult this time has been for Nadia."

"And Dylan," I said.

"And Dylan, of course." Tim's lips twitched, making his smile appear like a grimace. "But why don't we step into my office so we can speak in private? I'd like to explain a little more about the situation to both of you."

I shared a swift glance with Fiona. I wasn't sure what *situation* Tim was referring to, but I certainly wanted to hear what he had to say. "That would be great. Thanks."

We followed Tim into an office filled with sleek wooden-and-chrome furniture. I knew, from pricing replacement desks and other furnishings for the library, that it must've cost a pretty penny.

"I'm sorry Nadia chose to be so rude," Tim said, gesturing toward two upholstered armchairs. "Please have a seat."

"Think nothing of it," Fiona said, gracefully perching on one of the chairs while I sat in the other. "She's naturally going to be on edge, all things considered."

"Yes, but . . ." Tim stepped behind his desk, which was piled high with documents and photographs. Remaining on his feet, he picked up a Venetian glass paperweight and bounced it from one palm to the other. "I'm afraid I have my own suspicions. It seems to me that Nadia is protesting a bit too much, and you know what they say about that."

I stared at him, the realization that he was throwing Nadia under the bus heightening my interest. *Why would he do that?* I thought. *Unless he's the guilty one and is looking to pin his crime on someone, anyone, else?* "What do you mean?"

Tim placed the paperweight back on the desk. "Oh, nothing. It's just that Nadia was at odds with her mother for quite some time before Wendy's death. She wanted to be made a full partner in the business, but Wendy wouldn't have it."

"You didn't mind?" Fiona asked, gracefully crossing her ankles.

I had to admit, her pose did show off her attractive legs to good advantage.

"Of course not. I'd have gladly shared the company with both Wendy and Nadia. But I'm afraid Wendy said she'd never take on another partner. At least"—Tim shrugged—"not while she was alive."

The swish of the building's front door opening and closing made me wonder if Nadia had returned. Tim Thompson must've had the same thought, because he moved away from his desk and crossed to the office entrance.

Audrey poked her head around the door. "There's someone here to see you, Mr. Thompson. A man from the county planning commission, asking about some updated plans?"

"Right, right." Tim grabbed up a roll of what looked like blueprints. "Sorry, I need to take care of this. But please, stay. I'll be back in a minute, and perhaps we could even make plans to go to lunch?" He flashed one of his insincere smiles and left the office.

"I don't believe I want to go to lunch with that man," Fiona said, rising to her feet.

I stood up beside her. "Me either."

"However, I noticed something on his desk I'd like to take a better look at." Fiona strolled over to the cluttered desk. She took hold of a piece of paper hanging out of one of the piles of documents and twitched it free of the stack. "There's a crude, hand-lettered message on here, and it's written in red ink. Looks rather ominous," she said, handing it to me.

"It is," I said, keeping one eye on the door of the office as I studied the document. Fiona was right—someone had taken a flyer advertising several of Blackstone Properties, including Mountainside Farms and Crystal Lake, and written over the text and photos with a thick red marker. "It's a threat." I held it up so Fiona could see the message.

"*You will die for what you've done*," Fiona read aloud. "Hmmm, not too subtle, is it?"

"Absolutely not. But it means that Blackstone Properties has received at least one threat recently. Which also means there's someone out there who may have murdered Wendy over a property dispute or something like that."

Footsteps made me swiftly fold the document and shove it into my coat pocket.

"You're keeping that?" Fiona asked, sotto voce.

I nodded. "Evidence," I mouthed back at her.

She shook her head. "Inadmissible, though, if we take it without a warrant."

"But maybe enough to convince Brad Tucker to get that warrant and search these premises," I said in a whisper.

We both spun around as Tim returned to the office. "Now, about that lunch," he said.

"Sorry, but we really can't," Fiona said, her tone sweet enough to draw bees. "Not today, anyway. Amy reminded me that my son will be bringing their twins home around lunchtime and we need to be back at their house before that. Rain check?"

"Of course." Tim looked from Fiona to me and back again. "Well, thank you for stopping by. Your kind thoughts concerning our great loss are most appreciated."

"It's the least we can do," Fiona said as she swept past him to exit the office.

I followed, offering Tim a quick good-bye.

When we reached the sidewalk outside the building, Fiona cast me a conspiratorial glance. "I believe that was quite successful," she said as she started walking toward the home-and-garden shop that had been our original destination.

"You certainly played your part well," I said, lengthening my stride to keep up with her. "I'm impressed. I promise I won't underestimate you in the future."

Fiona fluffed her silk scarf until it looked like a flower poking up from her collar. "Really, Amy. You should never have done that in the first place."

Chapter Nineteen

After Richard dropped off the twins and rushed back to the theater, Aunt Lydia called, asking if we'd like to come over to her house later in the afternoon.

"Hugh will be here to help me wrap gifts, and I thought Nicky and Ella might want to help as well. In fact, if you want to bring over your gifts for everyone except the children, we could make a party of it."

"Are you sure you want the twins' help in this process?" I asked, recalling my aunt's beautifully wrapped gifts from past holidays and birthdays. "They think the more tape, the better."

"It's fine. They can do their best, and after we're finished wrapping, I'll provide hot chocolate and coffee and some cookies." Aunt Lydia coughed delicately. "With all the stress in the family right now, I just thought it would be nice to have a fun activity we could share."

"Sounds great," I said, realizing she was right. "Have you asked Scott to drop by? I'm sure he'd enjoy the break."

"He'll be here," Aunt Lydia said. "See you around two, then."

I asked Fiona if she wanted to join us, but she said she'd prefer to stay back and rest. "I also have some letters to write," she said as we cleaned up the dishes from lunch.

"You still write letters? Again, I'm impressed."

"Never could get comfortable with texting or email," she said, drying her hands on a kitchen towel. "It seems so impersonal."

"I won't argue with that." I stacked a couple of soup bowls in the dishwasher. "But if you change your mind, we'll be next door. I imagine we'll be using the sun porch, so you can just cross over from the backyard, where we have that arbor connecting the two properties."

Fiona thanked me but said not to expect her. "By the way, did you share that information we discovered this morning with your law enforcement friend?" she asked as we left the kitchen and walked into the living room.

"I tried but haven't been able to speak directly to him yet. I really didn't want to leave a message about something like that, so I just told him to call me as soon as he has a chance."

"I hope it will prove helpful," Fiona said, before heading upstairs.

Later, I had Nicky and Ella help me carry some gifts over to Aunt Lydia's house. Nicky suggested that we use their matching little red wagons, which I thought was a brilliant idea. "Like a train full of presents," I said as we pulled the wagons across our backyard.

When we reached the enclosed sun porch at the back of my aunt's house, Ella dashed up the short flight of steps and banged on the door. "The gift train is here!" she called out.

Hugh poked his head out the back door. "My goodness, how charming. Lydia, come here—you need to see this."

My aunt appeared behind him. "How clever. Who thought of this?"

"Nicky," Ella and I said in unison, while Nicky shouted, "Me!"

Hugh and Aunt Lydia helped us carry the packages from the wagons into the sun porch, where a long folding table filled the middle of the room. A child-size craft table that my aunt always kept on the porch for Ella and Nicky sat off to one side.

Numerous rolls of wrapping paper, gift bags, tissue paper, and ribbons and bows were piled on one end the long table. "I thought the children might prefer to use gift bags and boxes," Aunt Lydia said as we placed packages on the other end.

"I know I often do," Hugh said with a smile. He was dressed more casually than usual, in a soft blue pullover sweater and jeans.

"Nicky and Ella, you can use your craft table. Your special scissors and markers are in the drawers, as usual," Aunt Lydia said.

The twins grabbed a few packages—small gifts for their kindergarten teachers and friends—and dashed over to their table while I supplied them with bags, boxes, and tissue paper.

"We didn't bring Mommy's presents," Ella announced, tossing her dark hair behind her shoulders. "We didn't want her to see them."

"Very wise," Aunt Lydia said, opening one of the rolls of gift wrap. "I'm sure your father will help you wrap those."

"He took us to buy them." Stuffing a small toy into one of the bags, Nicky frowned. "I wanted to get something different, but he said maybe Mommy wouldn't really like a stuffed giraffe."

I shared an amused look with my aunt. "Just like I suggested that Daddy might not enjoy that box of Legos."

"Oh wait, we need some music." Hugh crossed to a small table set against the stone wall that had once been the exterior of the house and turned on a portable audio system.

Christmas carols blasted the room. "Very festive, dear," Aunt Lydia said, "but perhaps turn it down a hair."

"Of course, of course." Hugh adjusted the volume and strolled back to the table. "I can't wrap your Aunt Lydia's gifts today either," he said to the twins. "Or yours," he added with a smile.

"You can do ours. We won't look," Ella said, earning laughs from all the adults.

We'd almost completed wrapping all the gifts when the doorbell chimed.

"That must be Scott." Aunt Lydia hurried down the hall to the front door. She returned after a few minutes with my brother.

"It's okay to come in, Uncle Scott," Nicky said. "We've already done your gifts."

"And Uncle Ethan's too," Ella added.

Scott's smile tightened. "That's great. I didn't bring anything to wrap, I'm afraid. Anyway, most of them are for the people in this room, so that might not have worked out so well."

The twins' gazes swiveled to him. "You got us lots of presents?" Ella asked.

"Maybe not lots," Scott replied, his expression softening. "But more than one apiece, I promise." He caught my eye and shrugged. "I don't have any other kids to spoil."

"So you're going overboard with mine, as usual," I said with mock severity.

"It's one thing that brings a little joy right now." Scott crossed to the table and briefly pressed his fingers against Hugh's shoulder. "How are you? I haven't seen you in quite some time."

"I'm great, thanks." Hugh turned and extended his hand to Scott. "You do always seem to be out of the country whenever I'm home, and vice versa."

"The unfortunate consequences of our work." Scott shook Hugh's hand, then turned to Aunt Lydia and gave her a quick hug.

"Look what I did!" Ella held up a gift bag plastered with at least five stick-on bows.

"Very nice." Scott circled around the larger table and strolled over to the shorter craft table. Kneeling down, he engaged the twins in a lively conversation, admiring their handiwork and hearing more than he'd probably ever wanted to know about their parts in the *Nutcracker.*

"He's good with them," Aunt Lydia observed in a quiet voice.

I nodded and tied off the bow on my final package. I knew that Scott would've liked to have children of his own, but as he'd once explained, it wasn't practical. "Both Ethan and I have dangerous jobs," he'd told me. "I'm not sure it would be sensible."

And now Ethan is missing, I thought, sorrow tugging my lips into a frown. Although my brother and I hadn't spent a great deal of time together as adults, the closeness we'd felt as children always returned whenever we were together.

"Well, you're just in time for cookies and hot chocolate, or coffee if you prefer," Aunt Lydia said, dusting glitter from her hands. "Why don't you and Hugh carry our finished packages into the parlor while Amy assists me in the kitchen."

"Can we stay out here?" Nicky asked as Scott rose to his feet. "I want to draw a picture for Daddy."

Ella clicked two markers together. "Me too!"

"Of course. As long as you stay inside and don't mess with anything on the big table." Aunt Lydia cast both Ella and Nicky the sort of look that had always cowed Scott and me when we were kids.

The twins vigorously bobbed their heads.

As Scott and Hugh carried all the packages—except the ones I needed to take home—to the parlor, I joined Aunt Lydia in the kitchen. She pulled out an oval holiday plate and instructed me to fill it with homemade cookies from her stash in the pantry closet while she brewed coffee and boiled milk for the hot chocolate.

I'd just arranged an assortment of mugs and spoons on a pewter platter when a couple of loud shrieks from the porch made me rush out of the kitchen to see what was going on.

Standing just inside the back door was a tall, muscular man whose familiar face looked far too gaunt and whose bare hands were covered in cuts and bruises.

"Amy," said Ethan Payne in a hoarse voice. "Where's Scott?"

Chapter Twenty

I called for my brother, who sprang into action as soon as he entered the sun porch. Scott threw his arm around Ethan's shoulder and guided him into the hallway, where Hugh provided support on Ethan's other side. As they slowly made their way down the hall and into the sitting room, I ushered the twins into the kitchen and placed a small plate of cookies on the table in front of them while Aunt Lydia provided them with mugs of hot chocolate topped with marshmallows.

"You two stay here," I told them, testing the hot chocolate first to make sure it was cool enough to drink. "Aunt Lydia and I need to go and talk to Uncle Ethan, okay?"

"Can't we come?" Ella asked, her words muffled by a mouthful of sugar cookie.

"No, it's big-people stuff. You know—boring." I gave them each a kiss on the tops of their heads and hurried out of the room, right behind my aunt.

Ethan was slumped on the suede sofa in the sitting room, Scott close beside him.

Never one to mince words, Aunt Lydia had barely stepped inside the room when she said, "Where in heaven's name have you been, Ethan? You've had us worried sick."

"He's been held captive, dear." Hugh, standing behind my aunt's favorite armchair, gripped the top of the chair with both hands. "Please, come and sit down. Ethan said he'd tell us the whole story once everyone was here."

"Held captive?" Aunt. Lydia sank into the soft cushions of the chair. "But how? And why?"

"The bigger question is by whom?" I said, sitting in the other chair that faced the sofa.

"That's the one I can't answer." Ethan's voice croaked like that of someone who'd spent hours yelling for help. *Which*, I thought, *he probably did.*

I studied him more closely. His short hair was plastered to his head, as if he hadn't washed it in days, and there were bits of debris embedded in his flannel shirt, while the hems of his jeans were caked with mud. "You came here immediately after you escaped, or they let you go, or what?"

"I escaped," Ethan said. "Sorry for the condition of my clothes and all, but I desperately wanted to find Scott, and he wasn't at home, so I drove over here thinking he might be at your house, Amy, or here, and then I saw his car out front . . ."

"It's no problem." Scott clasped one of Ethan's hands. "No problem at all."

"Of course not," Hugh said. "It's just a little odd, because, well, you're a strong fellow, Ethan, and well trained in how to handle emergencies. How did someone get the jump on you?"

Ethan dropped his head back onto the top of the sofa cushions. Staring up at the ceiling, he exhaled a gusty sigh. "They played on my love for animals, dogs in particular."

"Someone sent him a text saying there was a dog trapped in an abandoned barn on a property near the Fields' farm," Scott said, with an anxious glance at his husband. "So of course Ethan went to check it out."

"Wait—the old stone barn?" I scooted to the edge of my chair.

"Yes. I was at the station, taking care of some paperwork, when I got the text. I couldn't tell who the sender was, but I thought I should check it out. I realized it might've been a prank, but since a dog was involved, I didn't want to take any chances." Ethan lowered his gaze and leaned in closer to Scott. "Hannah was actually in charge, in terms of supervising our volunteers on any other calls, so I thought it would be okay to just slip away and check it out."

"You didn't tell Hannah where you were going?" I asked.

Ethan shook his head. "I didn't think it was necessary. I just drove home fast as I could to grab my emergency kit and to make sure Cassie was taken care of, then rushed over to the property. The private road that led to the barn was pretty overgrown, but my vehicle could handle it. I parked the truck under a shed roof overhang behind the barn and looked around for the person who'd texted me, but I didn't see anyone."

"I suppose you didn't hear a dog barking or anything?" Aunt Lydia asked.

"No, but that just made me more concerned." Ethan cast Scott a sidelong glance. "I know I should've been more careful, but I thought the dog might be in real trouble, or even close to death, if it had stopped barking. So I decided to climb inside the barn to investigate."

"Were the entrances boarded up?" Hugh's dark eyes were fixed on Ethan's face, and I could see his sharp mind processing each new fact.

"Yeah, but there were spaces where an animal could've gotten in easily enough. I yanked off a couple of loose boards to get inside and used my cell phone light to look around." Ethan stretched out his legs, wincing as if the action caused him pain. "Didn't see anything at first. But then I heard a rustling noise over in one corner. When I got there, I saw a door I figured led to a tack room or storage space or something. I thought maybe the dog had crawled inside and the door had closed behind them, so I opened the door and stepped inside." Ethan inhaled a deep breath. "That's when someone hit me from behind."

"Someone ambushed you?" Aunt Lydia lifted her pale eyebrows. "Didn't you hear them coming up behind you?"

Ethan tightened his grip on Scott's hand. "No. They must've moved really quietly, and I was focused on finding that dog . . . Anyway, they hit me pretty hard, with some heavy object. My cell phone flew out of my hand, and I guess my attacker must've grabbed it when I fell forward on my hands and knees. Everything went blurry at that moment, and before I could get up, they closed the door behind me."

"You didn't get knocked unconscious, did you?" I asked. "Because you should be at the hospital right now if that was the case. Concussions are nothing to mess with."

"No, no. I was never out cold. I mean, my head hurt, but I knew from my own work at the station that I probably wasn't concussed."

"But we're going to get you checked out anyway," Scott said.

"Sure, but not just yet." Ethan's gaze swept over me, Hugh, and Aunt Lydia. "And that's where I've been, locked in that room. Because whoever it was must've brought along a padlock and used it to fasten the latch that was already there."

Aunt Lydia looked stricken. "All this time without food or water?"

"No, my captor left me some water. And even a little food, in a cooler. I mean, it didn't last the whole time, but it was enough to sustain me."

"So they didn't necessarily want you to die," I said, casting a swift glance from Hugh to Scott. "It was planned to keep him out of the way for a while, not to kill him."

"Sounds like it," my brother replied. "Although it certainly wasn't a healthy environment."

"Yeah, there was just a bucket for waste." Ethan made a face. "I had to kind of zen out to deal with it all, to tell you the truth."

"How did you get out?" I asked. "I guess you were looking for ways to escape the whole time, but it must've been difficult."

"Which is why my hands look like this." Ethan pulled his fingers free of Scott's. As he held up both his hands, I could see that his fingernails were broken, his palms scabbed over, and his fingertips scratched raw. "Not very attractive, I know."

"That doesn't matter. All that matters is that you're safe now," Scott said, gently clasping Ethan's hands again.

"I'm guessing you were forced to tear off a few wall boards to get out of there," Hugh said.

"The cooler actually came in handy for that." Ethan shot a glance at Scott. "I used the lid like a hammer. It was hard plastic, so it didn't break right away, and when it did, I used the pieces like pry bars."

Scott met Ethan's gaze with a look of love that made me catch my breath. "Good thinking. I always said you were a lot smarter than people gave you credit for."

"Well, I don't know how smart it was to fall for that scam about the dog and get locked in there in the first place," Ethan said ruefully.

Releasing his grip on Ethan's hands, Scott leaned in to kiss him. "That was your kindness," he said, sitting back. "Whoever it was knew about your love for animals and exploited that."

"But why?" Aunt Lydia rose to her feet. "That's what I don't understand. Why would anyone want to hold you captive in the first place, Ethan?"

"I think it was a diversionary tactic, my dear," Hugh said. "Don't you agree, Scott?"

My brother narrowed his dark-brown eyes. "It certainly kept the focus on Ethan in terms of Wendy Blackstone's murder."

"Right," I said. "The authorities thought Ethan had disappeared because he was on the run. They were sure he was trying to evade the law. It made him look like the guilty party."

"Which allowed the real killer to escape scrutiny." Scott snapped his fingers. "That's it, I bet. That was the plan. I'd put money on it."

Ethan managed a wan smile. "Not too much. We aren't that flush with cash."

"I know you're exhausted, but there is one other thing I'm confused about," I said, focusing on Ethan. "Hannah mentioned that you were quite late in getting back to the station the night Wendy Blackstone was killed. She felt like she'd eventually have to tell the authorities that, which wouldn't do you any favors, especially in terms of them considering you a top suspect. So what were you doing, exactly?"

"Oh, that was another stupid move, I guess." Ethan leaned in closer to Scott. "I was just so angry after my run-in with Wendy at the festival. Not in any condition to see anyone, I'm afraid. I felt I needed time to cool down before I headed back to work. I should've called Hannah, of course, but I just took off in my truck and drove for a while. I ended up parking near one of the mountain trails and hiking for a good mile or two in the dark before I decided I'd better get back to the station."

"You need to tell Brad Tucker that," I said. "Just to clear up that confusion."

Ethan nodded. "I will, I promise. I certainly don't want to make Hannah look like she was lying or anything."

"So now what?" Aunt Lydia asked as Hugh stepped out from behind the chair to stand beside her. "You need to be checked out at the emergency room, for one thing."

"He should go to the sheriff's department first," I said. "Let them see the condition he's in. That will help bolster his story."

My aunt swept one of her fine-boned hands through the air. "But they're likely to lock him up immediately."

"No, Amy is right. I should go and report to the sheriff's office. Even if they do hold me without bail, at least they'll get me medical care. I know Brad Tucker will insist on that." Ethan slid forward and attempted to stand up. As his knees appeared to buckle, Scott leapt up and grabbed his arm to steady him.

"We'll go now," Scott said. "I'll drive you there, then come back for the truck later."

"Don't worry about that," Aunt Lydia said, reaching out to clasp Hugh's hand. "We'll make sure your truck gets back to your house, Ethan. And if you leave the keys to your house, we can check on Cassie too."

"Thanks, that would be a big help." Ethan fished a ring of keys out of his pocket and tossed it to Hugh. "Cassie's met Lydia, at least, so she should be okay with you entering the house."

"I'd come along, but I need to get the twins home and make sure they're rested. They have dress rehearsals tomorrow and Thursday and then the premiere on Friday night," I said.

"That's right, they're in the *Nutcracker*. I was hoping to see that," Ethan said, his smile fading.

"We have tickets. We'll be there," Scott said firmly. "What could keep us away?"

Ethan shook his head. "In my case, a prison cell."

Chapter
Twenty-One

S cott called me Tuesday evening, letting me know that he and Ethan were finally back home. Fortunately, despite questioning Ethan's story, Brad hadn't ordered him to be held at the jail. He'd simply requested that Ethan stay at home until the sheriff's department could check out the old stone barn and see if there was evidence that he was telling the truth. Ethan had also gotten a good report from the medical team, who'd said that while he was suffering from a lack of proper food and water and sleep deprivation as well as the wounds to his hands, he was otherwise in decent shape. "It's the best possible news, all things considered," Scott told me. "Of course, he needs rest and time to heal, but he doesn't have any really serious injuries."

I finally got a message from Brad, but it was not encouraging. *Stop by Thursday around eleven and we can talk*, he texted.

Thursday!!! I texted back, feeling the need to use extra exclamation points. *My info is too important to wait that long.*

Sorry, will have to, Brad shot back, before ignoring my following three texts.

I finally gave up, but fumed to Richard when he got home late Tuesday night.

"Better Thursday than never," he told me, yawning and rolling away from me, then immediately falling asleep.

Of course, he was right, and by the time I left for work on Wednesday, I had calmed down enough to logically consider my plan of attack for the Thursday meeting.

I was thankful to have Fiona available to watch the twins on Wednesday. It was the only other day I was scheduled to work during the week, since Sunny, understanding the complications presented by our hosting Fiona as well as Richard's and the twins' rehearsal schedules, had graciously volunteered to take on extra shifts.

Samantha was already at the circulation desk when I arrived.

"I just want to warn you," she said as she turned on the desk computer, "that we might get some gawkers in here today. You know, people curious about what's going on with the Blackstone case."

"You mean people who want to know more about my brother-in-law's possible involvement?" I asked.

Samantha fiddled with the computer mouse. "Exactly. Since the news last night reported his reappearance, I expect we'll have some folks who'll want to question you about that, especially because the information offered was pretty sketchy."

"You mean nonexistent." I pulled a few returned books from the desk book drop. "Yeah, I'm not looking forward to the interrogations I'm likely to face today."

"Well, I was thinking"—Samantha straightened a stack of flyers beside the computer—"maybe I could cover the desk by myself today, with help from Denise and Bill during my lunch hour and story time. I don't mind, and they said they'd both come in if we called them. That way you can take care of some administrative work in the back. That *is* something that always has to be done." She gave me a wink. "I'd only call you out to the desk if a patron was asking for help with a real reference question, not just being nosy about your family."

"That's very nice of you," I said.

Relief must've been painted across my face, because Samantha just smiled and patted my shoulder. "No problem. I know you'd do the same for me if necessary."

"I most certainly would," I told her fervently.

Freed from the public desk, I spent a few hours at my computer workstation in the staff workroom, processing interlibrary loan requests and handling other back-office tasks. I was deep into organizing some budget reports when my cell phone rang.

Noticing that the call was from Fiona, I experienced a frisson of anxiety until she immediately responded to my greeting by saying that Ella and Nicky were fine.

"I just wanted to let you know that I talked with a few old friends this morning, and they provided some interesting tidbits about Blackstone Properties," she said.

"What might those be?" I asked, marveling at Fiona's continued interest in helping me.

"It's all rumors, or maybe even ghost stories," Fiona said, amusement brightening her voice. "But there's a lot of tales connected to one of their projects, the one called Crystal Lake. If you remember, it was featured on that flyer that had the threat scrawled across it."

"Oh?" I straightened and rolled my task chair back from my desk. "What kind of stories?"

"Some people say the whole area around the lake is haunted. A lot of foolishness, of course, but I think there's occasionally a nugget of truth behind such tales."

"I agree. So why do people claim it's haunted?"

"That wasn't entirely clear, but it seems some people think that a couple of people were killed when the lake was constructed. One of my friends said she heard it was a few of the workers, but another one said it involved residents from the area."

"Interesting. Thanks so much for sharing that, Fiona. I think I'll go on a research hunt and see what else I can find."

"Happy to help," Fiona said in a tone that surprisingly made me think she was telling the truth. "And don't worry about rushing home, Amy. The children showed me where you stored the instructions and supplies for doing their makeup and Ella's hair for tonight's rehearsal. I can take care of that before Richard drops by to pick them up."

"Well . . . thanks again," I said, so flabbergasted that no other words came to mind. I cleared my throat. "I should be able to get back in time to help you, but it's good to know it will be taken care of in case I'm delayed."

"No problem at all," Fiona said, before wishing me a good day and ending the call.

I stared at my screen for a moment. "Will wonders never cease, indeed." I asked aloud as I laid down the phone.

Inspired by Fiona's comments, I decided to try a few more searches focused on Blackstone Properties and its Crystal Lake development project. At first, all I retrieved were more of the promotional materials that the company had generated, but when I added in some terms referencing the history and folklore of the area, I discovered a more intriguing item.

It was an article written for a local paper, discussing an older couple who were refusing to leave the small farm that had been in their family since the early eighteenth century. The husband, Gregory Hurst, was quoted as saying they'd have to be dragged out in chains, while his wife, Trudy, pleaded with local officials to block the development. "We've been on this land since long before any of these Blackstone folks were even in the country," she told the reporter. "It isn't right we should have to move for some latecomers."

The photo that accompanied the article showed the Hursts standing in front of a log cabin with two sagging clapboard extensions and a porch that looked like it was being held up by stacked stone pillars and prayers. I peered closer at the photo but couldn't discern much about the Hursts' appearance, other than their well-worn clothes and the distinctively stubborn set of their shoulders and jaws.

Reading over the article again, I noticed that the Hursts, like all the people who owned property in the area slated to be flooded to create Crystal Lake, had been offered a "substantial settlement" by Blackstone Properties. Apparently, everyone else had agreed to accept "well over the tax value of their property," but the Hursts were still fighting their eviction.

I checked the date of the article and did another search—this one to uncover any articles referencing Crystal Lake by the same paper and reporter and published over the next year or so.

"Bingo!" I said when I finally found a follow-up report on the Hursts. I read through the short article quickly, noting that the Hursts had eventually bowed to the pressure exerted by both Blackstone Properties and local officials.

At least they made Blackstone shell out a bit more cash, I thought as I read that Greg and Trudy Hurst's payout had been substantially increased. According to the article, the couple had told Blackstone's management team that they planned to buy another farm farther west, but, having cashed their settlement check, the Hursts had provided no forwarding address. There were some rumors among the locals that the Hursts, whose only child, a daughter, had died a few years previously, might have moved closer to their only remaining family—a son-in-law who'd made a career in the army and a grandchild. But the reporter clarified that this information was not substantiated, as no one had been quite sure where the son-in-law was living at the time.

I sat back in my chair. *Could the son-in-law have carried enough resentment over the treatment of his wife's family by Wendy Blackstone and her team to want to kill her so many years later?* It seemed a stretch, but I'd encountered seemingly unlikely motives before.

Samantha cracked open the door to the workroom. "Sorry to bother you, but there's someone here I thought you might want to talk to." She widened her dark eyes. "It's somebody called Tim Thompson," she said in a softer voice. "He said something about a donation to the library, and I assumed that was always worth a conversation."

The coincidence of my researching Blackstone Properties and Thompson's appearance in the library wasn't lost on me. "More wonders," I said to myself as I stood up. Not wanting to embroil Samantha in my latest adventure in amateur sleuthing, I waved off her questioning gaze and said I'd be out in a second.

"How ironic. Just the person I wanted to see," I said as I strolled out of the workroom and faced Tim Thompson across the desk. Turning to Samantha, I added, "Go ahead and take a break. I can watch the desk while I speak with Mr. Thompson."

She murmured, "Thanks," and headed off toward the staff break room.

"You wanted to see me?" Tim's face expressed his obvious confusion. "That's odd. I had the distinct feeling that I hadn't made a good impression on you, Ms. Muir."

"Yet here you are, offering to donate something to the library," I said. "Personally, I find that a little peculiar as well."

Tim smoothed one lapel of his elegant beige wool coat. "Not at all. Blackstone Properties always likes to support community services in the locales where we build our developments."

"You haven't gotten final approval to build it yet," I pointed out.

"No, but I'm sure we will. There's a delay, of course, what with poor Wendy's death and all the issues surrounding that sad occurrence, but I'm confident everything will be resolved in due time." Tim flashed one of his overly bright smiles.

"I'm sure you think so," I said, fighting to keep my tone neutral. "But perhaps we should wait to discuss any sort of donation until things are settled. As I'm sure you're aware, my brother-in-law, Ethan Payne, is currently under suspicion in your business partner's death. I would hate for people to misconstrue your company giving money to the library as some sort of . . . well, payment for my silence on certain topics."

Tim's smile froze into a grimace. "What topics might those be?" he asked at last.

"I don't know, maybe the protests and other problems your projects have encountered in the past?" I registered the barely controlled fury contorting Tim's face. "I've been doing a little research, and it seems things have not always gone smoothly for your company. In fact, they almost never have."

"What nonsense. Naturally, there are always issues with developments as ambitious as ours. But we have always prevailed. Legally," he said, stressing the final word.

I took a breath before deciding to simply leap into deeper waters. "But you've made a lot of enemies along the way. At places like Mountainside Farms, for example. Or Crystal Lake."

Tim peered down his narrow nose at me. "Again, we handled all the difficulties with those projects in a fair and legal manner."

"Not everyone may have thought so," I said, crossing my arms over my chest. "Like the Hursts, or the Jensen family."

That scored a hit, I thought as Tim's face blanched to the color of bone.

"Where did you hear those names?" he asked in a strangled voice.

"I told you—I did some research. I'm a librarian. It's what I do," I said.

"Research, my foot. You've been talking to Dylan, haven't you?" Tim's eyes narrowed to slits. "That boy is disturbed. In the past he's seen conspiracies and cover-ups lurking behind every comment I, Nadia, or Wendy ever made. He needs help, not encouragement for his fantasies."

"I have spoken with Dylan, but—"

"Enough." Tim sliced the air with his hand. "I'm not interested in hearing more of this nonsense. I came here in good faith to offer a donation to your library, and what do I get? Unfounded accusations, that's what. I don't need to hear anything else from you, Ms. Muir. Good day." He turned on his heel and stormed away, shoving the front doors so hard that they clanged back against the doorframe.

"I take it that didn't go so well?" Samantha asked as she returned to the desk.

"Oh, I don't know," I said with a little smile. "I learned a few things that might be extremely useful. Now, if you'll excuse me, I think I'll go and add them to the list I'm compiling for my meeting with Brad Tucker tomorrow."

Samantha's eyes brightened. "You found out something that might help Ethan?"

"I certainly hope so," I said.

Chapter
Twenty-Two

With my notes and the threatening flyer I'd filched from Blackstone Properties in hand, I felt prepared for my meeting with Brad on Thursday.

"I hope you can convince him to broaden his investigation." Fiona carried a plate full of pancakes over to the kitchen table, where Ella and Nicky were seated on either side of Richard.

They were all still in their pajamas, having slept late following the Wednesday evening dress rehearsal. Fiona had volunteered to make breakfast when we realized I'd have to leave for my meeting before they were ready to eat anything.

Richard, nursing his second mug of coffee, looked up and met my gaze with a weary smile. Like the twins, his hair was adorably tousled and his eyes were a little glassy.

"When do you have to go in today?" I asked, leaning in to peck his cheek. "Do I need to cart the kids over later, or can you all drive in together?"

"I have to be there early and can't leave today, so I'm afraid you'll need to drive them to the theater," he said, clasping my fingers. "Sorry." He lifted my hand and pressed a kiss into my palm. "I'll make it up to you."

"I'll remember that," I said with a smile. "Ella and Nicky, behave for your dad and grandmother, okay? I need to leave now, but I'll be back in plenty of time to deal with your hair and makeup today."

Nicky, stabbing a pancake with his fork, waved it through the air. "Karla said that Grandmother did it really well yesterday."

"Yes, you both looked perfect for your roles." I glanced over at Fiona, who'd returned to the griddle she'd set up on one of the kitchen counters. "I mean, if she doesn't mind, maybe she should help again today."

"I don't mind," Fiona said without turning around.

I shared a raised-eyebrow look with Richard. "Well, all of you need to rest up today. Daddy included," I added, pointing a finger at him.

"I'll be fine as soon as this caffeine kicks in," he said.

"All right, see you later." I blew a kiss to the kids and Richard and thanked Fiona for handling breakfast, then headed into the living room.

After shoving my notes and the flyer into my soft-sided work briefcase, I pulled on my fleece jacket and knit gloves. Fosse and Loie lifted their heads to stare at me from their comfortable, cuddled position on the sofa. "You guys behave too," I told them, receiving, as usual, yawns and no promises.

Arriving at the sheriff's department ten minutes ahead of my appointment, I waited in the decidedly utilitarian lobby. Unlike the one at Blackstone Properties, this waiting area was neither stylish nor comfortable. Constantly shifting my position on the hard orange plastic chair, I looked through my notes, avoiding the gaze of the deputy stationed at the battered metal desk that guarded the entrance to the back offices.

Exactly on time, Brad stepped out into the lobby and gestured for me to join him.

"I don't think I've ever seen your new office," I said, trotting behind him as he navigated a rabbit warren of cubicles.

"It's hardly new. Just mine now." Brad ushered me into a room that looked like it hadn't been updated in decades.

"The seventies have called and want their style back," I said, surveying the wood-paneled walls and well-worn patterned carpeting. Although the entire decade was before my time, I recognized the overabundance of wood, dropped acoustic-tile ceiling, and brown-and-rust color scheme from photos in the reproductions of Sears catalogs we kept in the library.

"Have a seat," Brad said, gesturing toward a rolling task chair set in front of a hulking wooden desk. Brad settled into a more comfortable-looking office chair behind the desk. Obviously, even he drew the line at spending much time in a chair that looked like it should be tossed in a dumpster.

The rolling chair made a distressing noise as I gingerly perched on its threadbare seat cushion.

"I see you brought your research," Brad said as I lifted my briefcase onto my lap.

"Just some notes, and one other thing you need to see." I pulled a few pieces of paper and the flyer from my briefcase before setting it back on the floor. "Found this just the other day." Jumping up from the chair, I slid the flyer across the pitted surface of the desk.

Brad's eyebrows rose to comical heights. "Found it? And how exactly did you do that? Did someone drop it into a library wastebasket?"

"Not exactly," I said, cringing as the chair squealed again when I sat back down. "You sure this thing can hold me?"

"Absolutely. If it'll support some of my burly deputies, it won't fall apart under you."

"I don't know," I said. "Maybe they just intimidated it into obedience."

Brad laughed. "Okay, now that we've broken the ice, what is this all about, Amy?" He waved the flyer at me. "Where did you really find this?"

"At Blackstone Properties' temporary offices in town." I held up my hand, palm out. "And before you start berating me, it was really my mother-in-law who spied it in a stack of papers on Timothy Thompson's desk and retrieved it. Without Thompson's knowledge, of course."

"Of course," Brad said.

"We just thought . . . well, we wanted you and your investigative team to know that Blackstone Properties had received at least one death threat. Now, I don't know if it was directed toward Wendy, Tim, or even Nadia, but it shows that someone out there was threatening them. Which means Ethan isn't the only one with a motive to kill Wendy. Not by a long shot. I have other information along those lines too, including some viable motives linked to Jaden Perez, Thompson, Nadia, and even Dylan," I added, shuffling through my notes.

Crossing his arms behind his head, Brad leaned back in his chair. "That won't be necessary. Despite your obvious lack of faith in our abilities, my team and I have discovered that Tim Thompson, Nadia Blackstone, Perez, and others should be looked at more closely, and we're conducting those investigations right now."

"Really?" I looked up from my notes. "But in all the news briefings, you seem so focused on Ethan."

"It's strategy, Amy." Brad dropped his arms and leaned forward, resting his forearms on his desk. "We've investigated Ethan's story and have found evidence to back up his claim of being held in that barn. Which has led me to believe he was kidnapped to cast more suspicion on him while the actual murderer escaped. Or flew under the radar, anyway."

"Oh." I stared into his clear blue eyes. "Sorry. I just thought . . ."

"That I was incompetent?" Brad tapped the surface of the desk with his index finger. "Listen, Amy—you know I appreciate all the help you've given the department in the past. But you really aren't a one-woman investigative team."

Two women, I thought, thinking of Fiona. "I realize that, and I apologize if I got it wrong. But I hope some of my research will still be useful. For background, if nothing else."

Brad sat back in his chair and looked me over. "Okay, tell me, then."

I detailed the information I'd dug up about Tim Thompson and Nadia as well as the protests and other issues surrounding the Mountainside Farms and Crystal Lake developments. "Who's to say one of the protesters, like Jaden Perez, or someone affected by those projects didn't kill Wendy?" I said in conclusion.

"Quite possible, and yes, some of this might be useful." Brad held out his hand. "Do you mind leaving those notes with me? I'll have one of my deputies look more closely at those developments as well as any other Blackstone projects."

I stood and placed the notes on his desk. "I appreciate that."

"But you should back off of this case now." Brad stood, facing me across the desk. "Seriously, Amy. For your own safety. You've seen what happened to Ethan. Whoever is behind Wendy Blackstone's death, they aren't messing around."

"Okay, but"—I slipped the strap of my briefcase over my shoulder—"why aren't you publicly declaring Ethan's innocence if you know he's not the culprit?"

"To draw out the actual killer, of course," Brad said. "We'll clear Ethan soon. Probably sometime tomorrow. But until then, we're allowing the perpetrator to think they've escaped suspicion."

"Hoping they'll grow careless and make a mistake?" I asked.

Brad flashed a weary smile. "Something like that."

"All right, I'll go now. But first, I'll apologize again. I should've known you wouldn't just jump to conclusions, about Ethan or anyone else."

"I did, actually, at first. I was convinced that Ethan was Wendy Blackstone's killer. But now"—Brad spread wide his hands—"we're unfortunately back at square one."

"Not exactly," I said. "You do have some other leads."

"Which your research may help. But please, call a halt to your amateur sleuthing now." Brad pressed his hand over the badge on his uniform shirt. "I promise we'll do our best to find the actual culprit or culprits."

"I know you will. But if you do need any additional research assistance . . ."

"I know who to ask." Brad glanced at his watch. "Forgive me, but I have to ask you to leave. I have another appointment in five minutes, and I'd like to grab a cup of coffee before that."

"Sure thing. Thanks again for hearing me out. And straightening me out," I said with a rueful grin. Wishing Brad a good afternoon, I left his office.

As I drove home, my thoughts swirled around the information I'd just learned. As soon as I reached the house, I'd call Scott and let him know that Ethan was no longer under suspicion. Of course, Ethan would have to lie low at home until Brad made a public announcement about his innocence, but at least he wouldn't have to worry for one more day.

I tightened my grip on the steering wheel. I should've called Scott before I left the sheriff's office, but I never used my cell phone while driving. *It will be soon enough when I get home*, I told myself.

Caught up in these thoughts, I didn't notice the vehicle tailgating me until I pulled onto the stretch of rural road that separated the sheriff's office from the main street leading into town.

It was the lights that alerted me. Head lamps flared in my rearview mirror and almost blinded me. It was a gray day, so someone turning on their lights wasn't odd, but it looked like they had their high beams on, which was definitely unnecessary. I tried to catch a glimpse of the vehicle in my side mirror, but all I could see were the lights and what looked like a chrome grille gleaming against a black or dark-gray paint job. I increased my speed slightly, thinking the driver was pushing for a faster pace on the two-lane road, but the car simply accelerated to match.

"What the heck are you doing?" I muttered as I tried to keep one eye on the road in front of me and still monitor the vehicle behind me. There was no reason for the driver to push me. I was already driving ten miles over the speed limit, and the road offered sections of broken lines, allowing them to pass if they were so inclined.

"There's no one coming in the other direction," I said, my voice rising. "You can just go around me if you're in such a hurry."

The vehicle still clung to my back bumper. I tightened my grip on the steering wheel, fearing that if I had to stop short for any reason, they would plow right into me.

Suddenly, the vehicle pulled up beside me, as if finally passing my car, but then did not keep moving ahead. Instead, they inched over the center line, forcing me onto the paved shoulder. I yelled several obscenities as they continued to push me to the side. Holding on to my steering wheel for dear life, I slowly depressed my brake pedal while guiding my car onto the grassy portion of the shoulder. As I came to a stop, the offending vehicle sped past me, flying down the road so fast I couldn't get a good look at their license plate. But I confirmed that the vehicle was a black SUV, emblazoned with a logo that looked like a multicolored shield inside an open-topped laurel wreath.

A Cadillac, of all things, I thought, recognizing the emblem. *A Cadillac SUV. Not a cheap ride, by any means.*

I sat on the side of the road for several minutes, allowing time for my hands to stop shaking. As I stared mindlessly through my windshield, my cell phone buzzed, alerting me to a text. I plucked the phone from its dashboard holder and stared at the screen.

Just a taste of what might happen if you don't stop nosing around, it said.

I dropped the phone like it was a snake poised to strike. After taking several deep breaths, I retrieved the phone from the floor mat and punched in the shortcut I'd set to call Brad Tucker.

"Hello, Brad," I said, when I reached his voice mail. "Please call me back. I know you said I shouldn't do any more investigating, and I haven't, but I think the Blackstone case might've decided to involve me, like it or not."

After completing that call, I texted Scott and shared Brad's information concerning Ethan before trying another number, again reaching voice mail.

"Kurt, I wonder if you have time to talk to me. I might need your help with something," I said.

He called me right back. "What do you need?" he asked.

"Help tracking down a vehicle that just ran me off the road. And maybe assistance in digging up a little more information on a couple of Blackstone Properties' former projects."

"Tell me about the vehicle, and I'll get right on that. Have you informed the sheriff's department as well?"

"I will. Just waiting for them to call me back. Anyway, it was a black Cadillac SUV. Late model, I think, though I'm no expert on cars. But it looked fairly new."

"Very well, I'll check with some of my contacts. As for the other thing—have you spoken with Mary yet?"

"Mary Gardener? No. Why would she know about Blackstone Properties?"

"Because she still keeps up with all the gossip and stories about happenings in the Blue Ridge Mountains, near and far. If the developments were, as I think, located anywhere affecting that region—"

"They were, and did," I replied.

"Then she may have heard something. It would be worth a visit, perhaps? I think I can arrange that for tomorrow morning, if that suits you."

The day of the Nutcracker *premiere*, I thought, frowning. "I think I can manage it, but I know you're taking Mary to the *Nutcracker* opening tomorrow night. I don't want to tire her out."

"Oh, she won't mind. Visits from friends actually revitalize her." Kurt cleared his throat. "Why don't you meet us at Mary's house around ten? It'll be best if you drive yourself, as I plan to take her to my house for lunch and a little pampering before we head to the show."

"Don't tell me—I bet you're going to have a hairdresser and makeup artist on hand to glam her up," I said, shaking out my fingers as the tension drained from my body.

"Just one person, but they are going to help her get ready. Winterfest is dedicated to her, you know."

"And deservedly so. All right, see you tomorrow at ten," I told him, before hanging up.

Brad called me back a second later. I shared the vehicle information I'd given Kurt, along with the wording of the anonymous text.

"Someone is definitely not happy with you sharing information with the department," he said, worry rippling through his words. "I'll have a deputy look into this immediately. Please be careful, Amy. It seems one or more individuals may be keeping track of your movements. Perhaps you should stay home tonight and tomorrow. Give us time to track down this vehicle and its driver."

"I have to attend the *Nutcracker* premiere tomorrow night, but I'll be traveling to the theater with Richard and Fiona and the kids, so I won't be alone."

"I'm sure that'll be fine. Just keep a lookout for that SUV, and call the department if you see any sign of it. Otherwise, stay home."

"I will," I said, which wasn't entirely a lie. Of course, I was referring to the first part of his statement and not the second.

I was still going to meet with Mary and Kurt. My fear had been transmuted into anger, and after hearing Kurt's comments about Mary's possible knowledge of secrets involving Blackstone Properties, I was determined to go to her house the next day.

Threats from anonymous cowards might make me more vigilant, but they weren't going to stop me.

Chapter
Twenty-Three

Richard was at the theater, taking care of some last-minute technical details, when I left the twins with Fiona to go to my meeting with Mary.

"If Richard gets back before I do, could you just let him know that I should be home by noon," I told her. "I'm sure I won't stay at Mary's too long. She's almost a hundred, and while she's in good shape, all things considered, I don't want to wear out my welcome."

"All right. I think the children and I will just watch some of their little programs," Fiona said with a slight roll of her eyes. "I'll try to keep them relaxed and calm before tonight."

"Good luck with that," I said, smiling. "If I may offer a hint, the animal programs are better than some of those animated ones. In terms of adult tolerance, I mean."

"I'll bear that in mind," Fiona said.

Like Kurt, Mary Gardener lived outside Taylorsford, farther up in the mountains, but unlike Kurt's elegant and historic estate, Mary had a small, one-story house. It had white siding and a low concrete porch covered with a simple roof.

I parked next to Kurt, keeping my distance so I didn't ding his expensive Jaguar sedan. Climbing out of my car, I paused for a moment to notice that Mary's siding had been recently repainted. *Probably paid for by Kurt*, I thought. I knew he helped to take care of the woman who'd been one of the only people to show him kindness when he'd been a young boy at the orphanage where she'd worked.

The front door was unlocked. I pushed it open and entered a small living room paneled in polished wood. Windows framed with lacy white curtains let in the clear winter light, while several paintings of flowers lent color to the dark walls.

I followed the sound of voices into the kitchen, where robin's-egg-blue solid-surface countertops provided a lovely contrast to the gleaming stainless appliances and pale-yellow walls.

The tiny woman seated in a wooden rocker next to a built-in electric fireplace was flanked by Kurt and a sturdy middle-aged woman I assumed was her live-in caregiver.

"Ah, there she is," Kurt said. Leaning in closer to Mary, he said, "Amy's here," in a loud voice.

"Hello, I'm Dany," the middle-aged woman said. "I don't believe we've met."

"Amy Muir," I said, extending my hand.

"Nice to meet you." Dany gave my hand a quick shake, then cast a glance at Kurt. "I'll go take care of the laundry, then, if you'll be here to stay with her. Just come find me if she needs any care you can't handle."

"I'm sure we'll be fine," Kurt said.

Dany nodded and left the kitchen.

"Amy? Amy Webber?" Mary, who was so tiny that her feet didn't touch the floor, lifted one of her arthritis-twisted hands.

"Yes, but it's Amy Muir now," I said, raising my voice to match Kurt's volume.

Mary's hazel eyes still sparkled as brightly as water in a shallow brook in her deeply wrinkled face. "That's right. I was at your lovely wedding. And to that gorgeous man. Didn't he dance? I remember dancing."

I crossed to her and clasped her knobby fingers firmly. "You remember quite well. And yes, Richard danced. That's his profession, you know, although he's mainly creating dances and teaching other dancers now."

"Oh lawdy, girl, I can barely recall my own name these days. But I do remember your husband. He's hard to forget." Mary's grip wasn't as strong as it had once been, but I could still read the canny intelligence in her eyes.

"You'll see him dance again tonight, at the *Nutcracker* performance," I told her, gently laying her hand back down onto the crocheted blanket thrown over her legs. "Along with our children, Ella and Nicky."

Mary looked up at Kurt. "Goodness gracious, are those babies old enough to be onstage?"

"Apparently so," Kurt replied, his blue eyes twinkling. "I know it seems impossible, but that's what happens when you're living the high life, Mary. Time just flies by."

"Oh, go on with you," Mary said, offering Kurt a smile that lit up her wizened face. "Now, young man—show some manners. Pull up a couple chairs from the kitchen table so you and Amy can sit yourselves down."

"Yes, ma'am." Kurt gave her a little salute before he strode away.

He paused beside me just long enough to whisper, "Just so you know, Blackstone Properties owns that black Cadillac SUV. Company vehicle, it seems."

"Not surprised," I replied as prickles of anxiety danced down my spine. *I bet Brad will discover the same thing*, I thought. *Which should definitely put Tim and Nadia on his radar.*

After he brought over two chairs and we both took a seat, Kurt jumped right into the reason for my visit. "Amy is interested in anything you may have heard over the years about Blackstone Properties. You know, that company that likes to build subdivisions and other developments on mountain land."

Mary waved her hand like she was swatting away a fly. "Them folks. They have no more thought for the land than a flock of turkeys. And we all know about turkeys," she added with a little wink. "They'll stand in the rain with their heads up and their beaks open and drown. Well, that's them Blackstone folks. Dumb as a box of hair."

I covered my mouth with my hand to stifle a laugh.

"You don't seem to think too highly of them, at any rate," Kurt said, his eyes as bright as his tone was mild.

"And why should I?" Mary shifted in her chair and fixed him with a fierce gaze. "Pack of vultures. Always sweeping in when folks are down on their luck and buying up property for a song. Then they cut down every blessed tree and bush and throw up their cardboard houses and call that a proper place to live." She snorted. "You bet I've heard plenty about them, from my friends also keeping the mountain lore alive. Them Blackstones don't care nothing 'bout the history of our land. They just want to strip it bare, like blamed locusts."

"So there could be a good number of people who had a grudge against them?" I asked.

Mary turned her sharp gaze on me. "I'd say so. Some more than others, I reckon."

"There was a family, the Jensens, who wanted to turn their property into an organic community farm and nature preserve," I said. "But Blackstone Properties swooped in and bought it out from under the Jensens' other investors. Blackstone turned it into some cookie-cutter development called Mountainside Farms. Did you hear about that?"

"Laws, yes. There was a big to-do when that happened. I think I even talked that over with you at the time, Karl." Mary pressed the back of her hand to her forehead. "Sorry, Kurt. You know I have trouble remembering your name change sometimes." She cast me a sly smile. "To me, he'll always be the whippersnapper I knew as Karl."

"It really doesn't matter," Kurt said. "Unless, of course, you make a report to the authorities, who still might be interested in what happened to young Karl Klass."

Mary chuckled. "I've got no cause to be speaking with the law. And I know better than to bring up such things. I may be old, but I haven't lost all my marbles yet."

"I'll say you haven't." Leaning forward, I gripped my knees with both hands. "But getting back to Blackstone Properties, do you think anyone in the Jensen family would've built up enough animosity toward Wendy Blackstone . . ."

"To kill her?" Mary shook her head. "I wouldn't think so. I never heard nothing 'bout them being violent types. Now, the Hurst family, that's a whole other kettle of fish."

I sat bolt upright in my chair. "The Hursts? You've heard of them too?"

"Which development was this associated with?" Kurt asked, casting me a sidelong look. "I don't remember ever hearing about people named Hurst associated with Blackstone Properties."

"You most likely wouldn't have." Mary tugged her coverlet up to her chest. "It was that Crystal Lake place. Fancy-pants lake development that destroyed a whole valley. Anyway, the story of the Hursts was kept pretty hush-hush. I only know because . . . well, I met someone who knew all the details. Or at least claimed he did. Great fiddler, he was. Met him at one of our folklore conferences a while back, and we got to talking and hit it off." Mary shook her finger at Kurt. "Not what you're thinking, young man. Just friendly."

"What did he tell you? I asked, grimacing when my words came out as a demand.

"Quite a story, believe you me." Mary closed her eyes, seemingly lost in thought. "A real tragic tale too."

I turned to Kurt. "Greg and Trudy Hurst had a farm in the mountain valley that Blackstone Properties flooded to create Crystal Lake. They didn't want to move, even when offered a substantial payment for their land."

Kurt, his expression growing thoughtful, sat back in his chair. "They fought the eviction?"

"Until the last minute, from what I read. Although they did manage to squeeze more money out of Blackstone Properties, so I guess that was something."

"Ha!" Mary's explosive exclamation caught both Kurt and me by surprise. As we turned to face her again, I noticed that her eyes glittered with what look like repressed amusement. "You think that's what happened, do you? Yes indeedy, that's what Blackstone told everyone, but it wasn't the truth. Not according to my friend, anyways."

"They didn't get the money?" I asked.

Mary's sparse eyelashes fluttered. "No, child—they never moved away."

I frowned. "What do you mean? The place was eventually flooded when Blackstone dammed a small river nearby. There was no way they could've stayed."

"There is one way." Kurt's face went still as stone. "If they were dead."

Mary licked her forefinger and held it up. "One point for you, Karl. You guessed it right the first time."

I leapt to my feet. "Wait—they died? But I found a newspaper article that said they moved farther west after cashing their settlement check from Blackstone."

"Of course you did, dear." Mary adjusted the folds of her blanket. "That's what Blackstone wanted people to know. Or anyways, so my friend said."

Kurt reached out and took my hand, pulling me back down into the chair next to his. "How did this friend know anything about the situation?"

"He was hiding out in the area at the time." Mary shrugged her bird-wing shoulders. "He was a fugitive. Had been convicted of some minor crimes, like petty robbery or drugs or such. Not sure what, to be honest. Anyway, he was living out there in the woods near the Hursts' farm. Used to pilfer a few eggs and things from them. He thought maybe Trudy Hurst knew but didn't care. Said the Hurts weren't ones for bowing down to the law, if you get my meaning."

"He saw something, then? Something that convinced him they were dead?" I asked.

Mary's sigh rattled her thin chest. "He saw them killed, dear. Said it happened when one of Blackstone's flunkies came to finally force the Hursts off their property. Blackstone was just about to raze the last of the buildings still standing in the valley so they could start the flooding process. My friend said he guessed Blackstone was getting mighty frustrated, and awfully worried too. Every day costs money on a project like that."

"No doubt," Kurt said.

"So what happened when this Blackstone employee came to evict them?" I asked. "Did the Hursts resist or something?"

"Quite fiercely, or so my friend said. He saw the guy driving up and hid behind a storage shed, where he could keep a lookout on the cabin. According to him, as soon as the enforcer roared up in his truck, Greg Hurst bursts out of his front door, brandishing a shotgun. He lowered his weapon before he ordered the guy to leave, though. Leastwise, that's what my friend claims."

I clasped my hands tightly together in my lap. "The Blackstone employee killed Greg Hurst?"

Mary rubbed her lower arms as if she'd been stricken with a sudden chill. "So I was told. Shot him in cold blood, my friend said. And then when Trudy Hurst ran out onto the porch to see what was going on, she was shot dead too."

I tried to form words, but my lips refused to cooperate, reducing my reaction to a strangled squeak.

Kurt crossed his arms over his chest. "So, according to your friend, Blackstone Properties just covered this up? I suppose they buried the two bodies on the property and then, when the entire area was flooded, they figured the crime was hidden forever."

"That's right." Mary rocked back in her chair. "My friend, he wanted to go to the authorities, but never felt he could risk it. He was still a wanted man. He changed his name later"—Mary sent Kurt a knowing look—"but he knew if he tried to report any of this to law enforcement, the whole truth, including his fugitive status, would come out."

"So we only have his word for it," Kurt said.

"True enough. But I was inclined to believe him." Mary turned her gaze on me. "Does this answer your questions, Amy? I know you probably want to know 'bout any other folks who might have had a gripe against Wendy Blackstone, if only to help out that brother-in-law of yours."

"Well, actually . . ." I felt the intense heat of Kurt's attention switch to me and reconsidered my next words. "Yes, this is very helpful, Mary. Thanks so much. The only thing is, there was a son-in-law and grandchild, wasn't there? I mean, I read that they were the only family the Hursts had left. No one seemed to know where they were living at the time, though. Do you think there's any chance they ever found out the truth?"

Mary lifted her sharp chin and stared directly into my eyes. "I know at least one of them did. My friend met up with the son-in-law some years later. He said he told him the whole story, just like I told it to you here today."

"What was his name?" I asked, rising to my feet again. "Did your friend ever mention the son-in-law's name?"

"If he did, I don't remember." Mary sank back in her chair. "He may have said, but it's slipped my mind. Sorry."

Kurt stood up and crossed to Mary's rocking chair. "It's all right," he said, leaning down to pat her hand. "Don't worry about it." He straightened and shot me a sharp glance. "I think maybe it's time for you to go, Amy. We don't want to exhaust Mary before tonight."

Mary waved him away. "It's fine. I'll be bright as a button once I have that fancy lunch at your place and get all dolled up." She looked over at me. "I suppose I'll be seeing you again tonight, Amy."

"I look forward to it." I crossed to her and clasped one of her hands. "Thanks so much for all of this information, Mary. I'm going to share it with the sheriff's department, if that's okay."

"Fine, fine. You don't have my friend's name, so you can't get him in any trouble. Anyways, I think maybe he'll be willing to talk to the sheriff now, but I'd want to give him a bit of a warning first, if you don't mind." Mary sank back in her chair with another rattling sigh.

"I imagine they'd be willing to give him immunity at this point," Kurt said. "But we'll let him come forward on his own."

Thanking Mary again, and promising to make sure to connect with both her and Kurt later, I left the house. Sitting in my car, I texted Brad, telling him I might want to speak privately at the *Nutcracker* performance.

No rest for the weary, he texted back. *But okay. At intermission, perhaps? We'll both be busy with our kids after.*

I agreed with this plan. Driving home, I rehashed Mary's story several times. It was clear that if this tale was true and Mary's fugitive friend had shared it with the Hursts' son-in-law, he, or perhaps even his son or daughter, could've had a reason to seek revenge against Wendy and Blackstone Properties.

If only Mary had remembered his name, I thought as I pulled into my driveway. But that was something Brad and his team could certainly uncover, given enough time.

Climbing the steps to the front porch, I realized Wendy wasn't the only person who could be held responsible for the Hursts' death. There was the enforcer, as well as Tim Thompson. Blackstone Properties itself could also be considered liable, which might have an adverse effect on Nadia and Dylan, if only financially.

I inhaled a deep breath of cool winter air, hoping Brad and his team had enough time, before it was too late.

Before the killer struck again.

Chapter
Twenty-Four

T raveling to the theater with two children who were hyped to the max was quite an experience.

"How did you do this by yourself yesterday?" I asked Richard.

He shot me an amused glance as he turned onto Smithsburg's main street. "I told them I'd keep them off the stage if they didn't settle down."

I glanced over my shoulder. Fiona, to her credit, was sitting in the middle of the back seat, between Ella and Nicky. I knew that couldn't be comfortable, but she'd insisted.

"We're going to have a long wait at the theater," I'd told her when we'd discussed the arrangements in the afternoon. "Richard and the kids have to be there early to warm up and get into costume and all that. If you wanted to ride in with Aunt Lydia and Hugh, I'm sure they wouldn't mind."

"It's fine. I'll go with you and Richard. That way I can help with the children," Fiona had replied.

Feeling that she was trying to express her gratitude to us for allowing her to visit the entire week, I didn't argue.

Situated on the main street, the Smithsburg theater was an old cinema that had been renovated a year or two before the twins were born. It could still show movies, and a local film society held an annual festival there, but it was primarily used as a venue for live performances of various kinds, from Richard and Karla's dance productions to traveling shows and the plays put on by the area's community theater troupes.

Richard parked in the paved lot behind the theater. While he and the twins used the door that led backstage, I directed Fiona to follow me around the building so we could enter through the main lobby.

"I thought the children might need help with their costumes," Fiona said.

"Karla has a contingent of dance moms lined up to do that." I used the extra set of keys Richard had given me to open one of the front doors. Painted a glossy crimson, the doors reflected their Art Deco heritage in their diamond patterned windows and chrome geometric accents.

"I'm surprised you aren't a dance mom," Fiona said as we entered the lobby.

I grinned. "No need. They have a dance dad."

Fiona slipped off her black wool coat as she surveyed the lobby. It was a glamorous space, a perfect backdrop for her elegant silver silk sheath dress. Marble columns flanked the doorways leading off the lobby, and the soaring pale-blue ceiling created the illusion of a summer sky. A tiered chandelier hung over the center of the lobby, where a restored tile mosaic evoked the floor medallions of ancient Rome.

"There's a coat check somewhere around here, isn't there?" Fiona asked.

"Yes, but no one is there yet." I crossed to a small room enclosed by a proscenium-style arch. "Maybe one of these keys will work."

It took several tries, but I finally found the key that opened the coat check. Taking Fiona's coat, I slipped off my own and hung them on one of the metal racks, collecting the matching number chip from each hanger.

"That's a good color on you," Fiona said as she tucked the chip into her purse.

I looked down at my full-skirted dress. It was a deep rusty orange that I knew complemented my dark hair and deep-brown eyes. "Thanks. Even though I love the cool colors, I don't look as good in them, like you and my aunt do."

"No, warmer tones suit you better," Fiona said. She looked around the lobby. "Is there somewhere to sit down out here, or do we need to head into the theater?"

I pointed toward another alcove framed by an arch. Within its shadowed space, a few small tables and chairs provided a place for patrons to sit after they'd purchased intermission drinks or snacks from the concession area. "We can wait over there. I don't want to go into the theater until the ushers arrive."

"That makes sense." Fiona followed me over to the seating area. "When do they usually open the auditorium?" she asked with a glance at her delicate silver wristwatch.

"About thirty minutes before the curtain. But things will start buzzing around here before that," I said, taking a seat across a small café table from her.

We made idle chitchat for a few minutes before Fiona pulled out her cell phone to check messages. I did the same, and we fell silent until the theater manager appeared. I explained about having been given a set of keys by Richard.

"Oh, Mr. Muir? That's okay, then," the manager said as she buttoned the jacket of her simple black suit. "He's always very responsible."

The volunteer ushers and coat check staff arrived soon thereafter. A few minutes later, when the manager opened the front doors, ticket holders began to trickle in.

I kept a lookout for our party. Spying Sunny's golden hair amid the growing crowd, I told Fiona we should go and join her.

"Hi there," I said, linking my arm with Sunny's. "You look gorgeous, as usual."

Sunny smiled. "Just a little thing I picked up secondhand," she said, flourishing one hand to show off the periwinkle-blue dress that hugged her sleek curves in all the right places. She turned to the man standing beside her. Although Fred Nash was only an inch taller than Sunny, his muscular build dwarfed her slender frame. As always, they made a lovely couple. Her pale skin, blue eyes, and blond hair provided the perfect contrast to his dark complexion, black hair, and chestnut-brown eyes.

"Hello, Fred. Long time no see," I said. "I think you've both met Richard's mom, Fiona, right?"

"Of course. Good to see you again," Sunny said, with Fred echoing her.

"Ah, there you are." Aunt Lydia and Hugh made their way through the growing crowd.

Hugh, looking dapper in an indigo suit, greeted me, Fiona, Sunny, and Fred. "Although I've seen too much of him recently," he said, indicating Fred.

"All their secretive investigations." Sunny's elaborately braided updo was pierced with an enamel hairpin that resembled a peacock feather. "Tracking down art criminals and the like," she told Fiona, who'd raised her eyebrows at Sunny's first remark.

"Oh, right. I'd forgotten that's what you do." Fiona pursed her lips.

Some things don't change, I thought. *She still doesn't approve of private investigators or others who might skirt her definition of acceptable professions.*

Aunt Lydia, who was lovely as usual in a blush-pink suit accented with a fuchsia silk blouse, held up a pair of tickets. "Shall we head to our seats? It looks like they've opened the auditorium."

"Wait a minute, what's all the buzz about?" Sunny asked, eyeing the crowd.

I realized she was right. The usual low rumble of conversation had given way to louder comments and exclamations of surprise. Turning to face the front doors, I noticed that a circle of onlookers had formed around the two men who'd just entered the lobby.

"It's Scott and Ethan," I said, waving my arm above my head to alert them to our location.

Fred stepped forward, clearing a path for my brother and his husband. "It seems not everyone has heard the news," he said as they joined our little group.

"Yes, that's right," Sunny said, raising her voice so her words would project out over the crowd. "Ethan Payne has been cleared of any suspicion in Wendy Blackstone's death. In case any of you wondered." The light from the crystal chandelier glittered off her peridot-studded silver bracelet as she flicked her wrist through the air.

Ethan, color rising in his cheeks, mumbled, "Thanks."

"No problem at all," Sunny said, patting his shoulder. Fred, beaming with pride, took her arm.

"Come on, love, let's take our seats," he said.

They led the way into the auditorium, sweeping past a few obviously shocked patrons.

The rest of us followed. As we strolled down the center aisle to find our assigned seats, I once again admired the renovation that had been spearheaded by arts administrator and current Taylorsford mayor Marty Stover. The stage, which had been expanded from its original size to cover a small orchestra pit, could easily accommodate the demands of live theater and dance performances, especially since the original movie screen had been replaced by a retractable version. Midnight-blue velvet drapes, behind an elaborate pseudo-Roman frieze whose plaster decorations gleamed with touches of gilt, were pulled closed to cover the stage.

Passing rows of theater seats, I noticed Brad sitting with his wife, Alison, and waved. I'd heard from Richard and Karla that their six-year-old son, Noah, displayed a real talent for dancing—an observation I wasn't sure Brad would welcome. *But unlike Richard's dad, he has shown up for his son's performance*, I thought as we reached our row of seats near the front of the auditorium.

More than a few curious stares focused on Scott and Ethan. Combined with idle chatter, this continued until the lights flashed, warning people to take their seats. As I settled back against the sapphire plush-velvet upholstery and focused on the stage, Fiona tapped my arm.

"I had some flowers sent backstage for Ella and Nicky," she whispered. "I hope that's okay."

"I'm sure they'll be thrilled," I said, but then held a finger to my lips as the lights dimmed and the orchestra launched into the opening bars of Tchaikovsky's score.

The curtains slid back, revealing a party scene that evoked a Victorian parlor while still remaining stylized enough to match the aesthetic of the production. Ella and Nicky, along with Noah and the other children, performed their roles with a charm and assurance far beyond their years.

It's a testament to Karla's skills as a teacher, and her and Richard's brilliant choreography, I thought as I shared a quick smile with Fiona, who appeared transfixed by the action on stage.

She leaned forward when Richard finally appeared as Drosselmeyer, the mysterious figure who gives the main character, Clara, the nutcracker that eventually turns into a prince. Dancing with his usual skill and elegance, Richard projected a slightly dangerous quality that made it difficult to determine whether his character was meant to be good or evil.

He just can't help it, I thought with a little smile. I knew that Richard hadn't planned to put himself front and center in this production, wanting the focus to remain on the younger dancers, but the moment he stepped into the scene, it was impossible to keep your eyes off of him. *Of course, that might just be me.*

As the first act ended in its flurry of snowflakes, the audience broke into loud applause.

"Ella and Nicky were so good, weren't they?" Fiona said as the lights came up for intermission. "Well, everyone was."

"Including Richard," I said.

"Yes, of course." Fiona fiddled with her paper program. Meeting my gaze, her expression grew serious. "He is a great dancer, isn't he? I wish I hadn't waited so long to find that out."

I wish you hadn't too, I thought, but simply smiled. "I'm sure he'd love to hear you say it." Surveying the crowd, I noticed Kurt standing a few rows back, near a section that had been designed to accommodate wheelchairs. "Excuse me, I need to go say hello," I told Fiona before heading up the aisle.

"Don't you both look elegant," I told Kurt and Mary, who was seated in a wheelchair beside him. She wore a red velvet dress accessorized with a pearl necklace and earrings. A velvet patchwork quilt in shades of green, gold, and red was draped over her lap. "Very festive."

Kurt, who was wearing a pearl-gray shantung silk suit I was certain had been tailored to fit his large frame, gave me a little bow. "Thank you. We thought the occasion demanded a little extra effort."

I bent down to clasp one of Mary's hands. "Are you enjoying the show so far?"

"Oh, laws, yes. It's splendid," Mary said, her hazel eyes sparkling. "That husband of yours certainly knows how to make an entrance."

"He does, doesn't he?" I gave her fingers a slight squeeze. "The children did well too, don't you think?"

"They were adorable. Such lovely little dancers," Mary replied.

As I stared to slide my hand away, Mary clutched my fingers. "Lawdy, Amy, I almost forgot again. I remembered that name, the one that slipped my mind earlier." She tightened her grip. "The last name of the Hursts' son-in-law, I mean. It was one of those Scottish names common in these parts. Campbell, that was it."

"What?" I straightened, pulling my fingers free. "You're certain it was Campbell?"

"Oh yes, dear. That was surely it. Duncan Campbell, I believe the son-in-law was called. Not sure about the child."

As Kurt and I shared a glance, I saw understanding flood his face. "Megan Campbell," he said.

"I need to find Brad." I cast my gaze wildly about the auditorium. "And Sunny." Turning back to Mary, I wished her a good evening and darted off, searching the crowded rows.

I found Sunny first, standing in the lobby chatting with a member of Jaden Perez's environmental coalition. Grabbing her arm, I pulled her to one side. "Where's Megan? Is she still at Vista View?"

Sunny, her blue eyes widening in surprise, shook her head. "No. As a matter of fact, she disappeared in the middle of the night. Or early this morning. Anyway, it was while the grands and I were asleep. And she didn't tell any of us thanks or good-bye or kiss my as . . . astrolabe." Sunny flashed an apologetic smile at an older woman standing nearby. "She stole one of our coolers too. I just discovered that today. I went out to the shed to find a pair of pliers and noticed the cooler was gone. I guess she took that with her when she flew the coop."

"I think she stole it long before last night," I said, remembering Ethan's mention of a cooler when he was locked in the barn. "But it's actually good that she's gone. If she shows up again, call 911 immediately."

"Why?" Confusion washed over Sunny's face.

"Because I think she's Wendy's killer," I said. "Sorry, I can't explain now. I need to find Brad."

"Over by the concession stand," Sunny said with a wave of her hand. As I dashed off, she called out, "You'll clarify all this later, right?"

The lights flashed, warning that the intermission was almost over. I knew I had to get back to my seat, but first I needed to talk to Brad.

I intercepted him as he was heading for the auditorium doors.

"Amy," he said. "I knew I mentioned talking at intermission, but we don't have time—"

I clutched the sleeve of his jacket. "I know, but you have to hear this. It's Megan," I said. "Megan Campbell. Jaden Perez's partner in Environmental Advocates."

"What of her?" Brad pulled his arm away.

"She's the killer. Don't ask me how I know, there's no time to explain, but it's her."

Brad stared at me for a moment before yanking his cell phone from his pocket. "Go inside," he told me. "I'll call in an APB on the woman, but only if you swear you have some evidence to back this up."

"I do. I honestly do." Other than the volunteers, we were the only people left in the lobby. I pressed my hand to my heart. "I swear."

Brad nodded and held up his phone. "Then I'll call. You get back to your seat."

I followed his command, although I was trembling from the adrenaline rushing through my body. Just as the lights went dark, I grabbed my program off the seat and fanned my face as I sat down.

"You cut that pretty short," Fiona whispered as the curtains opened.

"Good reason. Tell you later," I said, before someone behind us made a shushing noise.

The rest of the production went by in a blur. I was glad I'd planned to attend all of the performances so that I could actually appreciate the second half.

Once Megan Campbell is in custody, I'll be able to concentrate on things like dancing again, I told myself, certain her arrest would occur before *The Nutcracker*'s closing night.

I hoped so, anyway.

Chapter
Twenty-Five

I thought I was the only one up by nine on Saturday morning, until Fiona appeared in the kitchen in her paisley-patterned bathrobe.

"Good morning," I said.

"Is it?" Fiona's voice sounded ragged, and her hair was pulled back into a simple bun rather than her trademark chignon.

I noticed she was clutching a wad of tissues in one hand and that her eyes were red rimmed. "What's wrong?" I asked, motioning toward the chair across the kitchen table from mine. "Here, sit down and I'll get you some coffee or water or whatever."

"Coffee would be good," she said as she slumped into the chair.

I didn't ask any more questions until I place a mug of black coffee in front of her and sat down with my own refilled mug. "Is someone ill or injured?" I asked, after taking a sip.

"No, nothing like that." Fiona shoved the tissues into the pocket of her robe and stared glumly down at the slightly oily surface of her coffee. "It's just that . . . well, last night was so lovely. I truly enjoyed seeing the children perform, and Richard too, of course. And all your friends were so pleasant to be around." She raised her eyes and met my questioning gaze. "Then, when we got home and I went upstairs, I received a phone call from Jim."

"What did he have to say? Confirming plans for your return home and then your cruise?"

"Yes, well, that was the issue, you see. The cruise." Fiona circled the top of her mug with one finger. "I didn't mention this before, because I'd already made up my mind, but he called earlier in the week and wanted me to come home Thursday. He had this idea that we could leave for our trip a few days ahead of time and tour Miami, where we were scheduled to board the ship, before the cruise. I told him I didn't choose to do that, because I wanted to stay until today. For the *Nutcracker* performance, among other things."

"I assume he didn't take that well," I said, studying Fiona's drawn face.

"He did not. Especially since he'd already booked a couple of nights in a Miami hotel."

"Without consulting you?"

Fiona shrugged. "As I've mentioned before, he always does that sort of thing. He calls it *taking charge*."

"I'd call it presumptuous."

Fiona stared over my shoulder, not meeting my eyes. "Of course, that's what it actually is. I've just grown used to it, I suppose. Normally, I go along with his plans to keep the peace, but this time I refused." When she focused back on me, I could read the resolve in her eyes. "I was determined to see Ella and Nicky's first stage performance. I didn't do that for Richard, you know."

"Yes, I know." I swallowed a gulp of my coffee.

"I regret that now." Fiona shoved a dangling lock of hair behind her ear. "Jim didn't want me attending any of Richard's dance performances, because he thought if we refused to support him, he'd eventually give it up. I used to argue with Jim about it but never really stood my ground."

"But you did this time," I said.

"Yes. I told him, when he called before, that I would not return home until today. He's been sending me angry emails and voice mail messages ever since. I was ignoring them until last night. I thought if I talked to him about how wonderful the *Nutcracker* was, how well the twins did, and how impressed I was with Richard and Karla's choreography and overall leadership . . ." Fiona pulled one of the tissues from her pocket and dabbed her eyes again. "It didn't do any good. I just got yelled at again. Told I was an ungrateful, unsupportive wife." Fiona blew her nose. "Unsupportive! As if I hadn't put up with all his cruel, self-centered nonsense for years."

"I'm sorry." I shook my head. "You shouldn't have to deal with that."

"No, I shouldn't." Fiona straightened in her chair. Holding her head high, she looked across at me. "Being here, seeing you and Richard and how you are together, and all the easy laughter and fun between you and with the children . . . well, I was just struck by the realization that I don't want to take that cruise. I don't even want to go home to Jim. Oh, I know I have to go back and sort things out, but I've decided it's time for me to make a change. A big one."

"You're going to leave Jim?" I asked, my eyes widening.

Fiona lifted her chin. "I am. He'll have to give me enough to live on, but I do have a little money of my own, so I think I can make it. I just need a small apartment and the furniture and things from my family. Just what's my own."

"Good for you." I stretched my arm across the table. "I know it will be tough, but I bet you'll be happier in the end."

"I know I will be." Fiona reached out and covered my hand with hers. "The only thing is, I don't want to go back and spend the holidays at home, with him. He'll be impossible, what with losing the money for the cruise on top of everything. Is there any way I could stay with you and Richard until after Christmas? I promise not to crash here too long."

"Of course," I said, clasping her fingers. "I'm sure Richard won't mind, and the kids will be thrilled. They've gotten very attached to you, especially after this week."

"First time I was really able to be myself, with Jim not being around," Fiona said. "I guess that bodes well for the future."

"I'd say so." Clattering footsteps on the stairs made me turn my head toward the hall. "I think that might be Ella and Nicky now."

Fiona smoothed her hair and dabbed under her nose one final time before stuffing the tissue in her pocket. "There are my stars!" she exclaimed as the twins ran into the room. "Come over here for a morning hug, both of you."

As she stood to greet them, she cast me a wan smile and mouthed, "Thank you."

* * *

After everyone had breakfast, Richard and the twins headed over to Aunt Lydia's house to wrap presents for me and Fiona, claiming they didn't want any peeking during the process.

"This is just a way to allow your mom time to decompress upstairs, isn't it?" I asked him as the children loaded the gifts into one of their wagons.

"Perhaps," Richard said, placing his hands on my shoulders. "Besides, don't you need to wrap my gifts?"

I wrinkled my nose at him. "Maybe I didn't get you anything."

"That would be okay, but I know it isn't true." Gazing down into my eyes for a moment, Richard smiled and gave me a lingering kiss. "Thanks for being so good with Mom, and basically, just being so good," he whispered in my ear when he pulled away.

"Thanks, but I don't know that I'm really all that," I said, tapping his lips with two fingers.

He grabbed the fingers and curled his hand around mine. "Oh, you are. In all the ways that matter."

With Fiona resting upstairs, the house fell quiet when Richard and the kids left. Having already wrapped Richard's gifts, I decided to take the opportunity to do some reading.

I'd just settled in on the sofa with my book when the doorbell rang. Swearing under my breath, I peeled Fosse off my legs and deposited him on the adjacent sofa cushion, where Loie was curled into a tight tortoiseshell ball of fur.

"Who's this now?" I muttered as I crossed the room and opened the front door.

The last person I expected to see was standing on my porch.

"Hello, Ms. Muir," Jaden Perez said. "Do you have a minute?"

"Um, sure. Come in." I noticed that Jaden looked rather worse for the wear. His normally silky dark hair appeared greasy and stringy, and there were dark circles under his eyes.

Jaden's gaze darted from the porch to the street and back again. "Okay. I just don't want . . . Well, I guess it's fine." He slipped past me hurriedly and reached out to slam the door before I could close it.

"Hold up, what's going on?" I asked, as Jaden appeared to be surveying our front room like a security expert looking for hidden dangers.

"Are you alone?" he asked.

"Pretty much. My mother-in-law is upstairs, but I believe she's napping. Anyway, I doubt she'll be down for a while." I motioned toward the seating area. "My husband and kids are next door."

Jaden dropped down into one of the armchairs. "I just didn't want to talk if there were too many people around," he said. "I know you've worked with the sheriff's department in the past—your friend Sunny mentioned that—so I thought you'd be a good person to talk to."

"Okay," I said, drawing the word out. I sat down on the sofa, earning baleful looks from the two cats. "You aren't allergic, I hope."

Jaden's gaze swept over Loie and Fosse. "No, fortunately not. I actually wish I could have a pet, but it's too tough, moving around the way I do."

"What did you want to talk to me about?" I asked, settling back against the sofa cushions.

"Wendy Blackstone's death." Jaden's dark eyes welled with tears. "The truth is, I know who killed her."

"What?" I sat up and swiveled my body to face him. "You should be talking with the sheriff's department, not me."

"I will. I mean, I plan to." Jaden yanked his fingers through his hair. "But I wanted an outside opinion on the whole thing. Like, what might happen to me."

"Were you involved?" I asked.

"Not in the beginning. I didn't know anything ahead of time, I swear." Jaden slumped in his chair. "But then I got pulled in, to help a friend."

"Megan Campbell," I said.

Jaden looked shocked for a second, then nodded. "We aren't romantically involved or anything, but we're close. Like brother and sister, I guess you could say. So when she came to me and told me what had happened, I felt compelled to help her."

I leaned forward, pressing my palms against my thighs. "What did she tell you, exactly?"

"She said she got into an argument with Wendy after Winterfest closed down that night. Everyone else had gone, including that Payne fellow, although we did see him fight with Wendy a little earlier. I know I originally told the authorities something a little different—that

Payne was still there when we left. The truth is, Megan asked me to say that, and I didn't see the harm at the time." Jaden cast me a morose glance. "Regardless of who left when, there was a lot of yelling between Wendy Blackstone and Ethan Payne, and he did grab Wendy, which is why Megan thought he was the right person . . . Wait, let me go back." Jaden exhaled. "The thing is, Megan told me that she and Wendy argued. No one else was around when this happened. I'd already gone back to the van to pack up some placards and stuff. Megan claimed she was just checking the grounds for any flyers that had been dropped. We don't like to leave any litter, of course."

I arched my eyebrows. "Environmental Advocates being your group's name."

"Yeah. Anyway, Megan told me that she ran into Wendy at the top of those stairs that lead down to the ice rink. They had some sort of argument, and in the midst of it, Megan claimed Wendy grabbed her. Then Megan tried to push her off, and . . ."

"Shoved her down the stairs?" I sat back, staring speculatively at Jaden. "So it was an accident, or self-defense, or both?"

"That's what Megan told me," Jaden said, misery painted across his face. "And I believed her."

"So why not go directly to the authorities? Why try to hide it?" I asked.

"Megan was afraid they wouldn't believe her. She had ties to Wendy and Blackstone Properties, you see."

"Ah, right. They instigated and then covered up the deaths of her grandparents."

Jaden shot me a wide-eyed glance. "You know about that?"

"I found out, with some help from friends, and my own research." I drummed my fingers against the sofa cushions, drawing a muffled meow from Fosse. "So what was the plan? Stay quiet and hope someone else, like Ethan Payne, took the rap?"

"I didn't know about that, I swear," Jaden said. "All I said I'd do was arrange for Megan to quietly leave the country and stay away until things cooled off. She had a valid passport, and we figured, since she didn't really seem to be on the sheriff's radar, she could just slip away. I have environmental activist associates in South America, you see. I thought Megan could go and work with them for a while, and maybe Wendy Blackstone's death would be declared an accident or something and it would all blow over."

"But it was declared a murder," I said. "The forensic experts found evidence of a blow to Wendy's head. Which led to her death just as surely as the fall."

"I know, I know." Jaden dropped his head into his hands for a moment. When he looked up, his pain was palpable. "I really did believe Megan when she said it was an accident. And then the sheriff was looking at Ethan Payne as the perp, and I said something to her, urging her to confess. To not let an innocent man go to jail. But she just said that he was a great distraction. When Payne disappeared, I thought it was simply a stroke of luck."

My fingernails dug into my jeans. "It gave you more time to make all the arrangements for Megan to flee the country."

"Which were complicated. Anyway"—Jaden sat up straighter— "I had no idea that Megan had anything to do with Payne's disappearance. I certainly wouldn't have supported that if I had known. She was acting peculiar, but I just thought it was guilt, or trauma from the accident." His lips twisted into a grimace. "Accident—yeah, that's a good one. There was no accident."

"You think Megan deliberately killed Wendy Blackstone?" I asked.

"I do now." Jaden stared up at the ceiling. "When Ethan Payne was cleared and the information about his kidnapping came out, I asked Megan if she knew anything about that. She just laughed in my face. Told me that she'd engineered the whole thing to keep the focus on Payne. It was almost like she wanted me to admire her for that, and when I didn't, she got angry. Demanded to know when I was getting her to South America. So I said maybe I wasn't now."

I pressed one hand against my chest. "What happened then?"

"She lost it. Started screaming at me. Said I'd betrayed her, just like the Blackstones had betrayed her family. Told me to forget about helping her. She'd take care of herself, like she always had. Claimed that her dad had taught her how to live off the land and she might just disappear into the mountains where no one would ever find her." Jaden pressed his hand to his forehead. "Then she threatened me."

"What? How?"

He met my intense stare without flinching. "She said she'd been keeping tabs on me and if I went to law enforcement with what I knew, she'd kill me. She swore she could—that no matter how long it took, she'd get revenge. Just like she did with Wendy Blackstone. She'd planned that for years, she said. Just waited for the right moment. And she'd do the same to me, just like she would, eventually, to Tim Thompson and Wendy's kids."

"Oh hell, that's not good," I said, rising to my feet and crossing to his chair.

Jaden stood up to face me. "No, it sure isn't. Maybe the woman isn't entirely sane, or maybe she's just allowed her anger and desire for revenge to overwhelm every other emotion. I don't know. All I'm sure of is that she's quite capable of killing again."

"I think you do need to go to authorities. Today. To protect yourself as well as others. And, to be perfectly honest, the sheriff's department knows about Megan's connection to Blackstone Properties and is looking for her as we speak." I laid a hand on Jaden's shoulder. "You'll have to face the music for your involvement in covering up

Megan's crime, but it you explain it the way you've told me and offer to testify, you may be granted immunity. Or at least, a very light sentence."

"It doesn't matter." Jaden looked down at me, determination replacing his earlier anxiety. "I can accept responsibility for my actions. I just don't want anyone else to get hurt."

"You know you'll have my support. Now, perhaps it's better if you leave. I don't want to have to explain everything right now to my mother-in-law or the rest of my family."

"No problem." Jaden cast a swift glance at the door. "My car's out front, parked on the other side of the street. I'll just slip out and go, before anyone else sees me."

"Good luck. And if you need anyone to back up your story, I'll be glad to tell the sheriff's department that you talked to me. That should help corroborate your confession and show that you planned to turn yourself in as soon as you learned the truth."

Jaden thanked me and headed outside. I locked the door and strolled back into the kitchen.

A minute later, as I idly rearranged the flowers that Fiona had bought for Ella and Nicky, I heard a bang that resonated throughout the house. I ran into the living room just as Fiona appeared at the top of the stairs.

"What was that?" she asked as another bang rent the air.

I knew that sound. I'd unfortunately heard it too many times before. "Gunshots," I said. "Call 911."

Leaving her fumbling with her cell phone, I dashed to the front door and unlocked it, using both hands to steady my shaking fingers. An older-model silver compact car sped away as soon as I stepped onto the porch.

"Hold on, help is on the way," I shouted as I flew down the steps to kneel beside the prone body of Jaden Perez.

Chapter
Twenty-Six

Reaching Jaden, I whipped off the sweatshirt I was wearing over an old concert T-shirt and pressed it against the wound in his chest. Although it was a relatively small bullet hole, the amount of blood was terrifying.

I was soon joined by Fiona, then Richard, who'd also heard the gunshots and squealing tires and had rushed out of Aunt Lydia's house.

"She's keeping the kids inside," he said, kneeling down beside me.

Fiona, her face ashen, waved the cell phone. "An ambulance should be here soon."

"Can you take over?" I asked Richard, who nodded and continued to apply pressure to Jaden's wound after I lifted my hands.

I yanked my own cell phone from my pocket, but my fingers, slick with blood, couldn't keep a grip. Swearing as the phone bounced onto the brown grass of the front lawn, I wiped my hands on my jeans. Finally able to hold the phone, I called Brad's direct line to let him know that I'd seen Megan Campbell's car leaving the scene of the crime.

"It's an older silver compact car with several dents and dings," I said in my voice mail message, raising my voice as the wail of sirens filled the air.

As soon as Hannah and a few of the volunteer medics jumped out of the ambulance, they shooed Richard and me away, suggesting that we go back into the house.

"We can take it from here," Hannah said, any trace of youth erased by her commanding professional demeanor.

Richard and I retired to the porch, where Fiona was already waiting. We anxiously watched as the EMTs placed Jaden on a stretcher and loaded him into the ambulance, which took off just as two sheriff's department cars roared up.

Brad jogged across the yard while a couple of deputies examined the scene. "Don't forget to set up a perimeter," Brad called out as he joined us on the porch.

"It was Megan Campbell. I'm sure of it," I said.

Brad looked me up and down, obviously taking in the blood that covered my clothes and Richard's hands and shirt. "I have an APB out on her already, and just added that vehicle you mentioned in your voice mail. I don't know how she's evaded our search thus far, but it seems she has some talents we were unaware of."

"Jaden told me that her father, who was career army, taught her survival skills."

"That explains a lot." Brad used two fingers to push his hat back from his forehead. "Okay, so tell me, Amy—what was Jaden Perez doing here?"

Richard looked down at me, his eyes narrowed. "I'd like to know that too."

"I didn't invite him, if that's what you're worried about." I started to brush back a straggling lock of my hair but then remembered the blood and halted my hand in midair. "He came to see me, uninvited and unexpected."

"To talk about what?" Brad asked.

"Something he was coming to tell you." I blew the offending strand of hair away from my face. "I'll share it now, since he can't, but I just want you to know that he was planning to confess everything today. I hope that will count for something."

"We'll see, but I'll keep that in mind," Brad said, pulling a small recorder out of his inside jacket pocket. "But for now, please tell me what he said to you."

Flanked by Richard and Fiona, I related Jaden's story.

"He thought it was an accident at first?" Brad asked, holding out the recorder.

"Yeah. That's why he agreed to help Megan. But he changed his mind over time, especially once he found out about her locking Ethan in that barn."

"And then, according to Perez, she confessed to deliberately killing Wendy Blackstone?"

"So he said." The blood was drying, creating stiff patches on my T-shirt and jeans. "Do you think Richard and I can go clean up now? I'm happy to come to the station to provide a more formal statement later."

"Of course, of course." Brad clicked off the recorder and slipped it back in his pocket. "If you can just give a brief statement to one of my deputies, Richard, that should be sufficient."

"Good, because I have another performance tonight," Richard said.

"But we will need more from you, Amy, so stop by the department sometime later today." Brad tipped his hat to us. "I'm going to see if the team has found anything yet. Please stay inside until they complete their investigation of the premises."

"Will do," I said. Turning to Fiona, I added, "Would you mind checking in with my aunt and the kids? Let them know what's going on." I lifted one blood-streaked hand. "But don't bring Ella and

Nicky home until I call. I think Richard and I should clean up before they see us."

"Good idea," Fiona said. She followed Brad off the porch, but while he joined the deputies in the yard, she headed across the driveway to Aunt Lydia's house.

"This is certainly not what I expected to happen this morning," Richard said, giving me a wan smile.

"It sure isn't what I anticipated either. Come on, let's wash off this blood and change clothes." I gripped his forearm with my fingers. "I really want to see the kids and give them a hug, you know? But not looking like this."

"Agreed," Richard said, patting my fingers with his free hand.

He opened the front door, using a clean portion of the tail of his shirt to avoid getting any blood on the knob.

Inside, the cats, who'd undoubtedly been frightened by the sound of the gunshots as well as the sirens, peeked out at us from under the coffee table.

"Sorry, guys," I told them as Richard and I crossed to the stairs. "Things should calm down soon."

Richard, two steps above me, looked back. "If only I could believe that."

*   *   *

Once we were cleaned up, I called Fiona to give her the all clear to return to our house, and Richard went back to Aunt Lydia's to collect Ella, Nicky, and the now-wrapped gifts.

While I waited for their return, Brad gave a quick call to update me on Jaden's condition. "They had to induce a coma," he said. "So we haven't been able to talk with him yet. That means we really do need your full statement, Amy."

"I'll come in after lunch," I said, feeling a frisson of concern over getting home in time to get the twins ready for the evening's *Nutcracker* performance. But then I remembered that Fiona was perfectly capable of doing their hair and makeup. *A benefit to having a more expanded family,* I reminded myself.

"Oh, and that black SUV—"

"Belongs to Blackstone Properties," I said. "Yeah, I know. It's strange, because it looks like Megan killed Wendy, so why would someone from Blackstone want to warn me off?"

"Probably to keep the truth about those deaths at Crystal Lake well and truly buried," Brad said. "But that's a lost cause now. I've already alerted law enforcement in the Crystal Lake area about two possible murders."

"Good," I said, before thanking him and ending the call.

When Richard and the twins returned, I discovered to my disappointment that Ella and Nicky were fascinated with the idea of someone getting shot in our front yard—a reaction I was determined to quash.

"This is not something to be excited about," I told them when they asked, for the umpteenth time, if I'd actually seen Jaden get hit by the bullet. "Mr. Perez is very badly hurt and in the hospital. That's not something you should wish on anyone."

Ella's sullen expression told me she disapproved of my lack of enthusiasm over these unusual events. Of course, what I didn't tell her, or Nicky, was that I had seen people shot in the past and had hoped to never experience that again. *Another hope dashed,* I thought as I sent them upstairs to read or play quietly in Nicky's room.

"They just want a story to tell their little friends," Richard said when I expressed my despair over our children's ghoulish natures. "They don't really understand the implications."

"I know, but I don't want to encourage them to find violence interesting," I replied, sitting down on the edge of our bed. "Switching to another volatile topic, you never really said how you feel about Fiona staying with us through Christmas."

"It's fine." Richard sat down beside me. "If it's okay with you, I have no problem with it." He cast me an amused sidelong glance. "She has seemed to have thawed out quite a bit lately."

"True." I reached over and took hold of his hands. "And what about her decision to leave your dad? I wasn't sure how you'd feel about that."

"I'd say it's about time." Richard entwined his fingers with mine. "I've never seen her as relaxed and happy as she has been this week, and I have to think it's because she's here without him. It's gotten me to thinking how he never encouraged her to do much on her own. I believe he's always seen her as his appendage—someone to be his mirror, or shadow, without any real life of her own."

"And now she finally wants one." I gave Richard's hands a squeeze before releasing them. "Of course, you know this means we'll probably see a lot more of her."

"That's okay." Richard rose to his feet. Crossing the room, he leaned against the dresser, facing the wall. "Maybe," he added, "I'm looking forward to having one actual parent for a change."

I stood and ran to him. Sliding my arms around his chest, I leaned against his back. "You deserve that, and more."

Richard covered my hands with his. "Thanks, sweetheart. And thanks for not holding a grudge against my mom. I know you've had plenty of reasons to do so."

"We all have our issues, don't we?" I stood up on tiptoe to kiss the back of his neck. "Besides, nothing makes me happier than to see you happy."

Richard spun around, breaking my hold on him. But he immediately took me in his arms and kissed me passionately. "I knew I was making the best decision of my life when I married you," he said when he finally released me.

"Glad you think so." I took hold of one of his hands and pressed it to my heart. "I feel the same."

Richard arched his eyebrows. "Oh, that *I* was making a good decision?"

"Right," I said, wrinkling my nose at him. "Just for that, you have to kiss me again."

"Such a tyrant," Richard said, before enthusiastically complying with my request.

Chapter
Twenty-Seven

My parents arrived early in the day on Christmas Eve, a fortunate decision, as it turned out. By midmorning it was snowing hard, promising a white Christmas, but also making travel treacherous.

As they often did, Mom and Dad elected to stay in one of the guest bedrooms at Aunt Lydia's house. Of course, with Fiona still visiting us, it was really their only choice. My aunt had also called Scott and Ethan as soon as the snow started falling and told them to come over and stay the night, since otherwise they "might miss all the family festivities."

"You can bring the dog," she'd told them. "I don't think anyone will mind."

So by early afternoon, Aunt Lydia's house was bursting with activity. Richard, Scott, and Ethan were assigned to keep Nicky and Ella—who were bouncing off the walls due to the combined excitement of Christmas, the snow, and Cassie—under some semblance of control. Mom, Hugh, Fiona, and I volunteered to help Aunt Lydia with food prep and other things. She quickly set Fiona and Hugh to work polishing the silverware in the dining room while Mom and I assisted her in the kitchen.

"It's not really big enough to accommodate too many helpers," she said, earning an eye roll from her younger sister.

"Just be honest, Lydia. You don't much like other people messing around in your kitchen," my mom said.

Aunt Lydia didn't correct her. She simply handed Mom a bag of potatoes and told her to get busy peeling them.

By late afternoon the snowstorm had stopped, leaving behind over a foot and a half of snow. Richard, looking a little haggard, poked his head around the kitchen door and made the suggestion that we all bundle up and take a walk before it got dark.

"Fess up, you just want to turn the twins loose outside to burn off some energy," I said.

He gave me a thumbs-up sign.

I had to admit that it was a good idea. Ella and Nicky needed some time to enjoy the snow, which wasn't that regular an occurrence in our area. Despite living at the foot of the mountains, we'd seen very little significant snowfall over the last few years.

As we all tugged on boots and other outerwear, Hugh asked me if I'd heard anything from the sheriff's department concerning Megan Campbell.

"Not really," I said. "I spoke to Brad Tucker again a few days ago, at the closing night of *Nutcracker*, and all he said was what's been on the news—the search for her is ongoing. They did find her car abandoned at one of the local trailheads, but there was no sign of her on or anywhere near the trail."

"I think that was a ruse." Scott pulled a white knit cap over his dark hair. "I bet she parked there and then walked to another location just to throw off the searchers."

"Probably hitchhiked or something and then caught a bus out of the area," Ethan said. "Judging by her ability to deceive and then get the jump on me, I wouldn't underestimate her."

Scott gave him a poke in the ribs with his elbow. "Are you saying someone has to be a genius to put one over on you?"

Ethan playfully bopped Scott's arm with his fist. "Okay, have your little joke. I know I was bested by a girl, and a rather physically small specimen at that."

"She just knew how to play on your good nature," Scott said, throwing his arm around Ethan's shoulders. "Mention a dog in trouble and you're putty in anyone's hands."

"Speaking of dogs, where is ours?" Ethan asked, looking around the sun porch, where we'd stored all our winter gear.

"Already outside with the kids," my dad said. "Don't worry—Richard and Hugh are out with them too."

After we were all dressed for the cold and snow, our entire group met up in the backyard, where Cassie was enjoying a romp with Ella and Nicky.

"They're going to be exhausted tonight," I told Richard.

"Good. Maybe they'll go to sleep a little early, so Santa can come before it's so late." He pointed to himself. "Because Santa would sure like to go to bed before midnight."

"We'll see." I patted the sleeve of his thick fleece coat with my heavy mitten. "They'll probably get a second wind around ten."

"I know," Richard said glumly.

"Who's taking the lead?" Aunt Lydia asked, her pink cheeks matching her rose-colored down coat. "Nick, you're already closest to the front. But remember, you have to blaze the path for the rest of us."

My dad shuffled his boots through the snow. "No problem. I'll just make like I have snowshoes on."

"You do have some pretty big feet," my mom said with a wicked smile.

My dad scooped up a handful of snow and tossed it at her, which started an impromptu snowball fight. Ella and Nicky enthusiastically participated until Richard grabbed Ella and swung her up on his shoulders. Scott did the same with Nicky.

"Easier for these guys to keep up this way," Richard told Fiona, who expressed some concern about his back. "And thanks, Mom, but though I am getting older, I'm not that feeble yet."

We set off, trying to stick to the sidewalk, although it was difficult to determine where the edge of the sidewalk ended and the road began. Of course, there were no cars or other vehicles on the street, so we felt safe either way.

There were only a few other people outside. "A shame," Hugh said. "It's so lovely. Like a wonderland."

I had to agree with him. The white-frosted limbs of the trees and shrubs created an elegant tracery against the clear gray of the sky, while the blanket of snow leant the lights and other holiday decorations an extra touch of magic. I drew in a deep breath of the crisp, cold air as the scents of pine and woodsmoke wafted through the air.

Cassie, who'd been trotting along beside Ethan, paused to investigate a squirrel that chittered at us from a branch not far above our heads. Ella reached up from her perch on Richard's shoulders and grabbed the branch, sending the squirrel skittering farther up the tree trunk and showering herself and Richard with a large dollop of snow.

Richard let loose a few words that horrified Fiona and made me giggle.

"You can't say those things in front of the children," Fiona said, brushing off the dusting of snow that had also fallen onto her wide-brimmed felt hat.

"Obviously, I can," Richard replied, but he then told Ella never to repeat them.

"Like that will work," my mom said, sharing a smile with me.

When we reached the edge of the business district, Aunt Lydia suggested that we turn around. "I know you younger folks could probably keep going, but I confess I'm feeling a bit tired."

"Me too," Hugh said, linking his arm with hers. "Trudging through this snow requires a lot more energy than regular walking."

As we turned around, a strong gust of wind caught Fiona's hat and sent it sailing.

"Go on ahead, the rest of you," I said, "I'll go after it."

I thought it would require only a few extra steps to grab the hat, which had settled on top of a snow-draped shrub. I stomped through a drift that reached my thighs, glad that the snow was still soft as powder. Reaching the shrub, I realized it was growing next to the brick building that housed the temporary offices of Blackstone Properties. I glanced over my shoulder. Although the rest of our walking party was moving farther away, Fiona had hung back.

"Don't worry if you can't get it," she called out. "It isn't worth a broken leg or anything."

"It's no problem," I said, giving her a wave. "Just a few more steps."

Right as I said this, another gust of wind blasted us. Catching the hat, the wind blew it off the shrub and sent it dancing across the snow and into the small parking lot behind the building.

Richard and the others, obviously expecting us to be following behind them, moved farther and farther away. I gnawed the inside of my cheek for a second, then continued to fight my way through the snow to reach the hat.

I'd almost laid hands on it when another gust blew it out of reach. As I swore under my breath. Fiona struggled through the drifts to stand beside me.

"It's certainly being difficult," she said, looking around us. "That's odd."

"What?" I asked, keeping my eye on the hat like a wildcat stalking its prey.

"There are lights on in the Blackstone offices," Fiona said, gesturing toward the back of the building with her black leather gloves.

"Maybe they're working. Some people do work on Christmas Eve." I took two steps forward, only to have the wind blow the hat away again. It landed up against the brick building, next to the back door.

"In this weather? And I forgot to tell you in the midst of all the hubbub today, but Emma, my hometown friend, texted me last night to say that she'd heard Blackstone Properties was abandoning their plans for a development here," Fiona said.

"Really? They're pulling out?" I asked as we both fought the snow to move closer to the hat.

"Apparently. So I'd imagine they'll be shutting down their offices sooner rather than later." Fiona held out her gloved hand. "It's snowing again. Let's forget the hat and head back."

I glanced over at her, noting the white flakes spangling her dark hair. "No, you need something on your head for the walk back. Anyway, it's stuck up against the brick now. I don't think it will escape again."

As we closed in on the hat, Fiona offered me her arm to help me navigate through a particularly deep drift. "Thanks. One of the many problems with being short," I told her, nabbing the hat just as the back door flew open.

Fiona and I stopped in our tracks. Illuminated by the lights of the office behind her, a young woman stood in the doorway.

Murder Checks Out

It was Megan Campbell. I recognized her immediately, even though she'd switched out her colorful glasses for a pair of pewter-wire frames and her curly rose-gold hair had been trimmed into a short pixie cut and dyed dark brown. She was wearing a camouflage shirt with khaki pants and a pair of short hiking boots.

And she was holding a gun.

Chapter Twenty-Eight

"Get inside," she said, brandishing the gun.

The one she used to shoot Jaden, I thought as I followed Fiona into the building.

Megan slammed the door behind us, locking it for good measure.

"Over there," she said, pointing with the revolver toward the office where Fiona and I had spoken with Tim Thompson.

I wasn't entirely surprised to discover Tim and Nadia in the office. The fact that they were tied to two sturdy wooden chairs and gagged was a little more unexpected, but not entirely, given Megan and the gun.

"What are you doing?" Fiona asked. I could read fear in the twitch of her left eyelid, but she was otherwise remarkably composed.

"I was about to exact some much-needed justice," Megan said, "until you two came barging in."

I opened my mouth to mention the fact that Fiona and I would've happily gone on our way if Megan hadn't forced us into the building, but one look at Megan's face silenced me.

Fiona had no such concerns. "We weren't doing anything except retrieving a hat. If you'd kept the door shut, no one would've been the wiser."

Megan walked up and stared into Fiona's haughty face for a moment before slapping her hard across the cheek. "Shut up. I know you were spying on me through the windows."

I made a slicing hand motion down low, next to my hip, trying to convey the need to stay quiet, but Fiona ignored me. Staring down at Megan, she delicately pressed her fingers against the red mark on her cheek. "I have no idea what you're talking about. We were out for a walk with family and friends, and my hat blew away. We had no interest in spying on anyone."

"Well, you're here now, so sit down." Megan shoved Fiona, causing her to stumble and fall into the desk chair. It rolled back, banging into the partition. "Don't move or I'll shoot you, along with these two."

Nadia and Tim, fighting their gags, made unintelligible guttural noises.

"Now you." Megan pointed the gun at me. "Sit in that armchair. I won't tie you up or gag you, but just know if you try to make a run for it or scream, I won't hesitate to shoot. Maybe not to kill, but I doubt you want to lose your kneecap."

I stared at her, astonished at her transformation from a quiet, seemingly meek environmental activist to this angry vigilante. "I'll sit," I said, inching my way over to the chair.

Megan's fierce glare slid from me to Fiona and back again. "You found out, didn't you? About what Wendy Blackstone and those two did." She jerked her head to indicate Nadia and Tim. "I know you talked to Dylan."

"Yes, but he didn't tell me anything about your grandparents," I said, lowering myself into the chair. "I'm not even sure he knew about that."

"Maybe, maybe not." Megan tapped the barrel of the gun against her palm. "But he knew something had happened—a tragedy connected to Crystal Lake. Something that his mother would do anything to keep under wraps. Poor little Dylan. He wanted to do the right thing but couldn't figure out how." She pointed the gun at me. "You figured it out."

"Through some research," I said. "That's all. Just research." I certainly wasn't going to mention Mary or Kurt or what Jaden had told me, although I suspected Megan already assumed Jaden had spilled the beans to me, since she'd tracked him to my house. "I did discover that there was a man who saw your grandparents' murders, and he told your father about it some years later."

"He told me too," Megan said. "I was just a young girl, but my dad never believed in coddling me. He thought I should know the truth, same as him."

"What's this all about?" Fiona asked, tightening her lips when Megan swung the gun around and pointed it at her.

"It's about my grandparents, Greg and Trudy Hurst. I used to spend summers with them, you know," Megan said, her eyes darting back to me. "My mom died when I was little, and my dad was working most of the time. He was in the army. Used to train soldiers in survival skills. That was his specialty."

"He trained you too," I said.

"Yeah, which has provided me with some very useful skills. They've come in handy, especially recently." Megan shifted her focus back on Fiona. "Anyway, I loved my grandparents. My dad was good to me, but he wasn't very warm or nurturing." She shrugged. "Not in his nature. So I liked spending time with Grandpa and Grandma. I loved the farm too. It was going to be mine one day. They said so."

Nadia, squirming against her bonds, kicked the leg of her chair.

Megan wheeled around, the gun pointed squarely at Nadia's forehead. "But then Blackstone Properties decided to take it all away."

"I can understand your anger at losing the land," Fiona said, her voice preternaturally calm. "But surely a business deal isn't worth killing over."

I caught Fiona's eye and shook my head in a silent warning. I knew I had to somehow reach out to Megan before Fiona inadvertently inflamed her even further. "But it wasn't simply a business deal, was it, Megan? Blackstone Properties took away much more than the land."

"That's right." Megan cast Fiona a withering glance. "I guess Amy didn't tell you? How Blackstone tried to force my grandparents to abandon the land that had been in their family for generations, and when they couldn't buy them off—"

"They had them killed," I said, lacing my words with as much sympathy as I could muster.

Fiona's gasp hung in the charged air of the room.

"No, they murdered them." Megan aimed the gun at Nadia and then Tim, then turned away slightly to look at me and Fiona. "Sure, it was another man who pulled the trigger, but he was sent by Wendy Blackstone and her company to do whatever was necessary. He was the killer, but he was just a tool." Megan met my anxious gaze with a smile that did nothing to calm me. "He admitted as much when my dad tracked him down, years later. He even said that he was sorry, especially for shooting my grandma, who didn't even have a gun. But he never came forward to tell the authorities the truth, because Blackstone Properties bought him off. After telling him that they'd make sure he'd be the only one who'd take the rap for the murders."

I nodded, thinking it best to play along and hopefully gain Megan's trust. "The Blackstones were just as culpable as he was."

"Absolutely. But they never paid for their crimes. He did," Megan added in an offhand tone, as if this information was as unimportant as a discussion of the weather. "My dad made sure of that."

Fiona and I shared a glance. I could see that she, like me, was terrified. I pressed my fingers to my lips to indicate it was safer if she simply stayed silent. She nodded.

"Your father exacted justice on him, then?" I asked.

"Yes. We buried him in the wilderness, where no one would ever find him. Just like Blackstone Properties buried my grandparents—all alone, with no one there to honor them or mourn. Their bodies thrown into a ditch and their unmarked graves buried under the depths of Crystal Lake."

"It was a terrible thing to do," I said. Turning my head, I noticed Fiona's amazed stare. She was probably wondering how I'd mustered the courage to play this deadly game with Megan.

But I knew it was driven by my fierce desire to live, and to save her life as well. I would not leave my children without a mother or force them to lose a grandmother. Because I refused to hurt them, and Richard, so tragically.

"Yes, it was." Megan crossed to the chairs holding Nadia and Tim. "Dad evened the scales with the shooter, but he couldn't do anything to make anyone else at Blackstone Properties pay for their crime." She glanced back at me. "He died, you see. Just last year. So it was up to me."

"And then Jaden Perez decided to bring your environmental activist group to Taylorsford, where Wendy Blackstone and her team were planning another development," Fiona said.

Megan stared down at the gun in her hands. "No, that was me. I discovered that Blackstone Properties was hoping to develop land near Taylorsford and convinced Jaden that our next protest should be held here." She cast Fiona a superior look. "That was clever, don't you think? I'd been thinking about my revenge for years, first with Dad and then by myself. I had my plan worked out, but it was only recently that I felt fate was on my side."

"That was very clever of you, using your connections that way," Fiona said in a hollow voice.

I shot her an appreciative glance. She'd understood the gist of what I was trying to do and was now playing along. "You knew Wendy would be at the festival and realized that would offer a perfect opportunity to confront her."

"To kill her," Megan said, with a lack of emotion that was more chilling than her earlier anger. "And now I have these two." Megan leveled the gun at Tim and Nadia, who whimpered and struggled against their bonds. "Idiots. They were in here, packing up their offices, getting ready to flee the area. I wasn't about to let that happen. It was so easy—I just strolled in. They never suspected a thing, not until I locked their front door behind me and showed them the gun. Then they quickly tried to throw each other under the bus, let me tell you. Such loyalty." Megan snorted in derision.

"They are quick to protect their own interests," I said, hoping to place Fiona and myself on Megan's side, at least in her mind. "You know, one of them even tried to run me off the road the other day. Then threatened me. I believe they wanted me to stay quiet about Blackstone Properties' involvement in your grandparents' deaths."

"Did they?" Megan casually clocked Tim upside the head with the gun. "That's for Amy," she told him sweetly as he groaned. "Your payment for my grandparents is yet to come."

Fiona's chair squeaked. I looked over at her and caught her making a tiny movement with her hand. It looked like she was pointing her thumb toward the back door.

I cast a surreptitious glance over my shoulder. There was a shadow darkening one of the windows. Whipping my head back around, I focused on Megan, who was tormenting Nadia by pressing the gun barrel against her temple.

Thinking a distraction was in order, I coughed. Megan made a half-turn to face me.

"Sorry," I said. "Tickle in my throat." I forced a smile. "You know, I think the cleverest thing you did was trapping Ethan Payne in that barn. That was a stroke of genius. It kept the focus on him while you waited for Jaden to make those arrangements to get you out of the country."

Megan stared at me, her nostrils flaring. "And it would've worked if Payne hadn't been quite so resourceful. Can't say I don't admire him a little for that, though. It just created a bit of a problem for me."

"Like Jaden did?" I asked, "He wasn't very loyal in the end, was he?"

"No," Megan said, her expression darkening. "He said he sympathized with me, but he didn't have the stomach for actually balancing the scales. Once he realized Wendy's death wasn't an accident, he lost his nerve. I had to keep an eye on him. When I followed him to your house, I figured he was heading to the sheriff's office once he left."

"So you had to silence him."

"I didn't want to do that. I just had to. I couldn't allow him to tell the authorities everything he knew. Not while I was still in the area."

For the first time, I heard real remorse in Megan's voice. "He isn't dead, you know. Just in a coma. The doctors say he'll recover eventually."

"That's good." Megan took a deep breath. "He can say whatever he wants when he comes out of the coma. I'll be long gone by then."

"Into the wilderness? Somewhere up in the mountains, where no one will find you?" I asked, keeping my tone light.

"That's the plan. But first"—Megan turned back to Nadia and Tim—"I need to carry out the punishment that these two deserve."

I racked my brains to think of something else to say that might delay Megan's plan. "What about us?" I asked. "My mother-in-law and I haven't done anything to you. Will you spare us?"

Megan, who'd trained the gun on Tim, lowered it an inch or two. "I may need to shoot you in the legs so I can get away cleanly, but I have no plans to kill you. Just like I won't murder Dylan. He's part of the Blackstone family, but he's had nothing to do with the company, and from talking to him about his plans in life, I expect he'll sell it off. So he can live too." She raised the gun again. "See, I'm no monster. I don't kill people unless they deserve it. I'm only interested in justice."

Nadia stopped struggling. She stared at the gun, her eyes wild and feral as those of an animal caught in a trap.

My head was spinning. I needed to do something, anything, to stop her from executing Nadia and Tim, but I didn't want to throw my life away on a foolish attempt at heroism. Because it wasn't just my life at stake—I was pretty sure that if I tried anything, Megan would shoot Fiona as well.

Just as I rejected the idea of hurling myself at her legs to catch her off-balance, a thunderous crack rang throughout the room, followed by a blast of cold air and snow. Megan spun around, aiming the gun at the now-open back door.

"Drop the gun," Brad Tucker ordered. "We have the building surrounded. You can't get away. Lay down your weapon, and let's conclude this peacefully."

Two deputies flanked him, weapons drawn. They inched forward until they were standing in front of me and Fiona, shielding us.

Megan, her face suffused with fury, leveled her gun at Tim's head.

"Don't be foolish," Brad said, his voice firm but calm. "We can take you out before you get that shot off. Put the gun down, Megan."

She hesitated for one more second, then dropped the gun and raised her hands above her head. The deputies rushed forward to secure her and the gun and then free Nadia and Tim, who were understandably in shock.

A burst of hysterical laughter made me turn to Fiona. She was hunched over, her shoulders shaking. "I'm fine. She needs help," I told the person bending over me. She looked vaguely familiar, but it took another second for me to recognize Hannah Fowler. "My mother-in-law—I think she's in shock too," I said, waving my hand toward Fiona.

Hannah nodded and hurried over to Fiona as I tried to stand. I got to my feet, but my legs, wobbling like those of a baby just learning to walk, threatened to drop me to the floor.

"Hold up," said a familiar voice.

Strong arms wrapped around me, lifting me back on my feet and keeping me there.

"How are you here? How did you know?" I asked as Richard turned me around so he could hug me to his chest.

"As soon as we reached the house, we realized you weren't behind us and also weren't anywhere in sight. So Scott and Ethan and I came back to figure out why. We could see enough of what was going on through the lighted windows to call 911 and get the sheriff's department and rescue squad here." Richard tightened his hold on me. "Just in time, it seems."

"She wasn't going to kill us," I said, my words muffled by Richard's coat. "Not me and your mom, anyway. I mean, that's what she said, but I don't know. She was going to shoot Nadia and Tim, and then . . . I don't know. I don't know."

Tears welled in my eyes and spilled over, drenching my cheeks and the front of Richard's coat. I leaned into him as he adjusted his hold on me so that we could walk out of the building.

Sirens wailed as one of the ambulances, carrying Tim and Nadia, took off. Another ambulance, its back doors open, still sat in the snow-covered parking lot. I noticed a slender, dark-haired figure sitting just inside the vehicle. Wrapped in a silver blanket, her legs dangling and an oxygen mask covering her face, Fiona looked up and met my gaze.

She gave me a nod. I prodded Richard with my elbow. "Your mom," I said. "She was very brave."

Richard gave my shoulder a comforting squeeze, then led me over to the ambulance, where we both wrapped Fiona in a warm hug.

Chapter
Twenty-Nine

I wasn't surprised when, early the next day, I heard shrieks from the room next door, accompanied by the sound of small children jumping on beds. It was Christmas morning, after all.

But after an evening spent getting checked over by emergency personnel and talking to law enforcement—not to mention fielding calls from concerned friends—I was not thrilled to get out of bed.

"You stay there," Richard said as he threw a robe on over his T-shirt and boxer shorts. "I'll take care of the kids."

"No, no. I want to watch their faces when they see their gifts from Santa." I sat up and swung my feet over the edge of the bed. "Just keep them upstairs until I can grab my robe and brush my hair."

"Oh, giving me the easy job," Richard said with a smile. He leaned in to kiss me and then pulled me to my feet. "Poor darling, you look exhausted."

"And I probably will all day. But what the heck, I'm alive." I crossed to our walk-in closet to grab a silky red robe I hoped would make me look a little more festive than I felt. As I brushed my hair, I examined it in our bathroom mirror, certain the adventures of the previous evening had added more gray strands.

Surprisingly, I didn't look any different than I had the day before, except for the paleness of my skin and the dark smudges under my eyes. I rubbed in a little concealer and added some color to my wan face with a light touch of blush and tinted lip balm.

When I walked into the upstairs hallway, I was met with more shrieking.

"Mommy!" Ella and Nicky shouted in union. They barreled into me, hugging my legs.

"Children, let go of your mother. You're making it impossible for her to walk." Fiona, tying the sash of her paisley bathrobe, stood in the doorway of Ella's bedroom. I met her concerned gaze with a smile.

"It's okay. We didn't get to see each other much last night. By the time you and I got home, Mom and Aunt Lydia had already fed the kids and supervised their baths. I barely got a chance to give them a hug and kiss before they fell asleep."

"We missed you, Mommy. And you, Grandmother." Nicky released his hold on me and trotted over to Fiona to give her an equally effusive hug.

"Daddy said we had to stay up here until he turned on the lights of the tree and gave the cats their breakfast." Ella looked up at me, her black lashes fluttering over her wide gray eyes. "But I think he's had time to do that, don't you?"

"Do you want to go downstairs for some reason?" I asked with feigned innocence.

"It's Christmas!" the twins shouted in unison.

"Really? Well, I suppose we should go see whether Santa brought you anything. Just be careful," I said as Ella and Nicky clattered down the stairs. "Don't fall," I called out, knowing they were probably already at the bottom of the steps. I offered Fiona a smile and gestured toward the staircase. "After you."

By the time we reached the tree, the twins had already discovered the bicycles that Santa had left—a gold-and-black one for Nicky and a silver-and-blue one for Ella—along with matching helmets. Richard, promising that they could try out the bikes as soon as the snow had melted, steered them to toys that they could use right away: a pair of saucer-shaped plastic sleds.

"After we open the rest of the gifts," he said, when the twins asked when they could try them out in the snow.

This led to some pouting, but this frustration was soon forgotten when the doorbell rang and my parents arrived, followed by Aunt Lydia, Hugh, Scott, and Ethan.

"Did you call them?" I asked Richard as Ella and Nicky were given the go-ahead to start tearing into the wrapped gifts.

Richard, handing me a mug of coffee, gave me a wink. "I did. It seemed to be the safest course of action."

"You are a wise man," I said, standing on tiptoe to kiss his cheek.

When Richard headed back into the kitchen to grab some coffee for the other adults, I leaned against the wall near the hallway, surveying the hectic scene. Ribbons, paper, and discarded gift bags littered the floor near the tree, providing Fosse and Loie with a wealth of items to pounce on and into.

To Ella and Nicky's credit, they didn't just focus on their own gifts but also carried presents over to the adults, insisting that they be opened one at a time so we could all see what everyone had received. It made for a raucous morning, but I didn't really mind. Seeing the joy on my children's faces as the gifts they'd chosen, with a little help, for their grandparents and other family members were exclaimed over and admired was worth a little chaos.

"This one's for Cassie," Ella said, handing a gift bag to Ethan.

"Perfect," he said when he pulled out a dog toy that looked like a flattened racoon. "I'm sure she'll love it."

Scott admired the gift before tucking it back into the bag. "I tell you what, why don't you give it to her when we go over to Aunt Lydia's for brunch? We didn't want to bring her over this morning, because we didn't think Loie and Fosse would appreciate that very much."

The twins thought this was a splendid idea. Leaving the dog's gift with Ethan and Scott, they dashed back to the tree and grabbed a small box topped with a white velvet bow.

"This is for you, Grandmother," Ella told Fiona. "Daddy helped us pick it out."

"Did he?" Fiona looked up and met Richard's gaze with a smile. "All right, let's see this gift. I'm sure it will be very special." She opened the box and lifted out a silver necklace. The fine chain held a pendant in the shape of a tree. Studding the branches were four gemstones.

"Those are Daddy and Mommy," Nicky said, "and the two that are the same are Ella and me, because we have the same birthday."

"Ah, birthstones," Fiona said, holding the necklace up to the light. "Well, that's lovely and perfect. Thank you." She leaned down to kiss Ella and Nicky before sitting back and putting on the necklace.

"A family tree. How nice," my mom said. She judiciously didn't mention that she'd gotten a similar gift for her birthday.

I leaned in closer to Richard. "You thought it was finally time to get one of those for Fiona, I see."

"Seemed like she might actually appreciate it now," Richard said, sliding his arm around my waist.

"Mommy needs her special gift from you, Daddy," Nicky said, rummaging through the remaining packages under the tree. He sat back, looking puzzled. "I don't see it. You know, the really special one."

"Oh, right." Richard shared a conspiratorial look with my mom and Aunt Lydia. "Now, where is that?" He reached into the left pocket of his robe. "Oops, nothing there. Maybe it's in the other one."

I stepped back, eyeing him with suspicion. "What's this? I can see some people in this room already know."

Mom and my aunt lowered their heads, hiding obvious smiles, while Hugh gave me a wink. Even Fiona, covering her mouth with her hand, seemed to be in on the secret.

"Ah, here it is." Richard pulled a long envelope from his right robe pocket. He brandished it through the air. "Not wrapped, I'm afraid, but I think you'll see why."

I took the envelope, casting a questioning gaze around the room before I opened it.

Inside were plane tickets and a sheet of paper outlining the itinerary for a trip to England and Scotland. I stared at it for a moment.

"Wait, this is the same time as that charity dance gala you're doing in London this coming summer?" I said, looking up at Richard in confusion. "But we said I couldn't go because of the kids . . ."

"That was until our mothers and your aunt volunteered to take turns staying with them so you can come with me. And also extend the trip so we can tour the places where some of your favorite authors lived," Richard said.

"Merry Christmas!" Aunt Lydia and Mom shouted in unison, their smiles radiating a smug happiness at the success of the surprise. They were echoed by Fiona, who also looked quite pleased with herself.

"We get to have both grandmas stay with us," Ella said. "And Aunt Lydia too."

Nicky bobbed his head. "Yeah, we think it will be cool. And you and Daddy can bring us back neat stuff."

"Okay," I said, and then burst into tears.

"It wasn't meant to make you cry." Amusement sparkled in Richard's voice. He pulled me into an embrace. "We just thought it was about time you got to do something you've always wanted to do. I mean, no time like the present, right?"

I hugged him, then pulled away and gazed around the room, taking in the bright faces of so many of the important people in my life.

"Quite a present," I said, thinking of the happiness of the day rather than the gift. "I do love it. But honestly, I love you all more."

"That's good, Mommy," Ella said. "Now can we play with our sleds?"

Acknowledgments

M y sincere thanks to everyone who's helped bring this book into being and supported the entire series:

My agent, Frances Black of Literary Counsel.

My editor at Crooked Lane Books, Faith Black Ross.

The Crooked Lane Books team, especially Matt Martz, Madeline Rathle, Dulce Botello, Rebecca Nelson, Stephanie Manova, Thaisheemarie Fantauzzi Perez, and Rachel Keith.

Cover designers C. Griesbach and S. Martucci.

My friends, family, and fellow authors.

Bookstores and libraries—the best institutions ever!

All the bloggers, podcasters, YouTubers, and reviewers who have mentioned, reviewed, and promoted my books.

And, as always, my amazing readers!

8/24 (4)